WHEN THE PERSON YOU PRAYED FOR BECOMES THE PERSON YOU PRAY WITH

From loving God alone to loving

God together

BY JOHN AND RONETTE JOHNSON

Table of Contents

Dedications   v

Chapter 1.   The Wedding of My Dreams   1

Chapter 2.   Home Is Sweet at Home   13

Chapter 3.   This Could Be Us   25

Chapter 4.   A Hug from Heaven   41

Chapter 5.   Fueled for a Fruitful Future   61

Chapter 6.   In Your Dreams, Dem   69

Chapter 7.   Maybe This Could Work Out   75

Chapter 8.   Embracing the Sudden Divine   97

Chapter 9.   A Love Demonstration   103

Chapter 10. Meet the Foxers   119

Chapter 11. Spring Break   143

Chapter 12. A Crazy Day at Kraze   177

Chapter 13. Unprepared Cries   191

Chapter 14. Waves of Deep Love and Safe Boundaries   217

Chapter 15. Treasure Discovered at Golden Leaf   245

Chapter 16. Heightened Love and Enlightenment   249

Chapter 17. A Promise in Progress   267

Chapter 18. Bold Moves   285

Chapter 19. Divine Beginnings   297

Chapter 20. Secured Secrets   331

Acknowledgments   347

About the Authors   349

Dedications

For **anyone praying for their future spouse:** *Never stop praying for the one your heart already loves, even after you meet them.*

For those **godly marriages,** *that love divine romance with a touch of passion. Continue praying together and keep it steamy!*

For **John, the husband of my dreams and my intimate prayers.** *Writing this romance novel with you has been like living a dream. Your loving heart and leadership inspire me every day. Thank you for loving me as I am; I simply enjoy being a soft wife while we live in God's favor together. I love you, my handsome husband!*

For **my wonderful wife, Ronette,** *you inspire me in countless ways. Your unwavering determination and eternally positive outlook on life contribute to your beauty, captivating me every day. Writing and growing alongside you has been both a joy and a blessing, which I am proud to be a part of and cannot thank God enough. I love loving you.*

To the reader,

Whether you're the one whose heart longs to be swept away by a profound love or someone already wrapped in the warmth of a beautiful relationship or marriage, we pray that God's incredible love surrounds you and grows deeper with each passing day.

May God's vast love surround you, becoming even stronger and more beautiful each day as you share your life with your special someone. May you feel this love deeply, see it reflected in your daily lives, live it wholeheartedly, and freely share it, even in life's challenges.

Or if you simply enjoy romantic stories, we pray our words bring you joy, laughter, and inspire your heart.

You may know us as @divineheartcouples on different platforms, mainly Instagram and TikTok. However, you've never encountered our writing on such a heartfelt and intimate level. Through this story and our words, you'll discover the depth of our romantic thoughts and feelings, sharing a deeper, more divine level of love.

Remember, you are amazing and Jesus loves you.

Sincerely,

Ronette and John

Chapter One

The Wedding of My Dreams

"Ah-choo!" The delicate fragrance of fresh blooms welcomed me as I stepped into the scene. In this brief moment, I treasured my wedding dress with pockets, a practical touch amidst elegance, reaching in for another tissue. Each step unveiled a burst of floral scent, playfully tangling with my shoes and weaving a bubbly tapestry beneath my feet. "Oh my! This walk feels endlessly beautiful, like a sign of forever," I whispered, moving toward the altar. My eyes then wandered to the handsome figure waiting, his eyes fizzing with admiration and confidence. A smile tugged at my lips and a gentle giggle slipped out as we shared a moment of connection. My gaze drifted over his regal double-breasted suit, a deep navy blue adorned with the glint of gold buttons that caught the light like tiny views of sunrises. Beneath the jacket, his perfectly pressed white dress shirt, casually unbuttoned at the collar, highlighted his warmth; even his brown shiny shoes seemed to harmonize beautifully with his expressive gaze. I inhaled softly, a gentle breath escaping as I fought to hold back my tears, determined not to ruin my carefully applied makeup.

Yet, as anticipated, the first tear slipped down my cheek, quickly followed by a second. It may have been a combination of both my allergies and tears of joy. Either way, if you could pin a joy emoji on my face, it would perfectly mirror my emotions. Suddenly, my tears began to flow freely, surging down my cheeks like a muddy river and landing softly on my fresh bouquet. I carefully dabbed at my lower lash line with a tissue, striving to regain my composure amidst the emotional torrent. Looking upward, I found my king waiting at the altar, his hands gently clasped together, rocking back and forth in eager anticipation. The warm sunlight poured through the window next to the altar, bathing my groom in a distinctive glow, as if he were standing under a spotlight, awaiting his moment with me.

I paused for a moment to absorb the breathtaking elegance of our beautifully decorated venue, feeling an overwhelming sense of joy. The sanctuary felt dreamlike, decorated with white hydrangeas that mirrored my bouquet, while delicate white balloons danced together gently above us. To top it all off, we were surrounded by our dearest friends and family, all of whom had guided us to this beautiful moment in our lives. As I gazed ahead again, I found myself lost in the depths of his warm eyes, unwavering and brimming with wonder. He shook his head in disbelief; as if I were the most exquisite woman he'd ever laid eyes on, his expression one of pure wonder at my grand reveal. I handed my bouquet to my maid of honor,

The Wedding of My Dreams

my hands nervously half-whirling as I inhaled deeply, feeling the weight of the moment.

Now, here we stood, face-to-face, hand in hand, our hearts racing in unison. "You look absolutely stunning, Narra," he whispered, retrieving a delicate white handkerchief from his suit jacket, his voice a tender melody wrapped in deep emotion.

The crowd of wedding guests erupted into sweet "Awws." The pastor started speaking and we took turns echoing his words. I couldn't help but chuckle softly, my cheeks tinged with pink.

"I can't believe this is really happening. I don't deserve someone as wonderful as you.

"Do you think we're ready, Narra?" he whispered, a hint of uncertainty in his voice.

"I believe it's time for the vows you've both prepared," the pastor stated with conviction.

"Narra, today, in front of these witnesses and, most importantly, in God's presence, I dedicate my love solely to you—profound and genuine, eternal and infinite, forever embracing the journey we undertake together. Through our sacred union, God has favored me with blessings I hardly deserve. It fills my spirit with awe that I am privileged to share my life with you each day, and now to have you as my wife.

"I vow to love you with the boundless love of Jesus Christ, my greatest honor to call myself your godly husband. I promise to nurture patience as you blossom into a Proverbs 31 wife, to uplift you emotionally, physically, and spiritually, and to be your unwavering rock, just as Jesus is our eternal foundation.

"Narra, each day spent with you is a beautiful reminder that my dreams have finally come true. I have what I've always wanted and prayed for.

"Thank you, God!"

Standing there for a moment, it seemed as if only he and I inhabited the room, a sacred silence enveloping us, until my maid of honor handed me a small, elegant black book. With eager anticipation, I opened it, skimmed through the pages to discover my vows; yet, to my dismay, the words were all blurry and some of the pages were blank.

"Narra … Narra! Would you like to read section thirty-nine?"

I found myself lost in thought, pulled back to the present by the laughter that filled the classroom. "Narra, are you alright?" asked Professor Govan, his voice tinged with genuine concern.

"Yes, I'm fine. I'm so sorry for drifting off," I replied, adjusting myself in my stiff wooden seat that felt more like a museum artifact than comfortable furniture.

"So, where were we?"

"Thirty-nine! Critical Perspectives!"

It was another daydream about my wedding day. As a passionate dreamer and hopeful romantic, I found myself increasingly preoccupied with thoughts of my future as graduation approached.

It was early September at Rovane University and the academic year was beginning, a few weeks into the semester. I had already showered and brushed my teeth and the room was infused with the pleasant aroma of fresh calendula herbs mingling with the subtle sweetness of organic rose water oil on my skin. As I prepared for class, I gathered my hair into a messy, curly bun, a touch of makeup barely there, whispering of simplicity and effortless charm. I chose a pale pink blouse paired with a waist-length chocolate cardigan, dark khaki skinny-fit pants, and camel-colored suede slip-on sandals—my fit for the day.

I began gathering my thoughts for my first class, slipping a handful of books into my pink bag, which I affectionately referred to as "my all-purpose bag." How blessed I was to share my journey with Sasha Pierre, my suitemate from sophomore year. Our friendship had blossomed beyond the university walls, with laughter and shared dreams weaving us closer through the years. This morning, as she lay snoring like a gentle cow, cocooned in her bed with her bedroom door open while classes loomed, I couldn't help but smile. Her slumber mirrored our bond: warm, comfortable, and steadfast.

I stood in front of one of our full-length mirrors, my heart swelling with gratitude. Reflecting on my journey, I whispered to myself, "I'm a senior at Rovane University, one of the top schools in Pennsylvania." It felt surreal, as if God's plans were unfolding—so close yet still distant. "Girl, this is it. You're so strong and you're almost there, Narra!" I encouraged myself, picturing the bright future waiting beyond graduation. In that moment of solitude, I remembered the words that uplifted me through challenges: "You're fearfully and wonderfully made."

And once more, I affirmed my strength with, "I can do all things through Jesus Christ who strengthens me."

I flopped down onto my fuzzy rose-pink throw blanket, draped over our cozy little ottoman just outside the shared bathroom of our mini dorm suite. Closing my eyes, I drew a deep, steady breath and sat silently for a moment. "God, You're so good," I whispered softly. "Dear Heavenly Father, thank You for this beautiful day, a gift woven with purpose, grace, and peace. I am grateful for your shield of protection over everyone, including myself, and our schools. Thank you, Holy Spirit, for guiding my way. I seek your comfort as I embrace this day. Grant me a humble heart, a spirit so free to learn and to grow, in Your love may I be. Father God, in all I do, let Your glory shine. In every small act, let Your light be mine. In Jesus' name, Amen."

"Amen!" Sasha yelled, clapping her hands in agreement. "I needed that." We both chuckled softly, my hand brushing against the soft fabric of my pink bag, brimming with essentials — a student ID, cellphone, a handful of books, keys, pens, and whispers of necessity. I opened the door and stepped out into the morning light, eager for my first class.

"Have a great day, Sasha!"

"Thanks. You too, Narra," she replied, her voice muffled as she pulled the covers back over her head.

As I walked across campus to class, I paused to appreciate the stunning scenery—the deep purple leaves of the cherry plum trees swaying gently in the morning breeze, offering a beautiful backdrop for my thoughts. These trees flanked my path, and with each step, I observed how their vibrant leaves had begun to carpet the ground in a captivating display of colors. It was indeed a sight to behold.

A lively energy thrummed through the air around me, with students and staff mingling to create a symphony of laughter and conversation that felt warm and inviting. Familiar faces— friends and professors—passed by, making the campus feel like a true community. The weather perfectly complemented this scene: a warm breeze wrapped around me as soft rays of sunshine filtered through billowing clouds, enhancing the cozy atmosphere.

At that moment, I couldn't help but think, *This is the most romantic time of year.* A flutter of excitement danced in my heart as I approached my first class—language and literacy, a subject dear to my English major and soul. Anticipation flooded me as I reflected on this year, marking the end of a beautiful journey through college. I longed to savor every second of my time here, especially after a year of navigating online classes while juggling my full-time job, saving for my first apartment, and planning for life post-graduation. Now, as the sun rose on this chapter, I was ready to embrace every opportunity that lay ahead, letting the warmth of campus life sweep me away into cherished memories that would last a lifetime.

Language and literacy have always been more than just subjects to me; they represent the heart of human connection and understanding. I enjoy exploring the intricacies of language and discovering how it shapes our thoughts, emotions, and relationships. Each text—whether a novel or an academic paper—opens a new door to insight and inspiration, allowing me to view the world through different lenses. As I delved deeper into these fields, I recognized their importance for my future. They provided me with the tools to communicate effectively, advocate for myself and others, and inspire change in the world around me.

I was also blessed with amazing parents; my mother and stepdad had always been my pillars of support, both financially and spiritually. Their wise, faith-driven guidance had shaped me, and now at 21, I felt poised to step into my independence. The foundation they had given me fueled my passion for English lit. I aspired to share this love and knowledge with others, perhaps becoming an educator or writer who would empower future generations to appreciate the power of words and storytelling as much as I did.

After finishing my first class, I stepped into the cozy new shop on campus, Tea and Treats. It was just a short five-minute walk from anywhere on campus. Sitting across from my friend and suitemate, Sasha, I noticed her eyes shining with excitement. "I can hardly believe graduation is almost here!" I said, settling into my seat. "It feels like a dream; I'm exhilarated yet aware of how much I'll miss college life. This journey has been beautiful, filled with unforgettable experiences and moments we've shared," I said as I enjoyed my drink. My enthusiasm remained strong.

And on top of that, I was tutoring a few young ladies through the realms of English literature twice a week after school. It was a meaningful act of sharing my knowledge; yet there was a bittersweet tinge to the thought of departing from this place soon. I want to make the most of these remaining months.

"Narra, I see a fire within you that ignites your dreams and aspirations. It's truly beautiful and inspiring to witness how filled you are with a profound sense of purpose and motivation. I've come to understand that, above all, you want to become the remarkable woman of God you feel called to be in this world. I admire your dreams of being a screenwriter or a writer of some kind. I envision a future where you own that quaint bookstore you've dreamed of, a haven where you gently share the gift of Bibles and books with those seeking solace and hope. Your generosity shines brightly, offering Bibles freely to all who seek them, even as you cherish the possibility of sharing other stories through sales. Your compassionate heart truly reflects the luminous spirit within you and that is one of the reasons why you will be a lifelong friend of mine."

"That is so sweet, Sasha!" I exclaimed, grinning from ear to ear.

As graduation drew nearer, excitement and nervousness swirled in my heart every day. I turned to Sasha, feeling warmth coursing through me. "I really hope we can stay in touch after graduation! It would mean the world to me. Just imagine, in the future, going on double dates when we're both in relationships and married and then organizing playdates with our little ones! I can't wait to hear all about your adventures, and of course share mine with you too. Let's promise to always cheer each other on, no matter where God leads us," I said, heartfelt emotions underlying my words.

With steaming cups of tea in hand and a shared box of sweet treats, Sasha and I strolled back to our dorm room, laughter dancing in the air. "How about that guy in the shop?" I chuckled, shaking my head. "I couldn't believe he actually asked for my number like that!"

Sasha burst into giggles, her eyes glittering with mischief. "I mean, who does it like that? It's almost like he thought you were a celebrity or something!" As we continued down the winding pathway, each step resonated with our shared memories.

"He certainly had the confidence of one!" I replied, taking a sip of my tea.

"I just can't get over how ridiculous it was. I thought you'd burst out laughing right then and there!" Sasha nudged me playfully, both of us reveling in the sweetness of the moment and the comfort of our friendship as we shared more stories and inside jokes on the way to our cozy dorm suite.

"At least I was nice to him though." I chuckled.

As we walked, Sasha stopped and said, "One last thing, Narr. Did you know that you're partly responsible for why I decided to download the Bible app a few years ago?"

"Wow, really?"

"Yes. I've been getting closer to Jesus and reading to understand as much as possible. It has all helped me become a better person and handle my anxiety and fears differently. I feel like I belong here on this earth and have a purpose."

"Amen, Sasha! All this time, I thought you were out here acting like a little heathen." I glanced at her with a serious expression and then we both erupted in spontaneous laughter.

"I have days when I need to ask God for repentance, but I promise I am getting better with my intentions. I'm no longer sleeping with anyone; I'm careful about who I date. I truly want to be better than how I grew up and what I've seen people close to me go through."

"Well, that's a start, Sasha! I'm proud of you."

As we entered our dorm, Sasha turned to me, grabbed her bag and a hat and said, "I have some studying to do with a friend. I'll be back in a few hours." I looked around at the scattered books while inhaling the soft, vanilla-scented air freshener in the room. I quickly grabbed my favorite gummy snacks and sighed. Settling onto my bed felt comforting; I realized I had the perfect opportunity to catch up on my studies and relax.

As I opened my textbook, Sasha's cheerful voice echoed in my mind, motivating me to focus and make the most of this quiet time, free from distractions. I really needed this time alone, and I also felt a nap would help me get some much-needed rest.

I began to contemplate my distractions during my classes lately. I'd noticed that my mind had been wandering more than usual, drifting into sudden daydreams. I started to wonder if the root of this distraction stemmed from my overwhelming schoolwork or the anxiety surrounding my impending graduation. Either way, those moments had become a perfect escape from the pressing weight of assignments and deadlines, evoking a gentle reminder of the future dreams I held dear, painting a picture of love and possibility. It was as if I were caught in a beautiful reverie, where the stresses of reality faded away, allowing my aspirations to take center stage.

Chapter Two

Home Is Sweet at Home

"Thank you, young man," she said, her smile a gentle dawn of gratitude as I helped an older lady carry her grocery bags to her car.

"You're most welcome, Ms. Kathy," I replied, feeling the warmth of the sun on my back.

"Did you say your name is Dem?"

"Yes, ma'am, it is."

"Well, Dem, I've got a granddaughter about your age. Would you like her number?"

I chuckled, the sound light and playful. "I'm sure your granddaughter is wonderful, but I'm currently focused on my studies and not looking to date right now." The older ladies always said the same thing, their intentions sweet and caring; yet I couldn't help but feel a bit amused.

It was a bright Saturday afternoon on October 18th and humidity had settled in, unexpected at this time of year. Experiencing mid-80s temperatures in October was indeed an unusual occurrence. The sun beamed down, forming a rich glow over everything as I cruised down the expressway after leaving the store to pick up a few things for the house. With the sunroof open, I immersed myself in one of my favorite worship playlists, each note blending seamlessly with the radiance of that beautiful day.

I was halfway to my destination—home—just an hour's drive from my school, where my parents lived northeast of Philadelphia, just outside the bustling city. This moment was special, marking my first visit home since the semester began, and I could already feel the warmth of my parents' excitement at seeing me again.

I made a brief stop at a local car wash in my amiable hometown of Whisby, eager to polish my car before heading home. As I drove the final three miles, excitement fluttered in my chest, each turn bringing me closer. I parked in the driveway, rolled up the windows, and gently closed the sunroof, every little action amplifying my anticipation. Just as I settled into the moment, my phone chimed with a cheerful ding from my dad, bringing a smile to my face even before I checked the message.

It said, *Son, the front door is already unlocked and open.*

As I glanced at my watch, it read 2:07 p.m. I felt a wave of relief—I had made it just in time. With my gym bag in one hand and a bag of items for my parents in the other, I stepped off the walkway and meandered across the freshly cut lawn, feeling buoyant and carefree, momentarily forgetting the delicate

Home Is Sweet at Home

blades beneath my feet in a playful act of rebellion against the meticulously maintained grass. I savored the thrill of my small transgression. "Oops!" I chuckled, a wide grin spreading across my face as I acknowledged my little misstep. At the front door, I kicked off my gym sneakers, careful to keep my mother's pristine floor spotless and free from grass stains.

"Hey, Dad!" I stepped inside through the front door, quietly closing and locking it behind me. I sank into my father's recliner, looking left and right then checking over my shoulder to admire the couch cover featuring his favorite football team—the world champions, the Philadelphia Eagles!

"E-A-G-L-E-S! Eagles!" We chanted together, laughter bubbling between us.

"Is this new, Dad?"

I stood up, giving him a firm handshake and a quick, tight hug as he joined me in the living room area.

"Is that my favorite son?" my mother shouted from the kitchen.

"Mom, I'm your only son!"

All three of us erupted in laughter.

I began sniffing the air like an eager puppy.

"Mmm, is that Mom's mouthwatering vanilla crumb cupcakes with cream cheese frosting?"

"It sure is, Son, and she made enough to feed the entire neighborhood!"

My dad and I exchanged knowing glances, shaking our heads and bursting into loud laughter.

"I'm sure there will be a few knocks on the door when word gets out about the cupcakes!" I chuckled. "It's cold in here. I know it's hot outside, but why do you all have the air conditioning set so low?"

"You know how your mom feels about it being too warm in the house, especially when the oven contributes to the heat."

"Yes, I sure do!" I said, empathizing with my dad. I had to deal with it all summer long. "How have you been, Son?" my father asked, his voice warm and inviting. "How's school? What has been the best thing so far in these first few weeks? And how are you feeling this year?" He leaned in closer, eyes flashing with curiosity and love. "I recall how last year you were still apprehensive about taking a year off before starting your freshman year of college. But I still believe it was an excellent choice, Dem. I wholeheartedly support your decision a hundred percent."

"Thanks, Dad."

His eyes still shining with pride, he said, "I see how much you've grown and it makes me so proud. Your adult journey is just beginning, and I'll be here cheering for you every step of the way." He added, "Watching you develop has been one of my greatest joys. I want you to know how proud I am of you. Your decision to take a year off to explore new paths and find your true self showed great courage. You've handled challenges bravely and I truly admire that persistence. I believe in you and your dreams and I'll always support you."

I smiled, feeling the warmth of his encouragement. It reminded me of the support that had always been there, pushing me to strive for my best and reassuring me that I was on the right path.

"Dad, everything has been going well so far. I'm learning new things and my grades are good. I'm having a great time working and earning some money! Oh, and I'm hitting the gym and enjoying myself a bit too."

"Just don't have too much wild fun. Be safe and make wise decisions. As I've told you over the past couple of years, avoid getting caught up with the wrong crowd or wrong kind of ladies. Be cautious about your choices at get-togethers and parties. I can't make the decisions for you, but I know you don't want any slip-ups, right?" my dad said, his eyes widening. "Also, make sure you get a new Bible. I know you like the Bible app, but there's nothing like a physical Bible. It'll be good for you."

I glanced at my father, murmuring, "That's the plan, Dad."

"Are you having sex, Dem?"

"Dad!"

"Just make sure you buy some condoms before heading back."

"Come on! What kind of question is that?" I asked, my voice sharp with a hint of frustration as I spoke through clenched teeth, glancing sideways in a silent plea for my mother not to overhear. The tension in my words hung in the air, raw and unfiltered, reflecting a moment of quiet rebellion and unspoken emotion.

"Dem, I know things can happen when you're young. You know, when I was your age, I had friends just like yours."

"Yeah, yeah, I know. I'm good, Dad!"

Even though I didn't want to hear it when my dad spoke of these types of things, I never got angry; I just felt a little uncomfortable. I listened and took these conversations as nuggets of wisdom and clear reminders. My dad wasn't perfect, but he was a standup guy.

I quickly changed the subject. "I truly miss being in church with all of you, Dad."

"That reminds me, Pastor Jack asked about you during Bible Study."

"No worries. I look forward to returning to church as soon as I can. It's been a while since I last attended, so I plan to start watching the service online again and will join in person when possible."

"Okay, Son. I hear you and that's a great start. There's no pressure at all. I know you've been busy settling into your dorm, completing class assignments, and working. I understand. However, I need you to take some action behind your words, young man. I raised you better than that." He added, "We Foxer men always keep it real. Remember, your relationship with God should always be your priority. Love you, Dem, and if you need anything, just let me know."

"Yes, Father!" He didn't like it when I used that term, but it was my way of getting back at him for those wild questions.

"Hi, Son!" my mom said in her soft, nurturing voice as she tiptoed into the living room, balancing a round tray of freshly baked cupcakes. "Try a cupcake and let your mother know if she's still got it! But be careful; they're a little warm." She carefully set the tray down on the coffee table, the gleaming glass cover dazzling in the light.

I bit into a warm cupcake covered in fresh, creamy frosting and I jumped up like an excited child, doing a happy dance, twirling around, and bursting into song. "Yeah, yeah, Mom's cupcakes! Yeah, yeah, Mom's cupcakes!" I sang. We shared a hearty laugh and wrapped our arms around each other, the warmth of the moment lingering like the sweet aroma of the treats. I wouldn't call myself a mama's boy, but my mother truly means the world to me. As an only child, I knew she wasn't rushing me, yet she had always expressed her excitement about the prospect of me one day having a wife and family. She dreamed of being a grandmother and hoped to see some little Dems and Demmettes running around. Her unwavering belief that I would make a great husband and father had always been a source of reassurance to me. My mom genuinely believed in me and always supported my dreams, encouraging me to pursue my passions wholeheartedly.

"You're a good young man and you love the Lord," my mother said. "I overheard part of your conversation with your father. I would love for you to come to church; if not tomorrow, perhaps the next time you are home. But please don't forget to start watching the service online."

"I won't forget, Mom! When does it start, around ten a.m.?"

"Nope, Dem," she said, sitting down and chuckling as she glanced over at my father to gauge his reaction. "Service begins at eleven fifteen sharp, Demery!" she added.

"Have you met anyone special yet, or are you dating someone? That's the one thing I haven't heard you mention, Dem."

"Nah, Mother Demi, not just yet," I said jokingly, squinting at her. "Yo, I just want to have a blast, live it up, and party hard!" I said with a laugh as I threw up my hands.

I could sense my dad's eyes slightly judging me.

"A woman like your mother only comes along once in a lifetime. I remember vividly the first moment I encountered her sweet eyes glaring up at me at Kimmer State University. I casually asked, 'What's up?' but before I knew it, she was making me cupcakes. How do you think she became a pro?

"All jokes aside, I'm thankful that God chose me to be her best friend and husband. This is generational love, Son. When you find your special someone, she will become more than just a partner; she will be your confidante, your joy, and your heart's most cherished companion."

"I don't know about all that yet, Dad."

"Just know that your mama and dad are only a phone call or a drive away. We're always here to talk and give you advice, Dem," my mom said, kissing me on the cheek.

"I love you, Mom!"

"Love you too, Son."

As she pulled back, my mom added, "I spent the whole morning cleaning out the basement. I organized your carpentry tools and dusted off the wood pieces you left behind. You really should see it; it's all neat and ready for your next project!"

She persisted, her eyes flickering with eagerness, "Some in the neighborhood and even some family members have inquired about when you'll craft more of those wood creations. They certainly enjoyed the last ones you made and they can't wait to see what you come up with next!"

"Oh yeah, about that, Mom. I still need to complete some orders for family members who were okay with waiting."

"That's amazing, honey!"

"I taught him well, didn't I?" my dad bragged proudly.

"I have some great ideas! Come on, Mom, let's go to the basement and check out what you've organized down there." As we headed to the basement, I was amazed to find that my mom and dad had gotten me new tools and equipment, along with some paint. They'd even purchased new tables and a light fixture! She truly understood me.

"I can envision it now—I'll run my own business out of here someday, Mom! Thank you, Mom and Dad! Everything looks great! I can't wait to return and get to work."

As I looked at my parents with grateful eyes, I was reminded of the strong belief in true love that they had instilled in me. Their often-unnoticed actions emphasized the importance of valuing marriage. Their relationship exemplified mutual respect and joy, showcasing the strength of their bond. Observing them face life's challenges together filled me with hope about what a loving partnership could be. Their mutual support inspired me to seek a similar connection in my future. I prayed to be with someone who shared these values, particularly someone who honored God and prioritized faith in their life. Even though I saw the beauty in their union, I was not rushing into anything just yet.

As we all gathered back in the living room, I turned to my parents and said, "Hey Dad, Mom, on a serious note, I want to share that my heart is currently set on school and enjoying time with my friends. This single life feels like an enchanting movie, filled with exploration, friendship, and fun while I embrace my inner party animal." They gave me a funny look, and I laughed. "Not to worry; it's nothing too crazy—just having a blast! I cherish the freedom of youth, making the most of every moment as I create beautiful connections and unforgettable memories with my friends. I want to fully immerse myself in this experience and relish it to the fullest before I take the serious step towards marriage."

I hesitated to share this with my parents, but thoughts of my future wife and the beautiful life we would create together often filled my mind. For many years, I'd been praying for her, hoping she would reflect the qualities I cherished in my parents: love, faith, and resilience. Though I might have been young, I felt it was not too early to envision the future, as God had granted me a glimpse of what was to come, and I trusted in His perfect timing. As I prepared my heart for her, I strove to find the right balance in my everyday life. Until that day arrived, I would continue to celebrate all that life offered while holding a hopeful glimmer for the future we would share.

Chapter Three

This Could Be Us

A soft whisper reached my ears. "Hey, did you notice the way Michael was looking at you?" Lena Julini asked, her eyes flashing with roguery. "It looked like he was peeling away your layers with his stare," she said with a spirited smile.

"What? I wasn't focused on him," I insisted, attempting to maintain a casual grin.

"Are you serious? Michael is absolutely breathtaking!" Her voice was a delightful mix of disbelief and approval.

"Oh no, he's walking toward us now! Don't look!" I glanced away, but then I couldn't resist glancing back at him. Our eyes met, igniting a stimulating connection that sent my heart racing.

"Oh my gosh, he's coming over here!" I whispered, nerves threading through my voice.

"How are you lovely ladies doing today?" His voice wrapped around us like a warm embrace.

"Hi, Michael!" we chorused, excitement bubbling within us.

"Have you given it any thought? Can I take you out or what?" he asked, sincerity etched into his charming smile.

"Wait, Narra, you had his number this whole time and didn't tell me?" Lena exclaimed, a blend of suspicion and excitement flooding through her. "I am totally shocked!"

"Yes, she has my number, and yes, she's going out with me— hopefully," Michael replied, tossing a flirty glance in my direction.

"I can speak for myself, Mike," I retorted playfully, a flicker of confidence in my eyes.

"You know, you could help me study for a test instead of us going out," I added, my tone light.

"Narra, just text me, okay? You're so beautiful inside and out and I'd love to hear from you," he said, his sincerity lingering in the air like a sweet promise.

Two days later, I found myself texting and talking to Michael. Our conversations flowed as we shared thoughts on almost everything. I purposely ignored my phone and texts, trying to remain focused on my classwork, but the guy was relentless in his pursuit.

A week later, we were together and a sweet romance blossomed between us, creating a delightful atmosphere of hope. He was a true gentleman, often holding my hand and kissing my forehead. This only deepened my desire for him, stirring feelings that I hadn't intended to entertain. Throughout my first three years of

This Could Be Us

school, I had been grounded and focused, but as a senior, I was beginning to let my guard down, cautiously choosing to open myself to romantic possibilities instead of shutting everyone out and declining dates. I couldn't believe I was falling for him; every time I caught him staring at me in class, I felt a flutter of excitement. This man wanted to get to know me, and I, too, wanted something real.

As night fell that Friday evening, I looked out from our balcony, the gentle wind barely whispering around me. The sky began to transform into a beautiful shade of deep midnight blue, wrapping the night in a light, romantic glow. I waited eagerly as I finally saw his car pull into the residence parking area near my hall, just as my phone chimed. His message was sweet and simple, letting me know he was there.

Hey, beautiful, I'm here.

I sent a text letting him know I was on my way. When he stepped out to open the passenger door, I was greeted with a wonderful surprise: a beautiful bouquet resting in the seat, a sweet gesture that made my heart flutter.

"You're so thoughtful, Michael," I remarked with a friendly smile, revealing my silver braces decked with blue-silver bands and inhaling the pleasant scent of the flowers as I held them closer to my nose. In that fairy-tale moment, after he returned to his seat and closed the door, I leaned in and gently kissed him on the cheek—something I wouldn't normally do, but it felt perfectly right in that moment.

"This is so sweet," I added, feeling warmth spread through me.

"I just want to make you smile, Narra," he said softly, his eyes graced with authenticity.

"Also, that black dress you're wearing truly enhances your gorgeous honey-brown eyes, especially as the sunlight gently kisses your face."

"You don't look bad yourself. We are looking good together," I replied.

Michael wore a sleek black suit that embraced his slender frame with a crisp white collar shirt and a black-and-mint-striped tie peeking from beneath it. His black shoes perfectly complemented his look. My long-sleeved black soft silk dress flowed elegantly, adorned with a delicate hint of chocolate at the hem and collar. I made sure to dress to impress, knowing this guy had a reputation for wearing some of the most stylish suits at our campus formal events. As young as he was, I was stunned at how impeccably he dressed. He exuded a charm that was irresistibly my type. I couldn't help but think he must have had a stylist or something as he always looked so sharp, even when dressed casually in jeans and a T-shirt. He paired his outfits with the coolest sneakers, like Jordans and other trendy brands. Mike truly knew how to own his look.

After a brief moment of gratitude, we set off to Fungoos, an upscale restaurant known for its exquisite food, one of Michael's all-time favorites. The expectation of the tasty dishes filled us with excitement. During the car ride, our conversation flowed effortlessly, as though we were two long-lost friends reconnecting after years apart. Michael possessed an undeniably comforting vibe, making every word exchanged feel easy and safe. I couldn't help but think, *This is the type of man I could truly see myself growing old with.*

Michael opened and held every door as we arrived, ensuring my hands were free before he took hold of them. In those moments, I felt like royalty when I was with him. We were seated at an intimate table, the atmosphere warm and inviting. The restaurant was unique, like none I'd ever seen or heard of. Perfect for a memorable evening. With our reservation, we had selected our meals in advance, ensuring that our dishes were served fresh and steaming from the grill when we arrived. As we settled into our cozy booth, I slid over as far as I could to be sure he could occasionally focus his eyes directly in my direction. It was only about ten minutes before a friendly server brought out our food and drinks, enhancing the heavenly vibes of the evening. The moment our plates were served, I looked up from my meal and caught Michael's kind green eyes, his smile broad and infectious.

"What's so funny?" I asked, curious about the glow in his eye.

"I know it's early between us, but there is something captivating about you and it inspires me to do everything I can to see you smile. Whatever it is, girl, you got it, and I am hooked!"

I couldn't help but notice how he always whispered the sweetest little compliments that sent cooling shivers down my spine.

We both laughed. "I agree it's quite early, but I'm truly enjoying where our connection is heading. I want to spend more time with you to deepen our understanding of one another."

"So, Graduation is approaching," he stated, his voice rich with intrigue and warmth. "Where do you see yourself in the next few years?"

"Personally or professionally?"

"Both."

"I find myself envisioning a beautiful future with you, Narra, and I hope I'm not moving too quickly in expressing these feelings."

I leaned back slightly, allowing a smile to form as I pondered my response. "I envision myself as a screenwriter or a creative writer. Ideally, I'll also own a charming bookstore where my stories and others can find a home."

He nodded eagerly, his eyes sparkling with belief. "I can see you shining brightly in whatever endeavors you pursue. Your imagination and your creative nature are truly admirable." His words ignited a spark of confidence within me. "And personally?"

"In a beautifully romantic marriage filled with divine purpose, one or two kids, content and joyful, alongside my loving, God-fearing husband. I want to be happy in Jesus no matter our circumstances!"

"I love that," he said as he took a sip of his drink, his eyes never leaving mine.

I looked at the bill, my breath catching in my throat at the total. "Such an expense, yet every dollar spent feels completely justified. This food is exquisite, Mike. Thank you for your kindness and sweetness; you truly make this moment unforgettable."

"There's more where that came from," he murmured with a playful glint in his eye.

"You make me feel like a queen."

"Stick with me; you'll never have to lift a finger or spend another dollar again. I've got you. I will take care of you."

"Michael Needan, you're just trying to outdo yourself, huh?" I said, teasing him, a smile brightening my face.

"Narra Needan. It has a lovely ring to it," he said as he gently sat up to settle himself comfortably. He took my left hand in his, his fingers lingering gently before he pressed a soft kiss to the back of my hand. Those words had a sweet, melodious ring to them and I loved every bit of the moment.

"I've never encountered such kindness before," I admitted, my cheeks warming. "And while I haven't dated much, you, sir, are truly exceptional. I admire how you present yourself, especially at your young age."

Michael displayed the calm confidence of a natural-born leader. Like me, he was majoring in literature and was incredibly articulate. He'd already secured a job and was just a few years older than I. Did I mention he looked like a male model? That man was undeniably fine, something out of a magazine type of fine!

♥♥♥

The next day, on a gorgeous Saturday afternoon, I drove to Mike's place so we could study together, a convenient excuse to spend some quality time with him. Our chemistry bloomed like never before in Michael's cozy apartment, tucked away off campus yet conveniently close. The atmosphere wrapped us in the warm embrace of freshly brewed coffee and soft, enjoyable music playing in the background. We engaged in genuine conversations, one of which explored deeply into faith and literature. As we sat at the sleek marble breakfast bar on black leather barstools, surrounded by our textbooks and laptops, the aroma of oven-baked garlic salmon now filled the air. We shared a sweet kiss that released a romantic vibe—a soft peck on the lips that lingered just a little longer than usual, soaking in the quiet intimacy of the moment. Although I valued our closeness and knew there were limits, he stirred something deep within me, igniting feelings I had never known existed. This man made me envision our future—our cozy home and the beautiful life we'd create together. In my daydreams, I even mapped out our wedding, every detail vivid in my mind. My mind was racing with thoughts. *I never knew I could experience puppy love like this, like I was back in high school, just months away from college graduation.*

After turning off the oven to let the food cool, he took off his stained white Rovane T-shirt, revealing his arms in a simple white tank top. With a sheepish smile, he looked at me and said, "Sorry, babe, I couldn't find an apron, so I need to take off this shirt. Don't want to be all in your face smelling fishy." We both laughed, our laughter mingling with another sweet kiss.

I felt the weight of his stare as he looked deeply into my eyes with those gripping green eyes during that moment and delicately grasped my waist to pull me closer, a silent exchange of sweetness that transcended words. I gently rested my hand on his back, my mind racing with the realization of, *This is as far as we can go.* I knew I had to regain my composure, quietly reminding myself, *The kissing has to stop, Narra.* His exposed arms only made it harder.

With a gentle sigh, he released me from his kind embrace like the gentleman that he was. I quickly reached for my pen, eager to jot down more notes from our studies. With a hopeful gleam in my eye, I asked softly, "Would you like to join me at church one Sunday?"

"Sure!" he exclaimed, a genuine sparkle of excitement lighting up his face. "Whenever I get the time, I would love to go with you."

"Okay, see you next Sunday?" I asked, detecting the anticipation in his voice.

He gently cupped my chin and looked into my eyes. "Narra, I think I'm falling in love with you." My heart melted almost as much as my body felt as I turned my entire body to face him and leaned into him as he pressed soft kisses to my forehead and neck. He whispered, "I'll let you know about church as soon as I figure out my weekend schedule," and then he gently lifted my head from his chest to capture my lips in a soft kiss again.

I slowly rose from the breakfast bar, my voice soft but firm with a sigh. "Mike, I really like this and I want it too, but we can't keep kissing like this." I faced him. Unable to resist, I puckered my lips in anticipation of one last sweet peck, but he softly reached out, gently taking my hands in his.

Looking into my eyes with understanding, he whispered, "I understand. You're right. We need to slow down a little." Rising smoothly, he gently pushed the barstool I was sitting on aside with his hands. Then he leaned in and kissed me again, his gaze full of affection. I wanted it, but my spirit whispered, *Absolutely not.*

"A lot," I added in a gentle but stern tone. We shared a nervous, knowing laugh, but I knew I had to leave—before things went further than I could handle. Not before I eagerly grabbed a to-go plate, though, like the foodie I am. Mike had prepared an exquisite meal: tender wild-caught garlicky salmon, creamy mashed red potatoes, and a sautéed zucchini medley with sweet onions and vibrant red peppers. He graciously offered me a taste of each dish before I headed out.

Mike and I often talked on the phone during the following week, sharing thoughtful conversations that revealed how much we had in common. It felt like he knew exactly how to connect with me—he was genuinely interested in my thoughts and ideas, which I found incredibly attractive and meaningful.

The following Saturday afternoon, I texted him to see if he could still join me for church on that Sunday. *Hey Mike, are you going to church with me tomorrow?*

He replied, *I'm sorry, but I have some important commitments tomorrow. Let's aim for next Sunday instead.*

Alright, Mike, let's try for next week, I responded, feeling an inkling of disappointment.

Two weeks later, after a short holiday break, Lena asked about my weekend on a Monday morning. "How did things go with Mike?" she asked, her face lit up with eagerness.

"Girl, let me share all the details! On that Friday evening, we went to Fungoos and it was a beautiful date night. He even surprised me with roses when he picked me up."

"Girl, shut up! Really?"

"Mike is so smooth."

"So, are you two together or what?"

"No, we are not an item, Lena, but we did share a few kisses during our little studies, but that's it."

"That's all? So now what?"

"He stood me up for church a few times and I am starting to think he has no interest in attending church at all."

"Isn't it funny that he didn't come to class today? It's like he's avoiding you." We both chuckled.

"As much as I like him, I cannot see myself being with a guy who is not a man of God.

Also, I'm not sure if he's looking for marriage. It seems as if he just wants a long-term relationship."

Lena said, "I'm not sure if Mike comes across as the husband type, but it's possible."

"It's a waste of my time if I'm not dating my future husband. I'm going to call him tonight to find out his reasons. I need answers."

"Narra, I don't blame you at all. You know what you want and need and shouldn't settle for less than that."

"I want to date my future husband forever—from the beginning stages to the end. And I need mine romantic and holy!" I exclaimed.

"Amen to that!" Lena said.

As the evening drew on, I found myself lost in thoughts of Mike when my phone rang.

"Hey Mike, I was just about to call you," I said with warmth in my voice.

"I've been thinking about you, Narra," he replied, his tone soft and inviting.

A blush crept across my cheeks, a smile playing on my lips. "I've been thinking about you too, Mike," I confessed, feeling a flutter of excitement.

"I cherish our conversations and truly like you—" he continued, his voice taking on a serious tone.

I interrupted him. "Before you continue, I need to clarify something: Jesus and I come as a package deal. I was designed to marry a man of God." I continued, "I know you aren't into God like that. You do not have to keep pretending just because you like me. I've been envisioning a beautiful future with you and did not want things to end with us."

"Me too, Narra. I don't want this feeling to end." He paused, voice unsteady with emotion. "I think I love you."

Sitting on my bed, headphones draped around me like a silent cocoon, I found myself immersed in a moment of quiet wonder. A gentle gasp escaped as I closed my laptop, my trembling hands instinctively rising to cover my mouth, embodying a sudden sensation of shock and awe. My heart fluttered, but I couldn't bring myself to respond—uncertain of what I truly felt in this moment of vulnerability and truth. "I was even considering introducing you to my family and friends—it feels right."

"Wow, Mike, hearing that makes me feel even worse! I can't believe we're in this situation," I said, a hint of regret in my voice.

"I'm sorry for not being straightforward and for avoiding you. That's not like me. I now see that dodging you and church was immature of me and I should have been honest from the start."

"Mike, God is truly wonderful and I hope you'll find your own path to Him. I never wish to impose my beliefs on you or anyone; for now, let's simply cherish the friendship we share."

"You're right, Narra. I'm not quite ready to fully embrace the idea of God and Jesus yet, but I cherish what we have. I'm simply not there yet."

"And I understand that, Mike. I truly believe you'll get there one day and I'll make sure to keep you in my prayers."

"Narra, you're so kind. Honestly, I want to be with you. Thank you for praying for me; I appreciate it and would never want to hold back the blessings God has in store for you. One day, you're going to make someone incredibly happy. I agree; let's nurture our friendship for now. Girl, you know I'll hold love for you still. Though this stings a little, I find comfort in your honesty, Narra. It serves as a bittersweet reminder that we must respect the path God has laid out for us."

"Oh, so there's a hint of hope in God after all, huh?"

"Yeah, I have to admit, there's something here."

"I'm genuinely happy for you," I replied, my tone unsteady yet firm. I knew deep down that we needed to end this now. I refused to let his sweet words draw me back in. I'd become wise enough to recognize my feelings and the importance of safeguarding my heart. My feelings were indeed valid, yet I had to exhibit discipline and sternness towards myself. I'd journeyed too far to revert to that naive girl who succumbed to a handsome man's charming, sweet words.

I took a deep breath and my eyes closed as I began to share my heart with Mike. "Let me tell you a little secret about myself: I've always felt a little different from others. I have this deep conviction in my heart that I will never settle for anything less than the beautiful promises that God has whispered to me. I'm waiting for that special love that the Bible speaks of—waiting for my husband, who embodies that divine love, to walk into my life and stay because we are aligned spiritually, naturally, and in many other areas."

As I spoke, Mike carefully listened and his curiosity piqued. "That's beautiful, Narra. You must have such an incredible sense of hope and faith. What do you imagine your future love would be like?"

I smiled, my vision coming to life in my mind. "In those quiet moments, God serenades me with sweet whispers of my future love. It feels spontaneous, like God is conspiring to show me glimpses of my husband. I envision a thoughtful man, a strong leader, a devoted prayer warrior." Mike remained quiet as I paused.

"He'd be a servant of the Lord, raising his hands in worship while staying grounded in the Word of God. A man of unwavering faith and integrity, whose inner substance shines just as brightly as his outward appearance. A spiritual soul who knows that keeping God at the forefront is essential."

Mike agreed, clearly moved by my passion. "You have a lovely vision of love, Narra. I believe that special person will see the light in you and help bring your dreams to life. It may be me or someone else. Only God knows."

"Yes, only God knows, and I'll continue to trust Him and His divine timing."

"I have no doubt it will happen for you. You deserve the same love that God has placed within you."

"Thanks, Mike. You've been a great listener and I appreciate you."

"All good, Narra. You taught me a lot on this one phone call."

"Mike, I pray that you will find what you are looking for and that you will find a relationship with God as well in Jesus' name, Amen," I prayed respectfully.

Chapter Four

♥

A Hug from Heaven

*U*sually, I would remain on campus on Saturdays, engaging in school activities and social gatherings. However, I needed to pick up a few things from home, and with church tomorrow, I decided to stay overnight with my parents and my ever-excited dog, who greeted me with enthusiasm even if I had just seen her a day ago.

My home was only a 45-minute drive from Rovane nestled in the charming suburban small town of Locakee, PA, just outside Philadelphia; living with my parents made it easy for me to reach all my favorite spots in the city. On that Saturday afternoon in mid-October, the air felt refreshingly crisp. The streets and grass were filled with swirling dances of hundreds of golden-brown, yellow, and vibrant red maple leaves. The leaves intermingled with earthy dirt and acorns, creating playful circles on the ground alongside oak leaves. As the wind whispered through the trees and the temperature dipped further, it felt as if nature was sealing the deal for a perfect fall day.

As I drove up the winding path to the Potter residence, excitement bubbled within me. I reached for my overnight bag and purse, throwing a glance at the passenger seat that had held my anticipation. I approached the door, and before my hand could knock, I spotted my dog through the vast bay window. She leaped and barked as if the scent of my perfume had already reached her senses, alerting her to my presence before she saw or heard me.

"Hi, my sweet Bonn Bonn," I whispered softly. I pressed the doorbell, announcing my arrival. After a brief moment, I dug my keys from my purse, the sound of metal on metal echoing my eager heartbeat. With a gentle turn of the knob, I unlocked the door and stepped inside, ready to embrace the warmth and comfort of being home again. My mom and stepdad sprang up from the sofa and rushed to me, arms wide open. I was welcomed with a huge group hug, a moment I always cherished.

"We're so happy you're home, Narra!"

"Especially this weekend!" my mom exclaimed.

As an only child, apart from our dog, my parents always seemed delighted to see me.

"Micah and Levi are flying in late tonight from Arizona to visit us. They'll be joining us for Sunday worship service and dinner tomorrow."

"And yes, Narra, the guest room is all set for them, so no worries!" my stepfather, John, assured me.

"I'm thrilled that we'll have a full house tomorrow. It feels like a special event!" my mom added excitedly.

"Oh, that's perfect! I haven't seen them since the wedding. How many years has it been since you two tied the knot?"

"It's been quite a while," my mother replied with enthusiasm.

The timing couldn't have been better. My stepbrothers, Micah and Levi, were both recent graduates and engaged to wonderful women. Being twins, they often shared similar life experiences. I always enjoyed chatting with them on the phone and imagining how the man I marry would be put to the test by them. That thought always made me laugh and reassured me of how much they cared about me and my future. Since they were just 24, a few years older than me, we could easily relate to one another. Having my stepbrothers join us for church was a meaningful experience. The excitement for our Sunday dinner after service made that weekend's visit all the more special.

I'd always envisioned myself marrying a man of faith who embodied kindness and integrity. I often found myself praying earnestly about the character of my future husband, whom I trusted God would bless me with. I dreamed of a partner who shared my values—someone devoted to God, our marriage, and the community. With Levi and Micah around that weekend, I anticipated a fun time, especially as I shared how everything had unfolded with Mike and me. Given their protective nature as my stepbrothers, I could only imagine their reactions to the situation. They might tease me about my dating choices or question what I saw in him. Their light-hearted teasing was expected to infuse our conversations with humor, creating unforgettable moments.

As I hugged my mother again, she asked, "Do you want anything to eat?"

"I'll get something later, Mom. I cannot wait to tell Levi and Micah about Mike."

"Yeah, Narra, I think they should hear about that one," she replied with a grin.

I grabbed my overnight bag, phone, and purse then headed to the basement. Thoughts of Mike lingered in my mind, leaving me to wonder if I made the right decision. I couldn't shake the feeling that I missed him or the idea of a man like him more than I expected. Lost in my thoughts, I stumbled over a dog toy. The squeaking sound, accompanied by my startled gasp and Bonn Bonn dashing quickly behind me, made my parents laugh.

Mike was a good man; he even briefly mentioned God during our conversation, which sparked a pleasing thought in my mind. However, I couldn't shake the feeling that I might be making a mistake in thinking so highly of him.

I gently closed the door—this was home. I spent most of my days unfolded within these walls, turning this space into my own little apartment. After sealing the door, I reached for a bottle of water from the mini-fridge—a modest convenience. Although I lacked a full kitchen and appliances, it was a blessing in disguise, guiding me to share dinners and precious moments

A Hug from Heaven

with my family, weaving us closer together through the quiet poetry of everyday life.

The basement had served as my haven for the past few years, a quiet refuge where I would weave my dreams amidst the shadows. During my past college days, I balanced online classes and a local job, all while living full-time within these familiar walls, journeying through another academic year. I loved being on the bottom floor because I felt I had all the privacy I needed—and so did my parents. My stepfather and mom bought this home a year after they married and it had become the coziest, most beautiful home I'd ever lived in. I loved to believe that my parents were living their best lives.

I threw my belongings onto the coat rack, which wavered like a fragile reed in the wind, nearly surrendering to gravity's pull. Collapsing sideways onto the bed, my phone clutched tightly in one hand, my feet hung over the edge, daring the void. I inhaled deeply, letting the silence swaddle me as I closed my eyes, seeking refuge in stillness. When I finally opened them, the wall clock's hands mocked me with the whisper of—three o'clock!

I must have been utterly exhausted from the drive and the busyness of schoolwork. But now I felt well-rested; honestly, that had been some of the best sleep since the semester began.

I sat on the edge of my bed, grabbed my phone and overnight bag in hand, and began to unpack my sparse belongings. Among them, my fuchsia ink pen and prayer journal caught my eye and I slowly pulled them out, eager to inscribe my thoughts.

This space was where I found solace and clarity. Here, I would pray, write, read the Bible, and study in peaceful solitude, free from interruptions. In this peaceful reverie, I could even cry without fear of being heard. I sometimes wondered if that was a good thing or a bad thing.

In the past, I had occasionally written down short prayers and thoughts. However, after considering that both my stepbrothers were engaged and visiting tonight, along with my power nap, an unexpected spark ignited within me—a desire to pray and to write. Today, a shift; reflections on past loves and heartache, challenging breakups that helped shape me. Through these trials, I'd drawn nearer to God, each hardship a stepping stone on my spiritual journey. This time, I was more mature, understanding the importance of divine order and God's timing. I recognized that my desires were driven by purpose. In recent years, God had gently guided me toward embracing the beauty of my singlehood. I had arrived at a profound realization: my relationship with God held greater importance to me than the pursuit of a husband or a wedding. Though it had been months since I last penned my prayers, my heart had remained engaged in prayerful conversations with Him.

A divine inspiration stirred within me, compelling me to write my prayers not just in silent reflection but as a heartfelt outpouring for my future husband. As I wove my words across the page, my eyes brimmed with joyous tears. With each phrase I read aloud emotion overflowed; a few tears slipped down my cheeks, pooling in the corners of my smile.

As I reached for tissues, some precious tears stained the open pages of my journal, leaving behind a tangible reminder of this moment and the deep feelings it evoked. I was wholeheartedly committed to delighting in a journey that pleased God, confident that He would lead me every step of the way.

My Dearest Heavenly Father,

You are not just a wonderful Father; You are the very core of love and protection in my life. You have shielded my heart from every danger, even those hidden from my awareness. In moments of difficulty, Your gentle guidance has been a beacon of love, cradling me in your peace and presence. For this, my heart swells with gratitude.

From the challenges I have faced, I find myself deeply thankful for the healing that has developed within me. My thoughts are clear, my spirit is settled, and my heart is pure and whole. I am filled with Your divine wisdom, love, and joy.

Father God, You have placed specific desires within my heart about my future husband and marriage, affirming them with Your approval and divine timing. As I wait patiently, please continue to cleanse my soul and heart. I recognize that I will always need daily renewal and refreshing and I am continuously growing as a child of God.

As I bask in Your divine presence, Lord, Holy Father, I whisper my deepest gratitude for the husband You have chosen for me—the one not flawless but lovingly crafted to be my perfect match. My husband reveres You and wholeheartedly trusts in Your divine plan. Though he bears flaws, he remains a great leader and a faithful servant of

Jesus Christ. Right now, he leans on You—a steady hand on life's winding road, especially when the path gets tough.

Heavenly Father, I am deeply thankful for the loving and kind man who shares a profound relationship with Your son, Jesus Christ. He embodies valor, faith, boldness, and strength, and his love enhances my life in indescribable ways.

I earnestly pray that my husband's heart thirsts only for You, dear Father, craving nothing of this world, and that he would not even be thirsty for me as his wife. May his fulfillment and joy be found entirely in You and may I serve to enhance what You have lovingly nurtured within him. I renounce the spirit of lust in the mighty name of Jesus, praying that he finds deep contentment in Your provisions, faithfully trusting in Your divine purpose for his life. May You fill him daily with an abundance of strength in moments of weakness. I stand firm against every demonic force that seeks to rob my husband of his focus, peace, joy, and confidence, in the powerful name of Jesus. I declare that he shall be the man of integrity You have called him to be. I profess that my husband will love deeply: first You, then himself, and finally me. Teach him the values of self-care, self-respect, and self-love so that he may develop discipline and share genuine love with others in the world. May goodness and mercy follow him all the days of his life, as spoken in Your Word. Peace knows his mind, joy knows his name, obedience knows his heart, strength knows his frame, and kindness knows his voice.

God, You know his spirit and soul, where genuine love and patience dwell. May grace and forgiveness be built within him, alongside the fruit of the Spirit planted firmly in his heart. Let him recognize that the same power that raised Jesus Christ from the dead dwells within him.

I decree kindness in his heart, safety in his days, and protection over his mind, body, and spirit. Shield his heart from all that is evil. I pray that You imprint Ephesians 5 upon his heart, gifting him wisdom and understanding, so that he may apply and operate as a godly husband even before we unite.

Teach him how to love as You do. Let him seek You, before and after we get married, irrespective of worldly opinions. May he place his trust in You and me as his wife, opening his spiritual eyes to discern what is of You and what is not. Lord, may he be blessed with discernment to seek guidance solely from spiritual leaders who are true followers of Jesus. As I recognize that we are all imperfect, I ask that You grant me the patience and grace to support my husband through every circumstance, especially through his growth and mistakes. Thank You, Father, for a husband who stands firm against societal pressures, prioritizing Your will and aspiring to be a leader in Your Kingdom.

I pray that he will prioritize You in line with Matthew 6:33: "But seek first the kingdom of God and His righteousness, and all these things shall be added to you." Father, I am profoundly grateful for Your divine protection over my loving and compassionate husband, a man who continually strives to love through You. Thank You, Father, for safeguarding his mental, emotional, physical, spiritual, and financial well-being. May he possess great wisdom, always considering your counsel and ways before making any decisions. Father, I am grateful for Your loving grace as my husband navigates through life's stumbles. As the apostle Paul reminds us in Romans, we all have our moments of weakness and fall short of Your glory. Thank you, Heavenly Father, for showering him with your daily grace and forgiveness. As we embark on this divine marriage, may we both extend that same grace and forgiveness to one another, nurturing our bond each day. Thank you, Lord, for being our most authentic example of love. May my husband grasp that the intimate connection You share with Your children is the perfect reflection of the love we are to embody. I am grateful for a husband drawn to your Word, remaining faithful to You and me, especially during tough times. Father, I thank You for the incredible man You are leading to me, in Your divine timing, as he walks the righteous path You've set before him. I pray for a husband who firmly knows his identity in Christ and discovers his God-given purpose in this life. I also uplift his friends in prayer, asking that they are genuine souls divinely connected to him. Please reveal any influences that stand against Your will for both of us, for they cannot stand in his way. I ask that my husband find a wise mentor who honors You and that one day he becomes a great mentor himself, guiding the younger generation and nurturing our future children. I declare he will be a wonderful father, instilling godly characteristics in our children to come. I pray You weave your heart, character, and patience within me as I aspire to be a Proverbs 31 wife—a woman of noble character whom my husband will cherish and appreciate. May compassion be a cornerstone of our relationship, eternally binding us in love.

Thank You, Lord, for protecting my husband's heart, mind, spirit, and body as he navigates life's challenges. I declare that worry, fear, doubt, and anger shall have no place in him. Surround him with those who uplift and hold him accountable, who will pray for him even as they witness his transformation into a stronger man. Resilient men

A Hug from Heaven

of faith will support him, and I pray he reciprocates the kindness he receives, nurturing his divine friendships. Teach him to protect me with the same fervor and passion with which You protect him. I trust in Your promise to secure his safety in all aspects of his life, granting us the strength to grow together in love and unity.

May our hearts overflow with compassion and gratitude as we commit ourselves to serving each other faithfully, fulfilling our divine purposes in this sacred union. I pray my husband leads me with profound love, grace, and discernment, nurturing the bond that we share. Teach him the spirit of humility, allowing him to embody discipline and holiness, as we journey together through life's joys and trials. Whenever temptation, anxiety, or sadness threatens his joy, Holy Father, empower him to rise above every challenge, sending each trial back into the pit of hell. Together, may we build a love that reflects Your grace, deepening in affection and unity with every passing day. May he seek help and godly counsel rather than worldly distractions, recognizing You as his one true provider and the source of all his desires, aligned with Your will. May he strive to please You above the opinions of others, guiding our marriage in a way that not only strengthens our bond but also draws others toward a relationship with Christ. Let him hunger and thirst for righteousness, aiming to maintain a healthy body, mind, lifestyle, and marriage, taking action; as we know, faith without works is dead. And Lord, may he always be handsome in my sight, his presence a source of joy and admiration.

Let prayer be the heartbeat of our lives, reminding us to pray together and for one another every day. The demons will tremble at my husband's unwavering faith and ability to pray. I pray he hears Your voice clearly, as Your Word reminds us in John 10:27, "My sheep hear My

voice, and I know them, and they follow Me." May our journey in
marriage draw us closer to You as we create a romance that mirrors
the divine love You have for us. Thank You, Lord! Hallelujah! I seal
these divine prayers in Jesus' name, Amen.

I got a text from my mom at approximately 10:40 p.m.

Micah and Levi are in the family room asking for you!

Yay! On my way, I replied.

As I rushed up the stairs, skipping a few of them, I could already hear their laughter echoing through the house. I could only imagine how excited they must be after their late-night flight. As I ran in, I was greeted by a warm group hug, feeling the excitement in the air. Micah was the first to share his news, and I couldn't wait to hear about the new women in their lives. I'd been hoping to be at their wedding, praying that I'd have a plus-one by then. While they unpacked, I helped them settle in, chatting away in the guest bedroom as we soaked in all the details of their adventures and the new chapters ahead.

"So, Narra, what's this I hear about the guy you were recently dating?"

"Yeah, he actually seems nice. It sounded like y'all were getting pretty serious."

"Nah, not that serious; I barely even touched the guy."

"Hmm…"

A Hug from Heaven

"I hear you were in love." They both laughed.

"Ha, ha, ha, I was not in love, but he gave me all the feels of something close to love."

"So, what happened?" they asked together, eyes flickering with curiosity.

"You're both doing that twin thing again!" Laughter bubbled up among us as we shared the moment.

I shared with them all about Mike and how he was a really nice guy, but just not the one for me.

"I liked him a whole lot, but he is not the husband or man for me. Enough about me! I saw both of your new wives-to-be on your socials, and they're both gorgeous."

"Yes, you'll meet them soon, Narra," Micah replied.

"They are eager to meet Dad and Mom, too," Levi added. "Okay, so your mom told us most of the details. Here's our take on it... Seriously, we heard you were hurt by it. Let's have a little heart-to-heart, shall we, Narra?"

Micah smiled fondly, saying, "Let's have a convo like we used to back in the day."

My eyes lit up. "Like a Q&A?"

Levi chimed in, his voice ringing with excitement, "Class is in session!"

"Did you love him?" Micah asked.

"No, I had love for him," I replied gently.

"Was he kind?"

"Mike is very kind."

"Were you friends first?"

"Still friends, but yes."

"Narra, you did the right thing. Who God has for you will not lack what you need in a husband," Micah said.

"You need God to be within your husband," Levi continued, and I nodded in agreement, a warm smile spreading across my face.

Levi stated, "I'm proud of you, Narra. You know your worth. You're a godly wife in progress, and God has what you desire."

"Oh, how these words fill my heart! You have no idea how much this conversation means to me. Earlier, I felt a twinge of loneliness and regret, thinking perhaps I'd made a mistake."

"Nah, you did well," Levi said, walking toward the door, removing his "Prayed For Pray With Apparel" hoodie. "I need to grab something cold to drink. Be right back!"

Micah nodded. "I've been through something similar before. The girl was stunningly beautiful!" he recalled, rolling his eyes dramatically. "She was soft, kind, and educated—truly, she had what I thought was the whole package. But she was missing a relationship with God. Not that it was the be-all and end-all. I would have given her more grace. Yet, I hadn't seen anything change; nor did she want to make any changes. It was her choice, and I could never force someone to change for me. They have to seek God for themselves."

"Amen, brother!" I agreed wholeheartedly.

"But then I found my fiancée, Lorianna—the future Mrs. Micah Potter. I'm so thankful God saved her for me," he said, his eyes shining with genuine happiness.

"That's beautiful, Bro," I replied, feeling the warmth of his love radiate.

"Bro, you and Lorianna are perfect for each other," Levi said as he walked back into the room, reaffirming the joy in Micah's heart.

"Yes, Narra," Micah assured me. "There's a guy out there for you—someone who will be just right."

"I can't express how grateful I am for you both, the living examples of what a young man of God looks like today. You've shown me your true selves—both your struggles and your strength—while demonstrating the divine truth of who God says you are."

"All good, little Sis."

The following day, as the church service approached, we gathered in anticipation to worship together, our hearts buoyed by hope. The Sunday service was a beautiful experience, filling my parents with pure joy. Back home, we indulged in more precious family moments. With a playful sparkle, Micah whispered, "Next time I see you, Narra, it might just be at my wedding."

"Oh really? That's in about four months. I never received a save-the-date," I replied, pretending to pout.

"My bad! I thought Mom would make sure you got it." He shrugged, a playful smile on his lips.

"I hope I'll have a plus-one with me when I show up," I said, a hopeful smirk spreading across my face. "But I'll keep you posted if anything changes."

That evening, I gathered my belongings and then I returned to campus early the next morning, just hours before my first class. I relished a brief moment of tranquility, treating myself to a delicious breakfast sandwich from a charming local café, feeling invigorated and ready to embrace the day ahead. As I prepared to see Mike in class, a bittersweet wave washed over me as I gently released the dream of us being together. After heartfelt prayers and cherished moments with my family, I had found solace in knowing that I was more than capable of nurturing my relationship with God, enjoying where I was in life presently, and dedicating myself to my studies as graduation approached.

"Hi Narra!" I heard as I settled into my seat a bit early, hoping he wouldn't be there, yet a part of me was glad he was. The classroom buzzed softly around us, the air filled with the anticipation of shared glances and unspoken words. My heart raced slightly, a mix of hope and nervousness coursing through me as I prepared for another day filled with the unpredictable ebb and flow of our connection.

"Hey, Michael."

"You don't know me anymore?" he asked, his voice laced with concern. "I'm sorry if I hurt you in any way, Narra."

"What do you mean, Michael? I'm fine."

"Why'd you stop answering my texts? I thought we would for sure remain friends."

"We are still friends: 'Friends with boundaries.'"

"I like that saying. All good." He chuckled. "But seriously, I'd love to make it up to you, Narra."

"I promise, I'm fine," I insisted, though my heart raced at his words.

"Narra, I still care for you a lot, more than I should," he murmured, his gaze penetrating my defenses. He was in sweet-talking mode again and the memories of his embrace swamped me.

Don't fall for it, Narra, I scolded myself silently.

"You are so beautiful and I can't stop thinking about you," he continued, his voice smooth and inviting. I tried to drown him out by burying my face in a pile of papers, flipping through pages as if searching for something crucial.

"Narra, I know you feel something more," he pressed, his tone earnest.

"Well, I'm actually feeling better about everything now," I replied, striving to keep my composure despite the flutter in my chest.

"Well, why won't you make eye contact with me anymore?"

I summoned the courage to look deep into Michael's eyes and said, "I'm okay now, Mike. Please don't worry about me or try to make it up to me."

"Okay, I got it, Narra, but please don't hate me."

"I would never hate you. I just need to stay focused on graduating, so maybe this is for the best."

"I completely understand," he said.

As class time drew near, I chatted with Lena to catch her up on a few things.

"Girl, Michael has been all over you. What'd you do to that man?"

"Nothing but cut him off and tell him we should just remain friends."

"Girl, he's asked about you. I think he really likes you, maybe even loves you. Y'all would make such a cute couple."

"Thanks, but I'm over it. Over him in the most humbling way. No bad feelings. We will remain friends."

Lena chuckled softly, her eyes alight with mischief. "Girl, you have to spill everything!"

"Lena, you crack me up! Michael is incredible, but as I mentioned a few weeks back, he's just not the one for me. I can see him being a wonderful partner to someone else someday, though. For now, I need to keep my focus," I replied, a touch of wistfulness in my voice, lost in thoughts about what could have been.

I hesitated to tell Lena about the deep yearning stirring inside me—to hug him and melt into his embrace. He was irresistibly attractive, so incredibly handsome that I found it difficult to hold his gaze; it felt like a magnetic pull drawing me closer, especially when I looked into those captivating green eyes. I had to be strong — it wasn't just the whole relationship with God thing. Michael was a distraction. He said all the right things and did some sweet things, but that didn't mean he was meant for me. Something vital was missing. Although I yearned for his embrace, we were not spiritually aligned. For now, we would remain friends and classmates. In the quiet moments of my heart, I trusted that God intimately understood my deepest desires. He knew precisely what I yearned for in each season of my life, guiding me gently towards love and fulfillment with every heartbeat.

Chapter Five

Fueled for a Fruitful Future

"*D*em, I need you to come home as soon as possible and meet me at the hospital."

My mom's frantic voice echoed in my ears, her words tumbling out quickly like a rushing river. It was a Monday in early October when I received that urgent call. "Mom, wait ... slow down. What's happening?"

"It's your father. He's in the hospital; he fell badly, and I'm on my way to see him right now at Angel's ER." Hearing the news about my dad and the worry in my mom's voice made it clear this was serious. A wave of nervousness and anxiety swept over me.

"Okay, Mom! I'll be there in about forty minutes." I could hear her sobbing quietly, and I fought back my own tears, saying, "I'm on my way. I love you, Mom. Everything will be alright."

After that talk with my mother, I decided to go home and stay through the weekend. I took a short break, a few days to breathe and to submit my assignments online in the upcoming days.

After gathering my laptop, keys, and a few personal belongings, I headed to the hospital.

At the Angel Medical Hospital's ER entrance, security's watchful eye greeted me. "Sir, could you tell me what room Robert Foxer is in?"

"Could I see your ID?" the receptionist asked in a gentle tone. I offered my identification and details, standing still for a heartbeat. "Demery Foxer?" I looked up. "Robert Foxer rests in room 303," she said, her voice a whisper of news.

Upon exiting the elevator on the third floor, I heard some vague sounds coming from a room. As I approached, the sounds became clearer—it was my mother praying for my dad. As the door was slightly ajar, I chose to stand quietly outside, respecting their moment of prayer. It was a powerful and moving experience. I could hear my mom specifically praying for my dad's physical, mental, and spiritual well-being. Her passion and sincerity reminded me of our discussions about the importance of companionship. In her prayer, I genuinely sensed the love of a Proverbs 31 wife, which is what I aspired to have in my own marriage one day.

Three days had passed since my father's return from the hospital to home, where he now rested, bathed in healing light. Today, I stood beside him and my mom, pillars of love and strength. My mother, a tireless soul, balanced the weight of her world— her career as a senior project manager at Waxy Tech and the tender care of my father. During those first two days after his return, I was her shadow—cleaning the yard, doing laundry, running errands filled with hope, and driving him to the doctor's visits while she managed her busy day. Waxy Tech, a beacon of innovation about 30 minutes away, was where my mother crafted her dreams amidst the hum of progress. In the initial days, I managed to find time to study and submit an assignment that was due. Additionally, I made it a point to read my Bible daily and enjoyed insightful conversations with my dad during our car rides. With today being relatively calmer, I chose to head to work at the ice cream shop early in the morning, which was typically when I would be in class. After finishing work, I headed to the gym. It was leg day, and I had an intense yet satisfying workout. I returned home just before evening and walked into the kitchen, where my Mom and Dad were having dinner. "I come bearing gifts!" I announced.

"Hey, Son! Did you have a good workout? You're walking like you really pushed it with those legs!"

"I whipped up some fresh vegan vanilla ice cream at the shop for you both. It's never been frozen—just perfectly chilled!" I chuckle and reply, "Yeah, Dad. Leg day beat me up, but I feel great!"

"Thanks, Dem! You're such a good son, always thinking of us," my mom replied gratefully.

"Of course, Mom! No problem at all."

"Once I take off this boot and get off crutches, I can go back to my regular workout routine." My dad had a small workout area in our basement where he regularly lifted weights, but he had to pause until he was fully healed.

After a refreshing shower and a hearty dinner of smothered shrimp and rice, lovingly prepared by my mother, I retreated to my prayer room for peaceful reflection before heading to campus in a few days. Observing my parents face challenges with calmness and kindness had deeply influenced me, inspiring ongoing reflections and a heartfelt desire to pray for my future wife and the marriage we would build together. I desired for my prayers to be selfless, guided not merely by my own wants but by genuine care and love.

I settled onto the soft carpet of my prayer room, holding my cellphone in my hand. As I opened the voice memo app, I pressed play to capture my heartfelt prayer, ensuring that the sincerity of this moment wouldn't fade away and could be transcribed later. I settled against the wall, slipping into a reclined repose, my arms lifted as tears traced silent paths down my cheeks. With a trembling voice, I poured out my heart: "Dear Heavenly Father, thank You for this precious day. I am deeply grateful for You never-ending grace and the forgiveness You provide for my sins each day. I treasure the fresh mindset and renewed heart that You grant me through my trust in You and Your perfect timing, oh Lord. Today, I offer a heartfelt prayer for my wife, inspired by Your spirit, dear Father.

"In this sacred moment, I humbly ask You to fill me with Your Holy Spirit. I pray for a woman who exemplifies boldness in her prayers and possesses a radiant spirit that brightens every space she graces. She has a compassionate heart and is deeply invested in the souls for whom You care, God. Her life is marked by unwavering obedience to You, Lord; this dedication has become second nature to her. When she speaks, may her words be gentle, flowing with the law of kindness, reflecting the love and compassion that You inspire in her. May she adorn herself with the bountiful fruit of the Spirit—love, joy, kindness, patience, and enduring grace. May she carry the wisdom of discernment in every chapter of her life, steering clear of counterfeit love and friendships that do not serve her well. I declare healing over her mental, physical, and emotional state right now, Father.

"Grant her the trust to lean into You and embrace Your divine plans. May she choose faith over fear in every decision. Speak tenderly to her heart, reassuring her that I will stand beside her when the time is right. May she embrace Your timing wholeheartedly, even if she hasn't in the past. Lord, gift her with a pure heart. Let her intentions concerning marriage and her career be bright and pleasing in your sight. I pray that my wife walks in boldness of spirit and that every encounter reveals Jesus's light shining through her.

"May she feel no anxiety or desperation for love, not even for me, her future husband. Shape me into the man she dreams of, the husband she deserves. May she lovingly nurture our future children, and may I be her unwavering support. May we parent as a harmonious unit, united in purpose and love, never against each other. Allow me to stand as the priest of our home, faithfully walking in Your footsteps and teaching from Your Word with a heart full of love. Father, mold us into true disciples, teaching us the depth of loving one another as You command. Let there be no secrets, no lies, but a true partnership in every respect. Together, we will build a safe and secure marriage, a loving home founded on You, our unshakeable foundation. May we both discover the beauty of sacrificing for one another, even in challenging times, and may our hearts embrace forgiveness daily as You have shown us, dear God.

"Help us, as devoted partners, to have a heart to serve You and each other, submitting with love and grace. May we be open to shedding the old ways of loving and living, welcoming Your divine truth found in the Bible. Together, may we build our lives upon You, creating a sanctuary of safety and health, cherishing and nurturing every precious blessing You have graciously granted upon us. Guide her journey, O Lord, and let our paths beautifully intertwine with Your Word, transcending worldly distractions. Reveal her inherent worth to me before I even lay eyes on her, and may I recognize the divine spark within her when our souls meet on this sacred journey toward righteousness. I pray that our hearts will cherish and treasure the moments spent in Bible study, prayer, and worshipping You together. She's a praying wife; I truly believe it. Thank You, Jesus! But may we understand what it truly means to worship You.

"Thank you for wrapping her in Your gentle grace as she grows. May she come to know her worth through Your loving embrace, understanding that her identity is beautifully intertwined with her relationship with You. I declare and affirm that all my heartfelt prayers will come to fruition in Your perfect timing, my Lord. In Jesus' name, Amen."

I made my way to my knees and reached for my phone to stop the recording. After saving my prayer, I began to worship God.

With my hands raised and no music playing, I was overwhelmed by His grace; tears of gratitude flowed as I reflected on my dad's improvement. I expressed my thankfulness for life and for the opportunity to know, love, and live for Him. I grabbed my Bible from the shelf behind me and started to read. Before I realized it, I began to drift off, lying flat again just to bask in God's presence. I woke up the next morning in my prayer room feeling refreshed, revived, and ready to embrace the day and everything the weekend had to offer.

Chapter Six

In Your Dreams, Dem

*T*wo days later, I returned to campus. After finishing our classes for the day, Benny, Chris, and I gathered outside my dorm, waiting for Aaron to join us before heading to the Fester Den dining hall.

As we leaned against the wall, my friend Chris Plemming, a senior I'd known since middle school, broke the silence. "You know, school is a bit harder for me this semester," he said, his expression a mix of hope and seriousness. "I feel overwhelmed by the growing amount of work, especially with all my physics papers." My friend Benny Reese, a junior, nodded in agreement. I also shared my struggles as a junior, mentioning that while this semester had been challenging, I was grateful for the moments spent laughing and hanging out with friends. Together, we navigated the ups and downs of our academic lives, finding comfort in our shared experiences. Chris asked, "Did you see Mr. Smith's shirt?"

"Yes, it looked like it was from the eighties," I replied.

"Nah, I missed it," Benny said.

"It was oversized and had boxy neon pink and green shapes. It was horrible."

As we joked and laughed together, my eyes drifted upward, and I saw the most beautiful girl I had ever seen walking gracefully by. It wasn't just her striking appearance that captivated me; it was the elegance and poise that truly drew me in. As she walked, her hair, initially secured in a neat bun, danced free when she removed her hair tie, flowing into beautiful curls that caught the sunlight. She wore a simple outfit: a fitted navy blue Rovane University T-shirt, complemented by classic light blue denim jeans that fit her perfectly, and cozy brown slides. A silver cross necklace, catching the light with every step, added a hint of grace.

In that moment, she radiated a magnetic charm, drawing everyone's gaze. Her presence was irresistible; it was not just her beauty but the way she carried herself with grace that captured not only attention but deep admiration. "Who is that?" I asked, my voice barely above a whisper.

"Who, the girl right there?" Benny replied, his eyes following my gaze, clearly having never seen her before but caught off guard by her presence.

"Yes, who is she?" My initial curiosity quickly evolved into an urgent desire to learn more.

"Who, Narra?" came a sarcastic voice from behind me, startling me. Though the tone was light, I could detect a trace of intrigue. It was my friend, Aaron WessWood.

"Aaron, you scared me!" I exclaimed, still trying to gather my thoughts.

"So that's her name?" I continued, feeling a flicker of hope ignite within me—the kind of excitement one feels upon discovering a hidden treasure on an otherwise ordinary day.

As I watched her walk, the sunlight painted her in various shades of gold, lightening her features and making her look heavenly. A sudden wind swept through, catching her curls and sending them skipping around her shoulders, and in that moment, it was as if the same wind caught me spiritually, my heart racing. My friends' laughter faded into the background as everything around me blurred into nothingness for a moment.

"Is she a freshman? What is her major?" I couldn't help but ask, grasping for any detail that could lead me closer to her.

"Narra's a senior," Chris interjected, finally breaking his silence. "She's been at Rovane since her freshman year, though I don't recall seeing her at all last semester."

I noted that she would be graduating soon. Still, an unshakable feeling lingered within me: she was different and there was a story behind her eyes—a narrative I yearned to uncover. As she turned slightly and glanced in my direction, our eyes met for the briefest of moments, but it felt like an eternity.

"Yes, that's her name. And please put your tongue back in your mouth," Aaron joked.

Benny and Chris both began laughing hysterically, bringing me back to reality.

"Yes, bro, you're basically drooling," Chris said, agreeing with Aaron. "She's definitely a baddie," he added.

"I've never seen her on campus before, but I'd love to see her again," Benny remarked. Aaron replied playfully, "The only chance you'll have to get close to her is if you're one of the twelve disciples. She's a 'church girl' who loves the Lord and is too holy to talk to us."

"I suppose I'm out since I don't go to church, but I do believe in a higher power," Benny remarked, shrugging his shoulders.

"Our Father, God, is the creator and Jesus is Lord and Savior!" I said, staring directly at Benny.

"Okay, Deacon Demery," Benny said, chuckling.

"Haha, good one! You've got jokes."

"Whatever, man, I'm hungry. Let's grab a bite to eat," Benny said.

"When are you not hungry?" I sarcastically asked as we all laughed out loud.

As we inched toward the dining hall, we passed a group of girls, one of whom was staring directly at me and smiling. She said, "Hi, handsome." I waved and said hello, then continued walking. Aaron and Chris started a flirty conversation with the girls.

"Can I talk to you for a moment?" Chris asked one of them.

She glanced at him with disdain and said, "No thanks, I have a boyfriend."

"What's your name?" Aaron asked a different girl.

"Jess," she replies. "Can I help you?"

"I'm A Wess and I was hoping to borrow your cell phone. Jess and A Wess have a nice ring to it!" he adds.

"What do you mean? Don't you have a phone? Everyone owns a cell phone," she replied with a hint of sarcasm.

"I left mine in my dorm."

With a slight smirk, she reluctantly handed Aaron her phone. "Thank you," he said, entering his name and number into her contacts.

"Call me!" he said, handing Jess her phone back. She smiled at his audacity.

We finally arrived at the Fester Den dining hall, laughing about our different methods of approaching girls. I was the more relaxed one.

"I think that girl back there liked you, Dem. Why didn't you get her number?" Aaron asked.

"I'm good. No, thank you. If I had wanted to, I would have gotten her number without a problem."

"Yeah, we all know you're picky about girls," Benny joked as we all sat down at our table after grabbing our food.

Aaron chimed in with a mouthful of cheese pizza, "Yeah, you think you can get any girl you want, huh? You've always been a little arrogant in that department. I blame your parents for spoiling you your whole life."

"Don't talk about my boy like that! It's not his fault!" Chris defended jokingly.

"Yeah, whatever you say," I replied. "But my mind is stuck on Narra. There's something about her that I just can't shake. I'm not even considering any other girls at the moment, no matter who they are."

"Oh, he even remembers her name!" Aaron said with a sarcastic tone.

"Even if it was Beyoncé?" Benny asked.

"Nope! I just found my 'Narra.'"

"In your dreams, Dem. She's out of your league," Benny said.

"Okay. Enough, y'all."

Chapter Seven

─── ♥ ───

Maybe This Could Work Out

"Blessed, Blessed." I sang along to one of my favorite upbeat gospel songs by Fred Hammond as it played softly from the speakers. My windows were down on both the driver's and passenger's sides of my sleek, charcoal 2011 Mercedes-Benz, a gift from my parents last year. When I pulled up to the gym, I snagged one of the last spots in the packed parking lot. Before I jumped out, I grabbed my gym bag from the back seat. As I rolled into the gym and headed to an available machine, I resumed my playlist on my phone and began my ab workout. I was facing a big glass window that looked out over the cardio area. With my clear, transparent wireless earbuds snug in my ears, they blended in seamlessly, making them easy to overlook unless someone was close by.

As I exercised, focusing on my arms, my gaze wandered to a pair of warm, inviting, honey-brown eyes quietly observing me. Every time our eyes met, she would shyly look away, a hint of bashfulness painting her demeanor. Her cell phone, dressed in a simple pink cover emblazoned with the name JESUS in bold, italicized black letters, teased at the nature of her personality. It seemed as though she was either deeply engaged in texting or carefully selecting her next song. Just as she readied herself to step onto the treadmill, taking care to watch her footing, our eyes met for a brief encounter. In that heartbeat, warmth surged through me, igniting a palpable spark of connection that was impossible to ignore. I couldn't help but smile broadly, my heart racing as I flashed a genuine grin. I was known as the bold one among my friend group, unreservedly proud of my faith in Jesus Christ and always willing to share my thoughts respectfully; yet, in her mesmerizing presence, a flutter of nerves took hold of me. She was elegant, truly stunning—the most beautiful woman I had ever seen.

Only a week before, I'd caught a glimpse of her at school while hanging out with the guys, but to see her here in the gym felt profoundly different—more intimate and personal. My heart raced and I found myself whispering, "Thank you, Jesus!" A wave of hope filled my voice, hoping that this encounter could blossom into something more, should she be single. Her disarming smile revealed the most beautiful teeth, made even more charming by her blue-silver band braces. As I tried to focus on her captivating face, my gaze inevitably roamed her entire form. I prided myself on my boldness, but I also knew the importance of respect in my interactions—a lesson deeply ingrained by my parents. Even as I wrestled with my desire to admire her, her beauty remained irresistibly alluring. Despite her intense workout, an enchanting aura radiated from her, evident in every graceful movement. When my eyes fell upon the word "hope" emblazoned on her shirt, a warm smile instinctively spread across my face.

I approached her corner, feigning a need to refill my water bottle, and softly said, "I truly hope you find everything you desire in your workout today." I couldn't tell if she heard me over her music, but to my delight, she turned toward me with a slight smile. After a brief moment of connection, she hopped off the treadmill for a water break. Sensing the opportunity, I decided to take her place on the treadmill she had just vacated, my heart fluttering with unmistakable anticipation.

"Hey!" she called out. "Don't you see my gym bag and my things? I wasn't finished with that machine."

"Oh, right. But you took too long, and I wanted to get in some cardio," I replied.

"I'm not done yet, and there are other machines available," she said, pointing slowly with a smirk.

"Okay, okay. I'm getting off now. My bad," I conceded.

"No worries," she responded softly as she walked to the side of the treadmill, gathered her things, and reached for her phone from the cup holder.

"Hey, I noticed you at school the other day, but it's the first time I've seen you at the gym—I practically live here," I continued, trying to keep the conversation flowing.

"Yeah, I've noticed you hanging out with Aaron WessWood and the crew, right?"

"Yeah, those are my boys! So, you've noticed me, too, huh?"

"Yeah, I definitely noticed you."

"You were checking me out, huh?"

We exchanged playful glances, the atmosphere buzzing with intrigue and attraction. Ignoring my flirtation, she replied, "I overheard you destroying— I mean singing— one of my favorite gospel songs super loudly just a few minutes ago."

"Oh yeah? I didn't realize I was singing so loudly." I chuckled, nervously glancing around before settling into her beautiful, soft honey eyes. This girl was melting me from the inside, leaving me stuttering. "So, how … how … how … come I haven't seen you here before?"

"Yeah, you shouldn't sing so loudly if you sound like that."

"As long as I sound good in God's ears, I'm all good."

"Is that right?" she softly murmured, lowering her eyes to meet mine as she studied me closely.

"Yes, that's right. The most important opinion about my singing is God's."

Narra smiled and nodded in agreement. "Hmm, that's actually beautiful. I love that," she said.

I felt like that was our moment. We both laughed heartily as we grabbed our gym bags and headed to the door. I hurried ahead to hold the door open for her. "Thanks, sir!"

"Sir?" I responded, taken aback. "Wait, I never introduced myself. My apologies. I'm Dem Foxer and I attend Rovane U!" I said, extending my hand for a handshake, my eyes never leaving hers.

"Yeah, I remember. I saw you on campus the other day. I'm Narra. Well, it has been a pleasure meeting you, Dem," she said, gently shaking my hand while maintaining eye contact.

We both walked in different directions toward our cars in the parking lot. I auto-started my car, realizing my music was cranked up a bit too high. The same song resumed playing from where I had left off on my phone. Narra turned around, her smile brightening when she caught me squinting against the sunlight while looking in her direction.

I quickly lowered the volume on my phone's Bluetooth and checked the rear-view mirror, hoping to catch another glimpse of Narra or at least see what kind of car she drove.

As I drove through the parking lot, I spotted her checking under her car's hood. *I have to make sure she's okay*, I thought, backing into a space next to her car.

"You need a jump?" I called out as I rolled the window down a little more. "I've got jumper cables in the back."

"Thanks, Dem, but my stepfather is handling everything for me," she replied, worriedly, typing rapidly on her cell phone. "I might need to get my car serviced. It's been giving me problems for quite some time now."

"Well, you know I won't leave you stranded here, Narr."

"Narr?" she replied in shock with a slight grin. "Oh, are we on nickname terms now?"

"Well, you called me Dem, right?"

"That's the name you told me."

"Now, can I give you a ride? I think we're both headed back to campus, right?"

"You got it. Good thing I saw you the other day, or else I wouldn't have been so quick to accept a ride from you."

"Don't worry, you're safe with me."

"Let me grab my things and lock up my car. My stepdad has an extra set of keys and will get it towed."

I hurried out of my car to help Narra with her things, then opened the passenger door for her. "Should I put these in the back seat?"

"Works for me," she replied with a low, friendly voice as she settled into my car.

"What a beautifully clean and lovely car, Dem," I heard, accompanied by the soft click of our seatbelts fastening, creating an intimate moment between us. Our eyes meet by chance, and a playful smile spreads on my lips.

"Oh, this old thing, but thanks, Narra! So, you never answered my question. Why haven't I seen you at the gym or on campus before?"

"Ha! You asked about the gym, not Rovane, but okay. Well, if you must know, I completed online assignments during the last academic year."

"Oh, cool. And the gym?"

"You are something else, Dem."

"I'm really interested."

"In me or the gym?"

"Both," I said, glancing over at her and then back at the road as we approached the main entrance of campus, the air thick with unspoken words and a lingering connection between us.

"I also need to know the name of your hall. I promise I won't stalk you or do anything weird. I just don't want you to walk too far with all your belongings."

"I'm at that one," she said, pointing at Stream Valley Residence Hall.

"Okay, so you're an SV girl, huh? I'm over at LV Hall."

"Lake Valley?"

"Yes, that's right. It's not far at all. I can't believe I've never seen you around here before."

"Well, to be fair, it's just the beginning of the academic year and there are quite a few new faces around."

"Also, I'll take care of everything with your car. I know a great mechanic who is available. I texted him before we drove off. He'll take care of it since he's close by."

"That's okay, my stepdad will be heading this way soon. You really don't have to do that; I'm good, thanks!"

"Narra, you can trust me. I got you, girl," I said as I looked at her, sitting in the residence parking lot close to SV hall.

"Okay, I feel like you won't take no for an answer."

"You catch on quickly!" I teased her with a playful smile, my heart pounding at the possibility of what could be between us.

"Here, please add your name and number to my phone so we can talk about your car situation," I said, handing my phone to Narra.

"Just ask me for my number, Dem."

I gazed at her with an adoring sense of possibility. "Narra Jones, may I have your number so we can talk later tonight? I'd love to take you out on a date in a few days," I said, striving to contain my excitement.

"You can totally have my number!" she exclaimed.

My eyes must have lit up like a Christmas tree.

"I'd love to chat about my car and I truly appreciate your kindness in helping me; it means a lot to me," she added, flashing a warm smile. "Wait, how do you know my last name? It sounds like you've been doing a little too much research on me," she said, a playful smile skipping over her lips as she raised an eyebrow.

"Not really. The guys mentioned a few things about you," I replied, matching her teasing tone.

"Wow, I had no idea they even knew my last name." Her eyes sparkled with curiosity.

"You seem too sweet and kind to be single," Narra said, her stare lingering on me.

"One thousand percent single," I replied, trying to maintain my serious demeanor, though warmth crept into my voice. "I know you mentioned one of your favorite gospel songs earlier. I'd love to hear more about the Christian songs on your playlist."

"Oh, you're speaking my language, Dem," Narra said, her enthusiasm palpable as she nodded eagerly.

"I'll talk to you in a few," she said, her voice laced with anticipation as she stepped out of the car, graciously allowing me to hold the door open for her.

"Okay, I'll call you later once I have more info about your car situation," I replied. Her smile lingered in my mind long after she had walked away.

A few minutes later, as I reached for my gym bag on my way to my dorm, I noticed Narra had left her headphones behind. I immediately texted her, letting her know I'd bring them to her after I showered and settled in.

Cool! Or you could keep them and toss them in my car. I have an extra pair with me somewhere; I just need to look around for them. But thanks! she replied, her kindness making me smile.

I'll text you in a little while to see if I can bring the headphones, I added, eager to help. It was just past 7:30 p.m. and I'd just finished showering, feeling fresh and invigorated. I took a moment to text Narra again: *I'll be there in a few minutes, if that works for you.*

Okay, that works.

Minutes later, I sent a second message, anticipation hanging in the cool evening air. *Hey Narr, I'm outside in the parking lot.*

Moments later, she appeared. I saw her rushing down a few steps near the parking lot toward my car with a warm smile, coming to grab her headphones, her RU navy sweatshirt contrasting perfectly with her white carefree shorts. As I was about to jump out of the car, she stopped me, pressed firmly on the door, and said, "I appreciate you, Dem. Any word about my car?" Her eyes glittered with interest.

"Yes, it's all good. It should take no more than two days. By the way, I need the keys to your car. Is that okay?" My heart was racing at the thought of prolonging our time together.

"How did I forget the keys? My apologies." Her laugh was light and genuine, like music to my ears.

"It's all good, Narr. I just wanted to find another reason to see you before the night ends," I replied, a hint of boldness in my voice and no doubt hope visible in my eyes.

"That can work. I'll stick around campus more this week to make sure I'm available to pick up my car," she said with a playful grin. "You're so slick with your words, Dem. And honestly, I kind of like it," she confessed, her voice teasing yet sincere.

"I'm trying my best," I replied, feeling warmth spread through me.

"Well, you don't have to try too hard," she countered, leaning in slightly, her presence warm and inviting, just like the glow in her eyes that drew me closer spiritually.

"Can I be honest with you, Dem?" she asked, her eyes secure within mine, drawing me in with a depth so profound that it felt like we were wrapped in God's presence together.

"Sure! Would you like to hang out for a bit?" I asked, keen to embrace this opportunity. I stepped out of the car and leaned against its cool surface while the evening air wrapped around us like a gentle lullaby. The weather was nice, perfect for a chat. We both found comfort leaning against my car, the hush of her residence wrapping us in quiet intimacy.

I noticed we both kept stealing glances at each other. "There's something about your presence that I felt from the moment I laid eyes on you," I whispered softly, my voice filled with warm courage.

"Well, okay then, what I'm about to say should not sound too strange," she said, reaching into the back pocket of her shorts to retrieve her keys. She detached the car key and its fob from the ring, gently handing them to me. The soft clinking of the keys added a lightness to the moment. "Honestly, I haven't stopped thinking about you since you dropped me off earlier. It's not only because you're helping with my car," she confessed, trying to keep her tone light yet sincere. "There's something about you that I can't quite put my finger on yet."

"I think I know, but I'll give you some time to ponder that. Haha," I confidently stated.

As I continued, I searched her eyes. "I know it's super early and we just met, but I really like you, Narr." I took her hands in mine, holding them gently as I stood in front of her, embodying my gentlemanly nature. I could see her blush deepening, her cheeks flushed with warmth and surprise as the moment hung between us, charged with unspoken feelings.

"I'm not this way normally, Dem, I promise," she said, her huge smile brightening the moment. "I feel something stirring inside me, just as you described.

"I'm honestly in shock," she continued, her voice trembling with excitement. "What's happening, Dem?"

"I don't know much about you, but I want you to know—" I paused, my eyes resting within the physical and spiritual connection of her gaze, "—I will never hurt you. I want to learn about you and who you are as a woman in Christ."

"That's so sweet, Dem. I can sense your faith; you're a man of God."

"You're right," I replied softly, raising the volume on my phone just enough for us to hear the gentle worship music softly filling the car, creating an intimate atmosphere.

Gently letting go of her hands, I stepped back to stand beside her, wanting to keep things comfortable. She smiled and said, "This is one of my favorite worship songs."

"I love this song!"

"Me too."

We began to sing together, gracefully swaying our heads to the rhythm, completely lost in the moment's intimacy. A group of people walked by, their laughter creating a joyful atmosphere, yet we remained absorbed entirely on our own little cloud of potential. Before we knew it, an hour had passed as we shared our favorite tracks, books, personal journeys with Jesus, and a few heartfelt testimonies about how God had been good in our lives. We noticed campus security quietly passing by, their alert eyes unblinking. Yet, they chose peace rather than cause any disturbance as we quietly enjoyed our moment.

Just then, Narra's phone buzzed—she got a call from her parents. "I'm sorry, Dem. I need to take this call." Her voice was laced with apology, but as she turned away, a delightful smile spread across her face, the phone pressed to her ear. There was a spark of excitement in her expression, hinting at our future love story.

"No worries, Narr. Just call or text me before you call it a night."

"Okay, I'll make sure to do that," she replied, speaking loudly yet trying to keep her voice down so as not to draw attention to us.

I woke up, showered, and prepared for my first class at 10:00 a.m. As I stepped outside, I immediately noticed my car was parked in my hall's parking area. I felt a brief moment of panic, worrying that it might have been towed and that Dem had to pay to retrieve it for me. As I narrowed my eyes, I spotted a white piece of paper tucked in the windshield, thinking I might have a parking ticket or fine.

Hey, Narr. I told you I would handle everything. It's all set, and your keys are in the glove compartment. The battery just needed a charge. Next time, let me give you a jump, girl! Please call me later.

Looking forward to seeing you soon. -Dem

In disbelief, I texted him. *Thank you so much, Dem. Talk to you later.*

Also, sorry I fell asleep after my conversation with my parents last night. That was not intentional.

I lingered in the car for a few moments, savoring the letter as I read it over and over. With each glance, I couldn't help but smile, enchanted by the way he already believed we shared something special. His choice of calling me "'Narr" felt intimate, and the way he affectionately referred to me as "girl" sent a warm flutter through my heart. I cherished every word. He had me lost in daydreams during class, craving more of his sweet notes, playful texts, and whatever else he might share. The possibilities felt endless, and my heart raced with excitement.

Classes had ended for the day, and I sank into the familiar comfort of our dorm suite, a permanent smile etched upon my face. As I tidied up one of the desks, our makeshift dining table, I embraced every swift emotion, convinced I had met the man of my dreams. Moving over to our cozy kitchenette, I paused while washing dishes, watching the frothy soap suds shimmering and dripping from the bottom of a small plate into the sink, caught in a moment of quiet reflection.

Sasha watched me with a warm smile. "Oh Narra, you look like you met peace and joy today."

I replied, "How did you know? Actually, it was yesterday." I blushed.

"I noticed you just a moment ago, cleaning with a grace that caught my eye. Your smile was super bright as you swirled the dishcloth in gentle mini circles across the dishes. For a brief moment, it seemed as if the cloth was tethered, stuck in place, almost as if it were glued to the surface—a brief pause in your effortless rhythm."

"Oh." I giggled.

"Sashaaaaa," I sang, my voice trailing off in a dreamy pause. "He is undeniably dashing! He's six foot two with a charming smile that captured my heart almost instantly. His sweet, deep, chocolate-brown eyes glisten with warmth and love, inviting me to explore his divine spirit every time our eyes meet. His dark brown hair, short and curly, perfectly frames his handsome face, enhancing his muscular build and sleek, toned arms—an impressive outcome of his unwavering commitment to the gym, where he rarely skips a day. And as an only child, he carries an irresistible charm and confidence that leaves me utterly mesmerized. And guess what?" Sasha's eyes sparkled with interest. "We bonded over Jesus and worship songs!"

"Oh my gosh! I love this for you, Narr. I look forward to meeting him."

"His name is Demery Foxer."

"Oh, I don't know him, Narr. How'd you two meet?

"We met at the gym. I haven't been to this gym in over a year."

"Was this yesterday?"

"Yes, yesterday is now eternal." I collapsed into a chair.

We both laughed. "Whoever he is, he must be a good one," Sasha said, her voice tinged with excitement and intrigue.

"I think he could be, Sasha!"

"I need more details, girl, about how you two met."

I didn't mind sharing most of the details with Sasha, but I decided to limit that information to just a few people so I wouldn't share too much with Lena.

"Girl, so I was working out at the gym, either on the treadmill or the elliptical—I can't quite remember which—I noticed a guy on another machine, focusing on his workout. He was doing something with his arms, I think, but honestly, I wasn't paying that much attention."

"Girl, I know you know!"

"Okay, it was arms!" I said, squirming in my seat. "I kept it cute, not trying to let him catch me staring, yet I noticed he was doing the exact same thing to me. Although he wasn't actively watching, I sensed his eyes following my movements as I exercised. Whenever our eyes met, I could feel those daring, divine eyes searching deep into my soul and my heart raced with a thrill I couldn't ignore."

"It was so dreamy," I remarked, momentarily closing my eyes.

"Oh, and he helped me with my car problems, getting it back early before class."

"I can't wait to meet him. I want to make sure he's a good guy for you, Narr."

A few weeks had passed, and Dem and I had gradually grown closer, exploring the beautiful layers of our connection. Not a single day slipped by without our laughter and heartfelt conversations, whether through texts or whispers over the phone. We'd cozied up together for online church services, shared delightful rom-coms, and then indulged in deep discussions that revealed our souls to one another. As I immersed myself in the romance of our encounters, I felt the depth of my adoration and gratitude for his unwavering kindness. To express these feelings, I started crafting sweet little love notes, which we liked to call "notes of love", and leaving them in unexpected places for him to discover at random times. The second note I wrote read, *And suddenly, it's your turn, and God makes it all happen for you.*

One of my favorite things was hearing stories from his childhood and learning about the deep involvement he had always had within his church. This aspect resonated with me. I'd noticed that Dem could be quite stubborn at times, overly kind, and he exhibited some traits of being an only child; while this can lead to clinginess, I share that trait too, although he would probably never admit it. Despite these quirks, I appreciated that he remained genuine and didn't pretend to be some perfect guy. This reminded me that, even as I was falling deeply in love with this man, he remained wonderfully human, just like the rest of us. This vulnerability added to his charm and made him all the more irresistible.

What truly captivated me about Dem was how distinct he was from others. He was unafraid to explore profound topics, diving into what mattered most with genuine sincerity. His emotional depth and unwavering consistency drew me in, igniting a spark that felt both exhilarating and comforting. Recently, he had expressed a desire to attend church with me. He discussed the beauty of marriage and shared his journey studying the Bible. Most recently, he had sought to understand the role of a loving husband. His dreams resonated with me; he longed for a godly wife like the one portrayed in Proverbs 31. Our exchanges of sweet prayers over the phone only strengthened the bond we were building, uplifting each other's spirits in the most heartfelt way.

He came to my dorm to help me with my studies and I happily reciprocated, especially since he didn't have a mate in his suite. He was extremely smart and his major in architecture seemed perfectly suited for him. Although he had his imperfections, it was undeniable that he was raised by extraordinary parents who instilled profound values in him, shaping him into the incredible person I was now beginning to know. I found myself completely smitten with him, even though we had yet to share our first kiss. Usually, I didn't take anyone too seriously in those days, but Demery was a refreshing exception. There was an enchanting quality about him that charmed me in a way I'd never felt before. We even met for lunch or coffee breaks between classes a few times. I shared a few little details about Dem with Sasha, but I hadn't mentioned him to anyone else yet. Several people had seen us together around campus on occasions, and we'd received our fair share of stares and smiles, which we expected. Dem mentioned a few things about his friends and that he'd had a few conversations about me with his parents.

After my second and final class, just before I had to teach at an after-school tutoring program, I found myself curious about what Dem was up to, so I texted him. He replied that he had to work that evening but promised to call me afterward. Once again, I was overwhelmed with emotions. Just the thought of him made me giddy and I couldn't help but let my mind wander to beautiful possibilities. I'm only human after all, and I was falling so deeply for him. He was starting to resemble everything I envisioned in my godly man, the future husband I'd always prayed for.

As I strolled across campus, my feet occasionally stumbling as I got lost in the vibrant glow of our old text messages, a bemused smile crept onto my face. "What is happening to me?"

I mused, reveling in the humorous absurdity of it all. "This is so out of character for me! Oh Lord, I need your help!" But oh, how I couldn't help but swoon over those charming images of us tucked away in my phone—each one a little love note from the past.

I stepped into my cozy dorm and sank into our charming little pink plush chair. With a flutter of excitement, I exclaimed, "Sasha! I've been thinking about Dem way too often between our texts and calls."

"Wow, Narra!" she replied, her eyes widening in surprise. "I've never seen you like this before. I've known you for a few years and heard about some of the guys you've dated, but it has never reached this level of intensity."

"I've never felt this way about anyone," I confessed, my heart feeling a rush of emotions.

"Dem is literally the sweetest, kindest, and most romantic guy I've ever met," I added, beams of warmth spreading through me. "Sometimes, I have to catch myself, having thoughts of 'it's too good to be true,'" I mused, a hint of worry creeping into my voice.

Sasha said, "I did a little scouting around campus and heard mostly good things about him."

"What do you mean, 'mostly,' Sasha?" I asked, my brow furrowed in confusion.

"No worries! There's no need to get all worked up; I just discovered that he works at Kraze and who he hangs out with," she reassured me, her smile comforting.

"Oh, thank God! I thought it was something worse." We both laughed, the tension lifting. "I'm already aware of his quirky friends," I responded, speaking lightly. "He's even mentioned how childish they can be at times. I guess we can't expect everything to be perfect, but honestly, I feel like I'm falling for him," I said, the warmth of blossoming love surrounding me as my heart swayed to a new rhythm.

Chapter Eight

♥

Embracing the Sudden Divine

*I*t was a frigid December night just before winter break, with the temperature hovering around 45°. I was bundled up in my chocolate corduroy puffer winter coat, while Narra looked stunningly warm in her long, midnight green peacoat. Though we had only known each other for a few months, I knew what I wanted, and God knew what I needed; we both believed in making ordinary days special, shunning the need to wait for holidays. Our connection was unique, guided by what we felt was a Holy Spirit influence.

After a delightful dinner at a nice restaurant, we decided to stroll around the town to enjoy the crisp night air before heading back to the car. The streets of Center City Philly were adorned with white Christmas lights, illuminating the bare branches of a dozen trees lining each side of the street. Some trees were wider and some taller, each showcasing its own charm. As we walked hand in hand, mesmerized by the enchanting cityscape, we admired the twinkling lights and each other, captivated by the beauty surrounding us. I halted near one of the brightest trees, my heart bolting with excitement as I produced a small red box wrapped in a silver ribbon. "Here you go, Narra." Her eyes glittered. "It's an early Christmas gift for you. It's light but filled with my thoughts and care."

"Oh, Dem, thank you. I also have something for you later."

Removing one of her chocolate gloves with her teeth, Narra delicately unfastened the box, unveiling a gold-chained bracelet inside. At first glance, she mistook it for a necklace, gently cradling it as her eyes traced the inscribed quote: "And suddenly, it's your turn, and God makes it all happen for you. - DHC." Her eyes lit up, flickering with tears of joy.

"Thank you, my wonderful, sweet man! This was one of the quotes I wrote on a note for you when we first began dating. How did you remember that? You're a dream come true."

"I know what you're thinking, but it's actually a bracelet, Narra. It doubles around your wrist," I explained.

"Oh wow, that is so beautiful, unique, and beautifully crafted! I love it so much. I'll wear it as often as I can."

"I have the same one, but I'll wear mine as a necklace," I replied, smiling from ear to ear.

"I love that we have matching quotes!" Narra exclaimed, excitement lighting up her face.

"I'm so glad you love it! This is our time, girl! Our love is truly blessed. Just don't give up on me as I'm learning and growing

Embracing the Sudden Divine

into the man God created me to be. Together, we will go with God's flow and allow Him to guide us on this journey. I desire to lead you with love, and that means letting God direct my path."

Narra leaned forward, her face inches from mine, her arms relaxed at her sides. I wrapped my arms around her, covering her in my warmth. "I promise I won't give up on you or us, Dem," she assured me.

She looked up at me and whispered, "I want you to be my best friend before you become my husband."

I spoke softly. "Please be patient with me. I'm not perfect; I make mistakes. I want you to know my feelings for you are genuine."

Staring deeply into her kind spirit through her eyes, I softly whispered, "I love you, Narra Jones."

"I love you, Demery Foxer," she replied, her eyes gleaming with joy before looking up at the sky.

"Look into my eyes, Narra," I said gently, my heart pounding with anticipation. I affectionately cupped her chin, tilting it just enough for our gazes to intertwine. In that precious moment, the sounds of cars and city buses around us melted away. Our lips met in a sweet kiss—a soft and reassuring peck that felt like a sacred promise. "I want you to understand that this isn't a fairy-tale where everyone knows how it ends. We are living in our real-life love story, where only God knows what unfolds, and we must trust Him and His timing." She squeezed me tighter.

"Narra, I want you to know that I have your back. You can trust me and rely on me. I'm a patient man; my father taught me well, and God isn't done working on me, but I can assure you that He's working in me.

"Right now, my priorities are clear. I'm committed to my relationship with God, striving to be a better person, taking care of my heart, and focusing on my studies. You rank pretty high on that list, girl." Narra listened intently, absorbing every word. I could only pray that she would trust the divine message that flowed through me to her, feeling the warmth of God's love surrounding us both.

"I wouldn't invest this much effort into us if I weren't sure about you, especially knowing you possess the qualities of a divine wife—my future wife." I was making a concerted effort to reassure her about my commitment. She hadn't brought up marriage recently, but I could sense that her thoughts often drifted to the future, which occupied her mind.

"I know you love giving me presents, but I want you to know that you're my greatest gift," Narra confessed.

"Narra, I love you. I've loved you since that very first moment we prayed together in my dorm after our first online church service. But I kept quiet, fearing you didn't share my feelings. In that moment, it felt as though time itself stood still."

It was as if Narra's heart soared at my words, a smile lighting up her face. "Wow, Dem. I love you too! I can hardly believe we've fallen in love so quickly." With eyes glowing, she glanced upward, her voice a soft whisper. "Thank you, God, for this incredible blessing," she said, as if seeking Heaven's approval of our newfound love.

Narra and I walked hand in hand back to the car, her enormous tote bag surprisingly concealing my early Christmas gift. As we settled into the vehicle, I activated the auto-start feature, warming up the car before slipping back in beside her. After fastening our seatbelts, Narra handed me a medium-sized box wrapped in brown paper, adorned with a bright red bow.

Curiosity bubbled inside me as I couldn't help but say, "I noticed you were carrying a bigger bag than usual. I had no idea! I'm in shock. No one ever gives me anything—especially not anyone I've dated. This is so unexpected!"

With an eager grin, Narra encouraged, "Open it! Open it!"

As I unveiled the gift, I was met with a vintage carpenter's tool chest, perfect for on-the-go woodwork, complete with a set of starter tools. "Wow! This is just perfect for me. You have no idea how much this means to me. I shared a bit about my love for carpentry and, incredibly, you've been paying attention to the little details." She smiled, her braces shining brightly. "You are truly amazing! I look forward to assembling everything once I find some free time tomorrow. At last, I can dedicate time to some small projects in my dorm!" A warm smile spread across my face as I realized the meaningful connection I had made with Narra. Our fingers intertwined as we drove off, and in that moment, I savored the excitement and possibilities that lay ahead for our future.

Chapter Nine

♥

A Love Demonstration

"*I*'ve had enough of papers, books, reading, and writing."

"Same! Let the fun begin!" Dem agreed.

Finally, the end of the week had arrived for us. It was a Friday in early March and I could feel winter loosening its grasp, making way for the promise of spring, just weeks away. The air had begun to warm ever so slightly, although the evenings still called for cozy denim jackets and winter boots. Festivities were in full swing around us with crowds of people, including alumni and a few famous faces. I was spending time with Dem around campus; we were still keeping our love private, but we weren't hiding it either. In that moment, we felt almost like best friends. The day was perfect—75° and sunny at noon, drawing many to campus to celebrate the university's 50th anniversary. Concerts, parties, and various gatherings filled the air, creating a vibrant festival atmosphere that began Tuesday night and would continue through Saturday. It was a gentle hush, even amid the noise. For a brief moment, all I could hear were the sweet songs of the birds and the soft rustle of the trees swaying in the breeze.

This charming bench, cradled among the branches of a nearby tree, was adorned with colorful flowers and white LED lights that outlined the entire bench and twirled around the nearby light pole, creating a warm atmosphere for the evenings. Dem and I often visited this spot whenever it was unoccupied, affectionately dubbing it the "bench of love," a name fitting for its deep red color. It felt as though we were nestled in the heart of a garden, surrounded by stunning blooms and lush, freshly cut grass. "I wrote you a poem!" Dem said with a big smile, clearly filled with excitement.

"Wait, you are full of surprises, Dem. You write poetry?" I exclaimed, my eyes widening in awe.

"I dabble a little, but it's nothing major or serious." With a shy smile, he pulled out a neatly folded piece of white paper and handed it to me. "It's called 'Sweet Narra,'" he said, beaming.

I engaged as he read:

Narra, Narra,

You're my super starra.

Parting with you is such sweet sorrow.

Some of your time I would love to borrow.

You stay on my mind.

I can't wait to see you tomorra.

I knew there was something special about you the first time I saw ya.

Our first conversation was like magic in the carra.

Oh, how I love you, sweet Narra.

I burst into laughter, the joy most likely evident on my face. Feeling a warm blush creep across my cheeks, I said, "This is so cute, Dem! No one has ever written me a poem and you memorized it without needing to read from the paper!"

"That's not all," he continued, offering me a finely carved cherry wood frame that bore the poem like a treasured plaque. "Now it can be your keepsake."

"Oh, your talent shines so brightly! Did you create this masterpiece? I'll cherish it, displaying it someday in our shared home. Until then, I'll find a special spot for it in my room back at my parents' house, keeping your gift close to my heart."

"You don't know us like that anymore, huh, Dem?' a passing friend teased as Dem and I relaxed on the bench beneath the tree. He looked up and realized it was Benny.

"Hey, Benny! Haha! This is Narra," he said, his eyes shining with excitement.

"Hi, Benny!" I waved warmly, my cheeks glowing with a hint of shyness.

Benny chuckled, his laughter filling the air as he began walking away. "Ha, um, I know who she is. You two lovebirds have fun!"

With a playful grin, Dem pointed toward the Reelindo stand, where the lively game of hoops was attracting a growing crowd. "I'll meet y'all there later, Benny."

All around us, vendor stands burst into life, showcasing beautifully crafted books, exquisite jewelry, and tempting food trucks, each one adding to the animated atmosphere. "This year marks the fiftieth anniversary," I said with awe in my voice. Turning to Dem, I said, "Experiencing this vibrant atmosphere during my senior year, partaking in such a jubilant celebration, fills my heart with boundless joy."

As he and I reflected on our experiences at Rovane, I texted Sasha. *Hey girl! Are you near the Sky Hall area? If you are, meet me by the red bench. I need someone to walk me back to our hall. Dem is heading off with the guys and I don't want him to have to walk me all the way, even though I know he already asked to!*

"Narr, I can walk with you super quick; it's no problem at all."

"Nah, she's coming with me! You've spent enough time with her today. See ya later, Dem! Have fun!" Sasha cheerfully declared, gliding in on her electric scooter, playfully tugging me along by the hand. With a bright smile, she folded her scooter and tossed it over her shoulder.

"Sasha, I had no idea you had a scooter!" I exclaimed, giggling.

"Yep! Just call me and I'll be there whenever you need!" Sasha sang playfully.

As I walked back to my dorm, I couldn't contain my excitement as I shared my poem with Sasha. "Narr, this is so cute and funny! You're so lucky!" she exclaimed, her voice bubbling with laughter.

"Nah, this isn't luck. It's all God, girl!" I replied. "Romance and holiness wrapped up in a beautifully flawed human! He can have my grace, Lord, as long as he's exactly who you designed him to be. As long as it's your will, Lord!" I said aloud with a beaming grin.

That evening, I decided to drive home to my parents' house for the weekend to visit my family and ensure I could attend church on Sunday.

After Narr left, I caught up with my friends Chris, Aaron, and Benny to join in the celebration. We were having a blast hanging out together. "Hey! A few of our friends are throwing a party off-campus later. Want to go with me?" Chris asked. At first, I felt uncertain and hesitant. However, the enthusiasm of those around me quickly captivated me. As I joined my friends, the atmosphere was electric with excitement and I could hear shouts like, "Yo, it's Benny Reese and the crew! A Wess, Dem, and Chris!" In that moment, we felt like celebrities, surrounded by laughter and fond memories. While I wouldn't describe myself as popular, my friends might have argued otherwise. A Wess and Benny Reese were well-known figures, and they seemed to know everyone. I suppose I found myself hanging out with fairly popular people, while I preferred to take a laid-back approach in our group.

It was pure joy—being out with friends, reconnecting with old faces, and reveling in the carefree moments. This was my kind of bliss, a celebration of life and friendship. But I only stayed for a little while. There were drinks, laughter, games, and the company of the ladies.

I wondered what kind of wild fun was going on in the basement. However, I felt a bit out of place, so I told the guys I had to head out early.

"Aww, he's going home to his 'campus wife,'" one of them joked, causing everyone to laugh.

"Yes, I am!" I laughed as I headed outside. "See you all tomorrow for the final day of celebrations!" My friends and I intended to attend a concert to wrap up Rovane's 50th anniversary celebrations, ensuring a fun experience for all.

The next day began beautifully as I awoke in my room at the Potter residence on a lovely Saturday morning. Warm sunlight streamed through the window, gently warming my face. I felt refreshed, my mind filled with delightful memories of laughter and celebration from the night before. Just as I settled into the peaceful atmosphere, my phone buzzed softly at 10:07 a.m., interrupting the bliss with an unexpected text from Dem.

Hey Narr, make sure to wear a lovely dress later. I'm excited to take you out on a date tonight. Please be ready by 6:00 p.m. Love you.

Just like that, we moved from bliss to bliss. Dem had carefully planned a romantic evening for us, intending to create a remarkable experience that would surpass anything we had shared before.

Later, as the sun dipped low in the sky, just after 6:00 p.m., the anticipation of the approaching daylight-saving time filled the air with excitement. Suddenly, my phone buzzed with another message from Dem.

Hey, my sweet Narr. I'll pick you up in about 20 minutes, he texted. A warm flutter spread through my chest at his words.

I replied, *Hi Dem, I'll be ready! Please park in the back. I'll slip out through that entrance tonight.* A soft knock on the door broke the moment, pulling me from my thoughts. When I opened it, I found Dem standing there. I had expected him to be in the car, waiting for me, but he seemed eager to spend a few moments with me inside. *There he is, looking effortlessly handsome and perfectly dressed, just like always*, I thought. Dem wore a chocolate-brown tailored suit with a crisp white shirt and no tie, exuding an air of relaxed sophistication. "You look incredibly handsome, Dem," I said, unable to contain my excitement.

"We look good together, don't we?" he replied, flashing a charming smile. I nodded in agreement, my coat already on as I felt eager to head out. My hair was neatly pulled up, framing my face beautifully. "Babe, I love the red lipstick," Dem said, gazing at me with an intent that suggested he wanted to kiss me, fully aware of the evidence that would smudge on his lips.

"Honey, I thought you'd wait in the car for me," I said, my heart racing at the sight of his charming smile.

"Yeah, right, Narr. I could never let you step out alone. I'll always be here, ready to stand by you, to walk beside you, to lead you, and to protect you. You are my queen and it's only right that we walk together hand in hand," he replied, his voice rich with unwavering attentiveness. As we stepped into the world outside, his words wrapped around me like a warm embrace, reassuring and comforting. I felt the strength of his presence beside me, a silent promise that together, we could face anything. This was more than just a moment; it was a testament to our bond, a shared journey fueled by love and loyalty.

"Wow, that's so sweet, Dem. I never really thought about it that way," I said, warmth flooding through me.

"Get used to it, my dear Narr," he whispered, leaning in to kiss my hand with a softness that made my soul soar as his eyes lifted, locking onto mine, as his lips parted from my skin.

As we drove to our date, I realized we were heading toward the gym—the same place where our paths first crossed. "I can't believe you ditched the festivities at the university today!" I said, surprised.

As I listened to him, all I could think about was how sincere his words felt. "My friends are all bachelors who thrive on the single life—rushing from one thrill to the next, living life on their own terms. But that isn't me. I know what I want now, and God knows what I need."

I longed to spend my free time getting to know Dem, and it felt like God had something special in store for us, and that something was Him.

"Look at you, so smooth with your words," I teased, a playful smile curling my lips, trying to lighten the mood. We both chuckled softly, the warmth of shared humor lingering between us.

"I can't help it, Narra. Whenever I'm with you, this romantic side just takes over me." He laughed gently, tossing a glance my way before redirecting his focus to the road.

"What's this surprise you mentioned?" I asked, allowing my curiosity to bubble over. My eyes sparkled with playful anticipation.

"You'll see in just a moment, Ms. Narra Jones," he replied with a pleasant smirk, his eyes flickering with promises. "Can I keep this one surprise for you?" His voice was laced with a gentle tease, yet love swayed softly in his eyes.

As we arrived, Dem smoothly glided into the parking lot of Kraze Creamery, the stillness surrounding us accentuated by the absence of other cars. The beams from our headlights cut through the night, illuminating the glass front of the building where the stark "Sorry We're Closed" sign hung ominously in view. Confusion played across my face, screaming perplexity and anticipation. "Dem, you know I don't mind being surprised by you," I ventured, my voice mixed with both excitement and anxiety, "just give a girl a hint every now and then," I added, wishing for a glimpse into his playful mind.

"This is the hint!" he retorted, his grin widening as he glanced at me, love bright in his eyes. With a flourish, I watched as Dem stepped out of the car to open the door for me. But in a moment of spontaneous fun, I locked the door from the inside, my smile beaming back at him as laughter burst from my lips. It was one of those random whims we indulged in—playfully punishing each other for the sheer joy of it.

"Okay ... yeah, this is what I get for not giving you hints." Dem chuckled, his laughter infectious, wrapping us both in the warmth of the moment. I unlocked the door, and as he tried to open it again, I quickly pressed the lock button once more. "Okay, Narr, what do you want to know?" he asked playfully.

"Give me a hint!" I replied eagerly.

"That's easy! Ice cream!"

I laughed as I unlocked the door, sharing a hearty laugh with Dem as he opened it for me. Stepping out of the car with both heels to the ground, I leaned in and planted a soft kiss on his cheek. As I walked toward the shop, I glanced inside, noticing everything looked perfectly ordinary. I continued my barrage of questions while Dem texted his manager to let him know we had arrived at the front door. Once inside, I spotted someone behind the counter. The staff guided us to a charming private area, where soft strains of piano music began to serenade the air, embracing the entire ice cream shop. The lights subtly dimmed, forming a smooth and warm glow that filled the space with an inviting atmosphere.

"May I take your coat, Ms. Jones?" he asked, his gaze tracing my figure appreciatively. He shook his head in awe, murmuring, "Umm, umm, I'm so blessed."

I was wearing my "one day all this will be yours" dress—a fancy, flared, midnight blue mini that hugged just above my knees. The dress was decked with a beautifully embroidered large blue rose that framed my chest. I paired it with delicate black sheer tights and cute black stiletto heels. Around my neck, a small silver cross hung, complemented by tiny silver hoop earrings. In that moment, I felt like the epitome of elegance and romance.

"Okay! It's giving cinnamon roll," Dem chuckled, as he admired the large rose on my dress. We couldn't help but burst into laughter as the romantic atmosphere wrapped around us. *It's too early for a marriage proposal. I only met him a few months ago,* I thought.

"I know what you're thinking, but we're not there yet! I want you to remember that you deserve the best, even on an ordinary date night. You should feel cherished every day and hold on to the belief that each date has the potential to turn into something truly special.

"Watch out, girl! With our kind of chemistry, you never know when the unexpected might happen. And the best part? I didn't have to spend much at all."

The setup was perfect, adorned with all the necessary ingredients, charming items, and gleaming equipment needed to create homemade ice cream. A dedicated teacher was poised to guide us through the delightful journey of making ice cream from scratch, offering step-by-step instructions with passion and grace. "Wow, I truly am speechless! This is so incredibly sweet," I exclaimed, completely awed by the experience. "Am ice dreaming?" I said playfully.

The scene unfolded around a lofty round table cloaked in a flowing red cloth that kissed the floor. Gentle LED candles flickered softly like whispers of light, forming sweet flames. The table was elegantly set with silverware and champagne glasses. To complete the mood, two laminated menus titled "Dem and Narra's Dreamy Date Night" lay invitingly on the table, hinting at a romantic dining experience. As I sat across from Dem on our date, laughing and talking; he surprised me by presenting a bouquet of fuchsia roses that he pulled from a box underneath the table. "You are full of surprises, Demery! You really don't need to do all this.

I'm just a simple girl. I don't need this," I stated, my surprise evident.

Dem smiled warmly at me. "I'm still going to do this because it's what I want to do for you. You deserve this, whether you ask for it or not."

"You really don't need to, though." My eyes began to water a little. I couldn't help but think, *This man's emotional intelligence is off the charts! Where did he come from?*

"You deserve every bit of this, Narra. Embrace it fully. Why shouldn't you live the soft, beautiful life you've always dreamt of right now? Why not you? God is unmistakably showing you the depths of His love." With each word, Dem's sincerity covered me like a genuine hug, encouraging me to let go of my reservations and accept the blessings being offered. This was my story; I reminded myself not to compare it to others' lives. I savored this present moment and all its sweetness.

After taking a moment to appreciate the scenery, Dem pulled out a chair for me, urging me to select whatever I wanted from the dinner menu; he then texted a staff member with our choices and as we awaited the preparation of our meal the fun began immediately. Dem shared his knowledge of making natural vegan ice cream from scratch, a skill he had learned during training a few summers ago from a professional teacher. We had professionals there that night to assist us in ensuring everything was perfect for our experience.

Wearing aprons, gloves, and hair nets, we were ready to select our own ice cream flavors. I chose all my flavors while Dem carefully noted each one for our creation. He turned towards me, his smile lighting up his face as he revealed all his teeth. With sincere affection, he said, "Narra, these three scoops of velvety vanilla ice cream represent the gentle softness of your love, the luminous nature of your spirit, and the silky smoothness of your skin. The luscious strawberry syrup mirrors the vibrant red lipstick you wear, adding a delightful sweetness to this creation. Meanwhile, the rich chocolate represents the sweetness of your soul, while the crushed chestnuts echo the beauty of your shimmering brown hair. The caramel captures the enchanting honey-brown of your eyes as they glimmer in the light. Each thick scoop of ice cream signifies the profound bond we share, all crowned beautifully with a cherry that seals our love and brings it all together." In a surprising twist, Dem named our creation "The Narr Barr Delight," promising it would become a permanent menu item.

After crafting our ice cream masterpieces, we took photos to capture the moment before placing the treats in the freezer for later. Once we had cleaned our workspace, we removed our hairnets, aprons, and gloves and began dancing together around the store. As Dem held me close during our dance, we shared moments of quiet, lost in the melodies streaming from his phone's Bluetooth.

"Dem, you outdid yourself tonight! I'm speechless." In soft whispers, we expressed our profound love for each other, hoping this cherished moment would endure forever. At one point, Dem took my hands, leaned in closer, and began to pray for me. He prayed for my heart, spirit, well-being, and safety, asking God to guide me towards the woman of God I was destined to become. His prayers encompassed my physical and mental well-being, my upcoming graduation, my peace of mind, and my ability to concentrate on my studies, celebrating every aspect of my happiness during this pivotal time in my life.

As dinner approached, soothing melodies filled the air and the staff served our meals alongside sparkling water. We shared laughter over funny memes on our phones, enjoyed one of the Narr Barr Delight desserts, and took the other to go. We had one final dance without music while the staff cleaned the restaurant in preparation for closing. I reflected on how Dem, with his old soul and maturity, stood out as a remarkable young man of God in my eyes.

"Sometimes, it's not about how much money you spend; it's about spending genuine, quality time together" - Ronette Johnson

Chapter Ten

Meet the Foxers

April had arrived. A romantic spring morning unfolded as dew glistened and gentle rain pattered softly, while the sun's warmth and the wind worked in harmony together. The pull of divine love emerged from the freshly turned soil, mingling with the fragrant air. Ushering in spring break, I informed my parents that Narra and I would be visiting. As I pulled into the driveway, I was pleasantly surprised that they weren't home yet. I called my mom: "Hey Mom, when will y'all be home? I've got Narra with me."

"Oh, my Lord! We cannot wait to meet her!"

"Son, could you give us about an hour?" my dad asked.

"An hour? Good thing it's spring break."

"My apologies, Dem," my mom replied.

"Yeah, we knew it was possible she would be coming, but we thought we'd be back by then."

"All good. Don't worry, we've got time. Don't rush. We'll be around."

"I am so excited to meet her!"

"I feel the same, Mrs. Foxer! Safe travels!" Narra shouted out.

"Alright, Narra. We have about an hour before they come home. Want to get ice cream at Kraze, burn some time, or hang around here?"

"I don't mind hanging around here until your parents return. I'm enjoying the lovely, hilarious photos of you and your family that are around. You were so cute as a baby."

"What about now? Am I still cute?"

"Haha, of course you are," she said, gently touching my chin while searching my eyes.

Dem is a true gentleman, full of hospitality. My heart yearned for his gentle nature and kindness each day. As we pointed out photos around the house, he shared the short stories behind each moment and the year they were taken. It was incredibly cute. The Foxers' home was a stunning, colossal masterpiece. As I looked around in awe, I took in the tall ceilings and expansive windows that filled the space with natural light. The pearl-colored walls gleamed and the fresh paint brought a crisp scent to the air. A beautiful modern fireplace added elegance to the room, complemented by green plants in several areas, while stylish light fixtures sparkled in every corner. Their three-car garage hinted at the wealth they possessed. Dem mentioned that his parents owned at least three other properties and that the house had been remodeled a few years ago into what they would consider their dream home. A seven-bedroom, five-bathroom residence featuring a large kitchen with a gigantic island, as well as luxurious marble floors and countertops. The expansive basement featured a rarely used movie theatre. A tall, white vinyl privacy fence surrounded the yard. The only thing missing was a sparkling pool, which seemed a bit extravagant for such a small family. Nevertheless, the comforting thought of always having a welcoming place to return to whenever we were in town felt like a dream.

"Wow, Dem! Are your parents rich?" I exclaimed, my mind racing with possibilities.

"Nah, well, maybe they are, but they never told me. Haha."

"I'd like to think you've never had to worry about struggles, huh?"

"Yeah, but my parents made sure I spent a lot of time in sports and with family. They wanted to avoid the only child syndrome."

"So far, I'd say your parents did a great job."

"Narra, can I show you something else?"

"Sure, Dem! I'm intrigued," I said, excitement bubbling inside me.

"Let me give you a quick tour of the house to help you familiarize yourself with everything and make the time go by more easily." He walked toward the stairs and said, "What I want to show you is upstairs."

"Upstairs? Where are you trying to take me?" I asked, slightly taken aback but still trusting that Dem was a true gentleman. He walked ahead, guiding me up the staircase. Suddenly, he stopped, reaching back with his right arm to take my left hand. "Close your eyes, Narra," he whispered.

"Why? Wait! I don't want to trip and fall!" I exclaimed, fear creeping in as I felt myself begin to stumble. He whispered, "Just take my hand and trust me to lead the way. I have something special to show you."

Dem guided me to an unexpected surprise upstairs. I had no idea what to expect, but I trusted him not to let me fall. As I giggled, I whispered, "What is it, Dem? You know I hate surprises."

"Almost there!" he replied softly.

We slowly walked down the hallway and I held on to the bottom of his shirt, inadvertently stretching it out with my free hand.

"I'm opening a door now," he said, quietly approaching a door decorated with a brown wooden sign that read "Peace of Mind" in elegant cursive. I peeked a little, careful to maintain my balance. He paused and instructed, "Open your eyes, beautiful." My eyes fluttered open. "Now open the door," he commanded softly as he flicked on the light switch. I turned the knob slowly, a breath caught in my chest. I exhaled, awestruck by the presence that filled the room, whispering, "Wow."

I looked around, taking in every detail, and was stunned to see pale yellow sticky notes neatly covering the freshly painted mint-green walls, with a few even stuck to the ceiling. At the back, I noticed a pile of books and notebooks resting on a small wooden shelf. As I continued my exploration, I gasped, "Wow, this is beyond beautiful, Dem." The first sticky note that caught my eye was written in dark green ink on a light brown sticky note; it read:

God, I trust you.

Love, Dem

The date was also noted on the paper.

We stood together, holding hands in his prayer closet—a surprisingly spacious walk-in closet for a childhood room. "This is quite a generous amount of space for a walk-in closet," I commented.

"Do you like it, Narr?"

"Yes, of course, I do! It feels like a dream."

"I built this prayer closet myself a few years back. At first, it was much smaller—it could only hold some of my childhood toys, shoes, and books. Two summers ago, I knocked down the wall and expanded the space. I always want to have a reason to visit my parents, you know? Haha."

Dem pointed to a yellow sticky note written in blue ink, which read, *God, thank you for my amazing praying wife, _____, who will love you first and always.*

"This is so sweet, Demery," I replied.

"Narra, this is where I initially prayed for you, even though I knew nothing about you, your name, or what you looked like," he explained. "I prayed for you, a godly wife. And as I'm with you now, I see the wife I prayed for within you."

Narra's eyes never left me, following my every move. I reached over her shoulder, grabbed my blue ink pen from the shelf and began filling in the blanks, writing Narra's name where I had previously written prayers about my wife on the yellow sticky notes. In that moment, Narra was speechless and clearly overwhelmed with joy. Her jaw dropped and she gently pulled me close for a hug. "Dem, I … I…Wow." She was lost for words.

Narra was in love with her purpose. She was in love with God's plans for her. That's one thing I had admired about her since our first meeting.

"There's no way this man is real!" Narra exclaimed, her eyes fixed on the ceiling as if seeking answers in the depths above. I turned to her, a warm smile gracing my lips, and said, "I know I'm not perfect, but I assure you, I am undeniably real. I'm so glad you see me for who I am, without any hesitation or thinking I'm weird."

"Why would I?" she asked.

"I just thought you would think I'm too soft or something. Haha."

Meet the Foxers

"No, not at all. You're actually strong. A man who openly prays and expresses his love for God, both publicly and privately, demonstrates true strength. And really, what's wrong with showing vulnerability from time to time?"

Right then and there, I asked, "You want to pray with me now? Narra, I would like to have you as my daily prayer partner before you become my wife."

"Wow. You really just know what to say, Dem. And absolutely," she said, standing directly before me, gazing up into my eyes.

Her eyes told a love story—it told our love story whenever I'd look into them.

Dem is in love with me! I thought as his eyes found complete safety within mine. A profound look of love filled both our expressions. Dem continued to hold my left hand and gently took my right as well. His fingers intertwined with mine, each one pressed perfectly between my own. With his eyes closed, he began to pray, creating a sense of peaceful intimacy between us. I closed my eyes slowly, a gentle smile forming on my face.

"Dear Heavenly Father,

"How wonderful and magnificent You are to us every day. I am deeply grateful for this day and the beautiful experience of sharing a prayer with my love, Narra.

"I ask in Your name, Jesus, that You guide us in nurturing our friendship first, helping us build a strong foundation before we take any serious romantic steps together. Please guide me to love her gently and to court her with the utmost respect. O heavenly Father, You comprehend our hearts and souls more profoundly than we ever could understand ourselves or one another. May we continually turn to You as the foundation of our relationship, seeking Your guidance in every moment. Grant us the wisdom to thrive in both life and love, embracing each challenge with grace. Heavenly Father, bestow upon us the gift of patience and the ability to shower each other with daily grace and kindness. May our journey together be enriched by Your everlasting love."

My eyes fluttered open slightly, catching a glimpse of Dem's closed eyes, his expression serious and thoughtful. He took a moment to pause before continuing.

"May Your love inspire and guide us as we navigate our physical desire for each other. Lord, protect us from harm and heartache. We express our gratitude, honor You, and bless Your magnificent name. In Jesus' name, Amen."

I chuckled and said, "Amen! I agree." We both burst into laughter, wrapping each other in a long, genuine hug.

"Just keeping it all the way real with God, you know?" At that moment, it felt as if destiny and strength were wrapping around me, bringing a profound sense of relief, relaxation, and safety.

"That was a fast prayer, yet still a very powerful one!" I voiced as I allowed myself to let go of him. He could hear the sarcasm in my choice of words.

"That's all we needed for this moment. God's timing, girl! We'll explore deeper together later on," Dem said playfully.

"Is it okay if I pray for you? Do you think I have enough time?" I asked, my heartbeat quickening as I glanced at the time on my phone. "Your parents should be here any minute now, but I feel the need to pray as well."

"No worries, Narr." His eyes flashed with trust. "I texted my mom earlier, letting her know I'd be showing my prayer room to you, hoping it would be a meaningful space for us.

"You have nothing to worry about. My parents trust me; they raised me right," Dem said, leaning in closer to my face. "I have never brought anyone home to meet them, so they know what this means. However, please do pray for me. I just got a text; they should be home in about ten minutes."

I felt a sense of urgency mixed with an electric intimacy between us, as if sharing this moment would bring our fates a little closer together. *This man is incredibly romantic, almost like something from a rom-com. It feels like he was sent to me directly from Heaven*, I thought.

"This is all new to me, Dem. I'm sorry if I seem a bit anxious." I paused. "No man I've dated has ever prayed for me. Ever."

He turned to me, his deep, sweet, chocolate-brown eyes focusing on mine, his voice soft yet firm. "Baby, this is real. I'm real. I meant every word. I'm not perfect, but I'm real. Even though I'm young, I am a genuine man of God. Men like me truly exist. Can't you see? Our union is already blessed, Narra."

I looked into his eyes once more, nodded in agreement, reached out and took his hands and closed my eyes. Then I began to pray.

"Dear Heavenly Father, my Alpha and Omega, the Creator of heaven and the earth, the one who performs daily miracles, bringing healing, provision, and protection into our lives. Thank You for showering us with Your grace. Thank you for this beautiful day and for this lovely soul named Dem, whom You have aligned with me in spirit before our paths intertwined. I cherish the opportunity we have to gather and uplift each other in prayer. I ask for Your divine protection over his parents as they journey home. May their light shine brightly as a beacon of hope for those they love and everyone they encounter along their way. Father, I pray that love and peace surround us as we meet for the first time today. Guide our hearts and minds in our interactions, for this is a sacred moment You have ordained. May Dem and I wholeheartedly embrace Your will in our lives, flourishing in the ways You envision for us. In Jesus' name, Amen."

"Amen!" Dem said with a smile as we embraced.

Right then, it felt as if our spirits fused, as though we had already become "the Foxers" in spirit.

Next to a tall navy-blue dresser, a folding chair was positioned just outside the intimate prayer closet. He opened the chair, gestured towards it with a soft smile and said, "This is for you."

With a playful leap, he flopped forward onto his neatly made bed, resembling a carefree giant child lost in joy. I relaxed in the chair, wrapped in the comfort of the moment, ready for a more profound conversation. The moment felt light and playful, with a hint of romance between us. "Why me?" I asked, curiosity evident in my voice.

"I'm not going to lie, Narr. I desire you deeply in every way, with every fiber of my being. As a human, my mind races with the countless things I crave to share with you… Oh, my!" He laughed softly, shaking his head with a mix of hope and amusement.

"I hope my sincere honesty fills your heart with joy, rather than causing any discomfort," he said, his eyes gleaming with truth, a tender smile bright on his lips.

"No offense taken here, sir! I want you to want me too."

Dem chuckled and said, "Please don't start with the 'sir' stuff again."

"Trust me, I've imagined wild scenarios about us countless times. Thank goodness you can't read my mind!" I said with a chuckle. He looked at me with an expression of love and I could tell from that look that he had fallen for me.

I continued, "I'm incredibly proud of us. I have so many feelings and emotions about various things. This proves that we shouldn't be alone in this bedroom right now. Look at us being strong together already," I said with a laugh.

"So … that sticky you pointed to? You think I'm going to be your wife, huh?" I smirked.

"Narr, why else would I invite you into my parents' house and into my precious prayer closet to share all my secrets with you? My love, you are destined to be my wife, and deep down, you know it!" Dem said with a hopeful smile, a hint of nervousness brightening his eyes.

"That was a bit of a serious question. Seriously, am I the only girl you've ever invited into your room? I'm just curious," I asked, my stare locked onto his as he returned it with his kind, chocolate-brown eyes, which I adored deeply.

"Narra, I've never met anyone like you. You're different, you're divine. You move differently in many ways and your spiritual movement attracts me to you," he said. "You're the only woman who has seen my prayer room."

"Hmm…" I mused with a playful raise of my eyebrow, my eyes firm in the soft, dim light. "So, someone has caught a glimpse of this cozy room but not the prayer room, huh?"

"Yeah, because there was no prayer room many years ago," he said playfully.

"I need to know you're serious about me. I can't afford to waste my time falling head over heels for you, only to find myself heartbroken when you run off with someone else—someone who probably doesn't even care about your soul," I said.

"Do you trust me? Even though we haven't known each other that long, I need you to trust me." He spoke in a stern yet gentle manner as he sat up on the bed. I looked up at him and saw honesty in his eyes. I shook my head gently and replied, "Yes, I trust you, Demery Foxer. But…"

"But what?" he asked.

One of the gifts that God has blessed me with is the ability to sense authenticity in others. Yet, in this particular situation, I found myself often confused. His smooth talk left me overthinking, igniting a whirlwind of emotions within me. I secretly nicknamed him "The Smooth Dude" for his undeniable charm, which captivated me during our conversations. Each smile he flashed felt like a quiet invitation, drawing me deeper into a connection that left my heart racing. The way he listened intently, his eyes sparkling with genuine interest, made me wonder if what lay beneath that layer of charm was something profoundly real. I shared the term only with Sasha and my best friend, Rya, who had moved to another country after 10th grade. She was my confidante, aware of all the guys I'd dated before. There were things I could tell Rya that I would never dare to share with my other friends or family; our bond was special. I, too, was someone she could rely on to share her secrets.

Dem loved it when I called him by his full name. He took such pride in the Foxer family name, and the thought that one day I would carry it too made me love saying it even more. "You're a real smooth operator," I teased, narrowing my eyes at him.

"What's that, Narra? You've never had a man like me? Praying together is as romantic as it gets."

"Hmmm…"

"As long as actions match words, everything's cool, right? I'll never be perfect, Narra, but I can be good enough for you."

His cell phone beeped. "My parents are finally pulling up in the driveway," Dem said, looking at it. "Let's head down to greet them as they arrive!" he exclaimed, his excitement infectious. We jumped up to walk down the stairs. Dem took my hand and guided me down as gently as he had guided me upstairs. We approached the front door and walked together towards his parents' car. Mr. Foxer opened the door for his wife and the first thing that captured my attention was her long, gorgeous, loose, wavy, pepper-colored hair, with a hint of salt, blowing in the warm wind.

"Narra!"

"Narra? That's all you see, Mom?"

We walked to the car, parked peacefully in the driveway, just beyond the garage, as my mom stepped out. Her eyes widened in surprise as she noticed Narra. With a warm smile, she extended her hand. "I'm Ms. Demi, but please, call me Mrs. Foxer. She's stunningly beautiful, Dem!" My mom looked at me then back at Narra and nodded, affirming Narra's beauty. "The pictures don't do her justice, Dem!"

Curiosity struck me about the photos Dem shared with his parents as I nervously yet excitedly hugged Mrs. Foxer after our initial handshake.

"So lovely to meet you. You are truly beautiful! Wow, you resemble your mother so much, Dem!" I exclaimed softly, admiration evident in my voice. "And your father as well! How have you been, Mr. Foxer?" I said as we embraced.

Mr. Foxer said, "Narra, we apologize for not being home earlier. You know it's the first few weeks of spring and I love taking my wife to her favorite spots to shop for fruits and vegetables and the lady just cannot help herself! She took a little longer than usual," he said with a grin.

"Oh, stop it!" Mrs. Foxer laughed out loud.

"Let us help y'all with the groceries." Dem and I grabbed as many bags as possible from the trunk and headed into the house. "Follow me to the pantry area, Narra."

"You got it, Dem," I said, struggling a little with the few heavy paper brown bags.

"I'll take that heavier one there, Narra," Mr. Foxer said, hurrying to help me.

"Thank you!"

Mrs. Foxer said, "I'm making dinner in a while. Would you love birds like to join us?"

"We might be heading out in a bit, but please save us some for later."

"Her leftovers are even better!"

"Always!" Dem agreed with his dad. Dem and I cuddled on the family room sofa, feeling the sweetness wrap around us like a gentle hug.

"Be in there in a few minutes," Mrs. Foxer said, the anticipation of her company bringing a smile to my face.

"Okay, Mom!" Dem shouted. When three minutes had drifted by, Dem's mom gracefully joined us, taking a seat on the sofa opposite, her presence lighting up the space.

"So, Narra. I've heard so much about you," she began, her eyes sparkling affectionately.

"All amazing things, of course!" We all laughed, a shared bond weaving between us.

"From what I've heard and the aura you carry, I can easily tell you are a lovely lady who values her love for Jesus."

"Yes, Mrs. Foxer. And you've raised a handsome gentleman who mirrors that same love," I reply, admiration seeping into my words. "Honestly, I'm in awe of the man he is already at such a young age." My heart swelled with pride, capturing the center of family love and admiration.

"So, what did you think of the prayer room?" Mr. Foxer inquired, his eyes glinting with curiosity as he joined our conversation.

I closed my eyes for a moment and said, "Oh my goodness, it felt like a beautiful dream. I had never imagined young men could create such sacred spaces, especially since he crafted it all himself."

Mr. Foxer grinned. "Yeah, I contributed a little, with the blueprint and some ideas."

"Ah, I forgot to mention that detail." Dem chuckled, his laughter warm and infectious. "I definitely inherited my carpentry skills from my dad; it's in my blood."

"Dem is truly one of a kind. You all raised him well."

"Yeah, we did our best. He has his issues, but we believe he'll grow into a remarkable man of God, learning and maturing from his missteps."

Issues? I thought.

"We strive to nurture in him a heartfelt love and compassion, as guided by God."

"Ah, Narra, Dem is truly a wonderful young man," Mrs. Foxer affirmed, her voice sweet-sounding. "Let me get started on dinner before it gets too late," she said, rising from the sofa. "Will you be staying here in the guest room or are you planning to head out?"

I kept a straight face, but I was surprised that the Foxers would let me stay overnight, even in the guest room. Their trust in their son was truly admirable.

"Mom, you act like I've never brought anyone home before," Dem said playfully.

"I'll probably return to my parents' place tonight, hoping to join them at church this weekend. But if that doesn't work out, I'll be sure to settle into the guest room later on."

"Alright then, Mom and Dad. Narra and I have a few plans," Dem announced, rising from the couch, and I stood up as well, making sure to shake their hands.

"You two drive safe!" Mr. Foxer said.

"It was a pleasure to meet both of you."

"The pleasure was all ours; we know we'll be seeing much more of you," Mrs. Foxer replied, laughter bouncing in the air. Dem took my hand, leading me toward the door. As we stepped outside, he paused in front of the driveway, a soft smile on his face, as if savoring the moment.

"Are you hungry? What do you feel like eating for dinner? Should we get takeout or dine in and then hang out in the city? I know a great place that serves both healthy options and delicious comfort food. Let's go to that spot, relax, and grab a bite to eat!"

My brows furrowed. "Wow! You must be really hungry; I can barely get a word in. But sure, let's go."

Dem narrowed his eyes at me and chuckled. "My dad mentioned that I can take his car tonight. I texted him earlier to ask, so it's ours for the evening."

"Okay! So, we are driving the black Audi with the black rims?"

"Yes, Narr, that one! My dad's new car is super cool. I helped him pick it out, as you know. It's much nicer than mine, which is why he gave me his old one," Dem said enthusiastically.

We collected our jackets, my handbag, and keys from Dem's car before settling into the Audi.

As we glided down the open road in the luxurious Audi, the cool spring breeze softly whirled through my loose curls as the sun began to set. With all the windows down, I reached over, lacing my fingers with Dem's, and he met my gaze with a sweet smile as the gentle worship music filled the car, wrapping us in its serene embrace.

Every moment with Dem made my heart flutter and deepened my affection for him. Yet, amidst this whirlwind of emotions, I couldn't help but wonder, *Is it too soon to feel this way for someone I've only just met?*

During the car ride, overthinking began to cloud my mind. *Is he truly the one for me or just another charming stranger skilled in sweet words, seducing me into a whirlwind of romance? Does he seek something more or is it merely a fleeting desire? What is it about his words that resonates with me? Sometimes, he captures my heart with the perfect sentiment, yet I find him falling short at other times. Perhaps, just perhaps, he isn't pretending to be someone he's not. I can't just be out here believing everything I hear from a man I barely know. Is this discernment or am I overanalyzing it all?* I thought.

My mind raced. *I can hardly believe this is real! Are my prayers being answered and are my dreams finally coming true? Am I too young for this? Will he truly commit to me at such a young age? I've never met a guy's parents before*, I thought.

He lowered the volume on the radio a little and looked at me briefly. "That went well, Narr. Even better than I expected!"

"Yes, I love your parents! They are amazing people."

We arrived at the restaurant, a charming little place in Philly called Nothing Beats Deets, just a 30-minute drive from Dem's house. The warm and inviting atmosphere perfectly complemented the delicious food we savored. Each bite we took was a flavorful experience, making our meal satisfying and truly memorable. As we indulged in those delectable dishes, we reminisced about our parents' love stories, sharing how their enduring romance inspired us. It was touching to reflect on the depth of their love and it added a heartfelt dimension to our conversation amidst the joy of our meal. After dinner, we parked in Center City and went for a walk. Walking together is something we often enjoyed; it was always a peaceful experience.

"It's such a lovely night. The moonlight skips across the leaves, don't you agree?" I remarked, smiling at Dem.

"Yes, just a little wind, but not bad at all. It feels perfect, like this moment is meant for us," he replied, squeezing my hand gently.

As we continued walking, my jacket wrapped around my waist, I felt the warmth of his presence. As we held hands, we lost ourselves in laughter and soft whispers. "You know," I said, looking into his eyes, "this night makes me realize how blessed I am to share these beautiful moments with you."

He smiled at me. "I feel the same."

Every step we took together felt like a step toward forever. We walked hand in hand, the environment around us softly dissolving as we shared our dreams and nurtured the love beginning to bloom between us.

After our relaxing walk, Dem drove me to my parents' house, where my car had been parked earlier that day before he picked me up. As he held the car door open, I stepped out and turned to look at him, a soft smile gracing his lips. "You want me to walk you to the door, Narr?"

"No need, I'm already right here." I chuckled.

"You're right. But next time, I'm walking you to the door even if it's just two feet away."

With a gentle wave of goodbye, a flutter of hope twirled in my heart, knowing our beautiful story was beginning. Once inside, I quietly walked to the basement door leading to my cozy apartment, where I was careful not to disturb my family. I tossed my keys, jacket, and bag onto the floor in a flurry then plopped down onto the bed. Unable to shake off the enchanting memories of the evening, I felt every sweet moment linger in my thoughts.

It was just after 10:00 p.m. when, after ensuring Narra was safely inside, I took a few moments to collect my thoughts, cranked up my music a bit, and in that moment of solitude, I realized I was in love for the very first time in my life. This feeling surpassed anything I had ever known.

As I drove, my phone rang—it was Benny. "Hey, Dem! What's up, man?" Benny said enthusiastically as his voice echoed through the car's speakers. "How's everything with you and Narra? We touched on it a bit last week, but I've got to say, everyone is shocked you landed the girl we all thought was too good for you!"

"Straight to the point, huh?" I said, chuckling.

"You both are the talk of the campus. Yeah, I bet you're with her at this very moment."

I laughed, my heart fluttering at the thought. "Yeah, I didn't pay much attention to what anyone said that day. I believe that what God has in store for me is mine, as long as I have faith and use discernment."

"Okay, Brother Dem! You're absolutely right. Honestly, we all thought she'd never look your way. I'm genuinely happy for you, I truly am, but I can't help but miss our special get-togethers with the guys. It feels as though you're drifting from us. We've all been wondering how you managed to pull one of the finest girls who ever graced Rovane!" Benny exclaimed, his surprise evident.

"Y'all really want to know what I've been up to, huh? Haha."

"Seriously, how did you get her? She doesn't seem like the type to be down to earth."

"Nope, not what you think at all. Narra is actually the opposite."

"So, she's not what we thought, huh?"

"Exactly. Narra has high standards, but I meet those expectations and she also aligns with my standards. She's a virtuous woman.

And yes, she's a young woman of God who loves Jesus. She's beautiful inside and out. That's the best part about her. Man, she prays for me and everything."

"Oh, I see what you mean. She's kind of like a dream girl, huh?"

"Man… Narra randomly writes me little encouraging love messages and hides them in my things, knowing how to uplift my spirit with her words. I often find them in my gym bag, in my car, or in a textbook that she knows I'm currently using for my studies. Who else would take the time to do such thoughtful things for me? She's a gem. Truly rare."

"That's dope, bro. I've never heard of anyone our age dating a girl like her. Dem got the gem!" Benny laughs.

"I'll let her know about the jokes y'all have. And thanks, Benny. Just don't go running your mouth about me or us. If you want to know something, just ask me," I said playfully, a hint of seriousness in my voice.

"It's just that the guy we all know is a man who loves hard, but we've never seen you this whipped, Dem. Don't forget about the bros! Enjoy your early twenties, bro. You still have more college life to experience, parties to enjoy, and fun to have. Plenty of amazing girls are out there; there's no need to rush."

"Ha, I'm in no rush, Benny!" I replied, my voice betraying a hint of nervousness. "I'm just really happy and I know Narra is the one."

"The one? Are you serious, Dem?"

"Very serious," I responded, ensuring my tone conveyed my claim's gravity. "Narr is different. She's not like any of the other girls I've dated."

"But you're just about to turn twenty-one. Isn't it too early to talk about a girl being 'the one'? No matter how wonderful she is or how happy she makes you, take a moment to breathe and slow down a little, bro.

"Anyway, the guys and I are having a gathering on Monday before we all head back to campus on Tuesday. We plan to pull out the grill and barbecue at my parents' house. I really hope you come through and hang with us like the old times."

"I plan to be there, bro, but I have to work at the shop that afternoon, so I may get there later on."

"Don't stand us up; we need you in the place, bro."

"I'll be there!"

Chapter Eleven

— ♥ —

Spring Break

A little after 10:45 p.m., a message from Narra lit up my phone screen. *Hey, babe, are you home yet? I just wanted to check in to see if you arrived safely. I know it rained heavily while you were en route and I was thinking about you.*

Smiling, I replied, *I'm all good, my love, just settling into the house. Although the drive took me at least another ten minutes because I was driving safely."*

The next text said, *Are you free to meet me at my church tomorrow? I would love to introduce you to my parents during the Sunday worship service.*

Hesitant but genuine, I replied, *Actually, I'll be at my home church with my parents tomorrow. It's been a while since I've attended in person, so that's where I'll be in the morning.*

Narra called me right away, her voice a mix of urgency and longing. "Do you absolutely have to go to service with your parents tomorrow? You can go anytime! It would mean a great deal to me to introduce you to mine before things get extremely busy. I don't know when we'll all find time again!"

I could feel her desire for connection and I responded gently, "Narra, relax. I promised my parents long ago that I'd attend Sunday service with them during spring break. But I can stop by afterward; I'd love to meet your family. Plus, I'd love for you to pack an overnight bag so you can come back to my house to stay over and enjoy the night with me."

"Yeah, I understand, and I kind of promised my parents the same," she replied in a tone that felt understanding yet wistful. "I need to stop being lazy and actually attend church in person more often. I've been so spoiled with watching online."

I tried to lighten the mood by saying, "Let's have a family fun night or something! My mom can't stop asking when you're coming back over. It's like she knows you already! She even cleaned the guest room to make it feel cozier for you. My parents adore you. They really do."

"Aww, Dem, those words warm my heart, knowing how much they cherish our connection. I can't wait for the two families to finally meet and create memories that will last a lifetime."

Her excitement is contagious and I can't help but smile, imagining the love and laughter that we all will have. "Alright, babe, have a good night and enjoy church."

"You as well, my love."

Sunday, my favorite day of the week, had arrived. I woke up early to get ready for church at Trinity Worship Center. I was excited to go with my mom, stepdad, and stepbrothers, who were visiting for a few days. I woke up early to read my Bible, currently focusing on the Book of Luke. After my morning scripture reading and a conversation with God, I took a shower, brushed my teeth, and removed my hair rollers, allowing my hair to fall beautifully in its curls. The day was a family affair and everyone was excited. I was particularly looking forward to Dem possibly meeting my family after church when he came to pick me up. I wanted to look my best, not just for Jesus and myself but also for him. Although we hadn't officially announced our relationship or gone public yet, we were clearly aligned about where we stood, enjoying our privacy and not hiding anything from each other or anyone. Just then, I heard my phone ping. *Would you like to join us for breakfast? I made enough for everyone in the house, plus your favorite, shrimp and grits*, my mom texted.

"Shrimp and grits sound lovely, oh my goodness," I whispered to myself. However, I knew I couldn't indulge in such a tasty meal just yet. Fortunately, I couldn't smell the delicious aroma or I might have found it even harder to resist.

No, thank you, Mom. I'm fasting until dinner time, I replied.

At church, I had a chance to catch up with all my friends and the people I'd missed dearly. One lady approached me and said, "I hear you have a new boyfriend. I can't wait to meet him."

"Wow, news travels fast," I said, glancing at my parents, my eyebrows arching as I chuckled, sensing the gentle irony of the moment. The sermon, titled "Contentment in Every Season," whispered softly to my heart. Exactly what I needed.

Today, in the warmth of my family at Living Word Ministries, I found nourishment for my soul. Murmurs of joy danced in the air—"Yay, Dem is back!" and "The Foxer family is in the building"—as we greeted each other, a chorus of familiar love and belonging. The Sunday message echoed within me, a soulful reminder to stay steadfast in my bond with Jesus. Each word resonated deeply, rekindling my spirit and reaffirming my divine devotion. As I continued to listen to the sermon, a gentle hesitation arose—a flicker of uncertainty about my romantic future. I started to wonder if settling down and getting married in just a few years was the right path. Could we be too young? My friends, Benny and the others, often urged me to explore more adventures before narrowing my focus to just one girl. Their words made me pause and consider if they had a point. Deep down, I longed to navigate my college journey with purpose, all while developing a genuine friendship and relationship with Narra—one that was free from complications.

After the church service, I talked with my pastor, whom I hadn't seen in months, about my relationship with Narra. He knew a little from what my parents had shared with him, but he hadn't realized that things had escalated quickly and they left the details for me to explain. Pastor Jack was easygoing and empathetic, always approachable for nearly any topic.

In the sanctuary, praise music continued to play softly. I approached the pastor and gave him a tight hug. "How are you, P. Jack?" I asked.

"Hey, D. Fox!" he replied with a smile. We both laughed. I then began sharing more about how serious things had become with Narra and me. "Pastor Jack, I'm completely in love with Narra," I admitted. "I feel a strong, undeniable attraction towards her. I want her—truly desire her in every sense of the word. But I wonder if I'm ready to take that plunge and settle down."

"But do you feel like you need her?" Pastor Jack asked, his voice steady. "Wanting someone is one thing, but can you envision a future with her? Does she have the qualities of the godly woman you've always dreamt of? Is she a woman of purpose?"

"She absolutely does! You'll see it when you meet her! I feel like I've hit the jackpot with her!" I couldn't help but let out a joyful "Woo, wee!" "Our friendship is blossoming; it lays the groundwork for a deep, lasting connection. Deep in my heart, I know she is meant to be my wife. I've been seeking guidance from the Lord and the signs are clear: she is the one. My future wife, the mother of my children, my eternal love and closest companion, sharing the same dreams I've envisioned for my future. I dream of marrying Narra within the next couple of years and every part of my being yearns to make that dream a reality. Perhaps it will come a bit later, but the anticipation of our shared future fills me with warmth and hope.

"While some friends, family members, and a few outside observers might feel we're too young to think about marriage and settling down, I truly believe that we are mature enough to make this decision on our own."

"Wow, Dem, I am so happy for you! Listening to you talk about Narra fills my heart with joy. I can't wait to meet her."

"Soon, Pastor … very soon!" I replied, our hands clasping in a warm shake, followed by a strong hug and shared laughter.

"Hope to see you back in the building in a few weeks, Dem!"

"I hope to be seen, but if not, you know I'll be watching online!"

Later that afternoon, after Sunday service, my parents and I enjoyed lunch that my dad quickly prepared for us. "Dad, this turkey BLT sandwich makes me miss being home more often," I said, my mouth full of lettuce, tomato, and turkey. "And this vegan bacon and mayo! I cannot tell the difference. Just how I like it—fresh wheat bread."

"Oh, that bread is very fresh! I baked it myself, honey!"

"Oh, Mom, you've really stepped up your game! Teach me how you do it; I need lessons."

My mom asked, "Is Narra still coming for family fun night?"

"She sure is!" I said with feigned excitement. "I just texted her. She'll be ready for sure when I get there, but I'll be meeting her family before we head back."

"Meeting the parents for the first time too? Well, that must be exciting! Are you nervous?"

"Just a little, but more excited. I'm meeting her stepbrothers as well. Hopefully, they won't hound me."

"You should be good. I'm sure Narra has spoken nothing but good things about you."

Walking toward the living room, I heard my dad say something in almost a whisper.

I leaned my ear a little closer in his direction, my hand hovering over it. "What was that, Dad?"

He asked, "What's wrong, Son? I sense you are not enthused at this moment."

"I'm okay, Dad," I said, lying. I wasn't okay and my dad knew it.

He gave me a deep stare. "Tell me later when you feel comfortable."

"Thanks, Dad!"

I pulled him to the side just before I headed to Narra's.

We talked in the living room while my mom was preparing the family's Sunday dinner.

"So, what's up, Son?"

"I have been going back and forth about something Benny said the other day."

"Is it about you and Narra?"

"Yeah, how'd you know?"

"Of course your best friend will feel a certain way when you find someone special who has all your attention, especially when you're genuinely happy. He knows things will never be the same."

"Wow, Dad! How do you know these things?"

"I was your age once and I had to change some things. My friends acted strangely when I met your mother. I went from being a bachelor to a husband really quickly." He laughed.

"I overheard some of your conversation with Pastor Jack at church. You told him you met someone special who loves Jesus. I did not hear much after that. His response of joy should tell you everything you need to know about your relationship with Narra."

"Yeah, Dad. I love Narra, but I haven't told her everything that's on my mind yet. I think I'll let her know soon though. I also believe we should slow things down a bit. I need to tell her I need to stay focused on school for now and she should do the same. I hope she understands. I'm still very interested, but I need some time before we get too serious. I know I want to marry her, but we need to take things a little slower."

"Just think carefully before relaying that info to her."

"You're right, Dad, I will.

"She strongly resembles a Proverbs 31 woman. In so many ways, she reminds me of Mom. I have no doubt she will be a loving wife and nurturing mother to our future children. I've shared bits and pieces about her previously with Mom, but there's so much more to tell.

"From the very first moment I laid eyes on her, Dad, I felt the difference in her presence. It was the way she carried herself that captivated me. Although I didn't know anything about her at that point, I felt as if I understood her spirit completely just by looking at her.

"Narra isn't materialistic; she finds beauty in the simple things in life. She's so thoughtful and I'm learning a lot about the simple things in life. We often surprise one another with our favorite candy bars—a sweet little gesture that highlights how well we know each other."

"The Reese's chocolate bar, huh?"

"Yep, Dad. She does so much for me, but it's the little acts of kindness that reel me in even deeper. Now and then, she bakes heart-shaped cupcakes and hand-delivers them to me at my dorm and fills my days with sweetness. Though flawed like us all, she is different, Dad, holding my heart gently in her hands.

"I am a romantic, much like you and Mom, and she illustrates that spirit beautifully. It's wonderful how deeply she shares my hopeful perspective on love. Everything flows naturally between us; there's no need for force or pressure, but we truly need a touch of space—a gentle pause to allow our hearts to breathe.

My dad said, "With how you are talking about her, I think you both will do fine after a break. You have nothing to worry about."

"With Narra, I'm exploring realms I've never ventured into before. We share new Christian songs we discover, crafting a unique Spotify playlist that binds our spirits. When distance keeps us apart, we communicate through texts, each selecting a song to feel close, an unbreakable bond beyond space and time. Even from afar, I sensed God's presence in her, though I never heard her voice or saw her face up close. Then, at the gym, I saw her—her warmth undeniable. Her kindness shone through every word, her gentle spirit echoing Christ's love. Narra is the woman God talked to me about."

"Dem, I've never heard you speak about anyone like this before! You're serious, huh, Son?" My dad was smirking, both shocked and delighted at the goodness of God in my life.

"I knew we sent you to the right school. You're not only getting an excellent education but also finding the woman of your dreams too! God is Good!" he said as we laughed together, filled with joy at God's blessings.

An hour later, I arrived at Narra's place, pulling up beside her house and parking behind her car. She greeted me at the door and hopped into my vehicle momentarily. "Hey, babe," she said, her voice laced with nervousness.

"What's wrong, Narr?"

"Fair warning, my mom might not be a fan of you at first."

"What do you mean? That doesn't make any sense. What did I miss? She doesn't even know me yet!" I exclaimed, my voice tinged with shock.

"No, it's not you exactly; it's about my grades. My GPA has dropped a little."

"Your grades? How? When? Why? What is my role in this?"

"She thinks we've been spending too much time together and that I've become distracted."

"Narraaaa," I breathed out slowly, stretching the sound of her name to emphasize my astonishment. "I don't even know if I should walk in there now. Why didn't you tell me sooner?"

"I didn't know how to tell you, Dem."

"You just could have said it, Narra. I could've helped you study for your exams at least."

"I just thought I could manage everything and raise my grades without making it a significant issue, perhaps hoping it would not be a huge deal."

"But Narr, you're graduating soon! And now your mom thinks I'm the problem? Haha, this is hilarious," I said, my tone dripping with sarcasm.

"My mom believes we need to slow down a bit so I can focus on my grades. I'm so close to graduating."

"Well, how do you feel about what she's saying?"

"Well … she's not wrong. We have spent a lot of time together."

"Okay, let me quickly gather myself to meet your family. I also need to tell you something later, but we can discuss it at my house. It can wait."

Narra looked up at me, a delicate mix of worry and trust in her eyes. In that passing moment, her expression conveyed that she knew our hearts were intertwined—she was mine and I was hers. As we stepped out of the car, our hands instinctively reached for each other, fingers locking together as we ventured inside, united and ready to face whatever awaited us.

"Hi, everyone!" Dem exclaimed, his voice breaking the anticipation before anyone could respond.

"Mom, Dad, Levi, and Micah, this is my boyfriend, Dem." I introduced him with pride lacing my words.

"Nice to meet you, Dem," came the welcoming reply, warmth in the voices of my family.

"We've all heard some truly wonderful things about you," my stepfather added, his smile genuine and inviting.

"Oh, I'm sure," Dem replied, grinning. "I've only heard great things about the Potters and I can't express how elated I am to meet you all finally! Also, congratulations, Levi and Micah, on your engagements and the upcoming weddings."

The twins said, "Thanks," in unison.

"Come into the dining area, make yourself comfortable," my mom said as she and Dem embraced warmly.

"Oh, is this Bonn Bonn?" Dem nervously chuckled, looking down at his feet where Bonn Bonn couldn't stop sniffing.

"Yes, that's my little doggie."

"Have you eaten anything yet, Dem?" my mom asked, her eyes filled with concern.

"Not yet," Dem replied with a smile, "but I've got dinner waiting at home that my mom whipped up for us. Thank you though!"

I smiled as I reflected on my mother's incredible cooking. "Yeah, my mom's food is truly delicious. I've already devoured some of it!" I gestured with enthusiasm as I recalled the baked chicken—so tender it practically fell off the bone—perfectly nestled among the fragrant rice.

As we all gathered around the large dining table right outside the kitchen area, I moved to the kitchen island. I delicately selected a piece of chicken I carved earlier. With a playful glint in my eye, I turned to Dem, inviting him to share in the feast. "Here, try this," I said, gently offering him a piece from my fork, eager to see his reaction. "Mmm, this is delicious," he murmured, chewing thoughtfully while making an effort not to speak with his mouth full.

"You two are simply adorable together. It's easy to see why Narra is so enamored with you, Dem. You're not only extremely handsome but a true sweetheart."

"Thank you, Mrs. Potter," Dem replied, a shy smile spreading across his face.

My mom added, "I've heard so much about you that I feel like I've known you forever."

"So, you went to church earlier, huh?" my stepdad asked.

"I did and the message was on time. Whenever I can't attend in person, I make it a point to watch online when I can," Dem explained, the warmth of his voice wrapping around us like a cozy blanket. I proudly looked at him, not only for being a man of God but also for the way he handled himself in unusual situations. I initially thought he would be upset with me, yet he managed to gather himself and meet my family as if nothing had happened. It was as if he were unaware of my mom's disappointment regarding my grades. In that moment, I couldn't help but think of how mature he was. I felt a sense of relief and calm and finally I felt safe enough to call him mine.

"You all have a lovely home," Dem said, looking around at the walls and decor.

"Thanks, Dem. I'm proud of you, young man of God. I've heard many great things about you, but make sure you treat my daughter well," my stepdad stated.

Micah added, "Yeah, we've heard nothing but good things. We won't grill you too hard."

"Nah, forget all of that. I'm ready to grill him now!" Levi laughed.

"Hey, it's all good. What do you wanna know?" Dem asked him.

"I just want to know if you are truly who you say you are."

"I need to know if you genuinely love, Narra. We don't want her to get hurt," Micah added.

"I assure you, there's nothing to worry about. I'll continue to let my actions speak louder than words. But I can promise you Narra means everything to me. She helped transform my life."

Dem kept raving about me. "We both add so much value to each other; we are truly gifts from God to one another. Narra has drawn me closer to Him in this short time together. I'm confident I've done the same for her as if we weren't already close to God. It only gets better now that I've found her. We share similar aspirations in life and are spiritually aligned."

"Alright, okay!" Levi exclaimed, looking at me and nodding in agreement.

"I told you, Dem is different. He really loves Jesus." I glanced at Dem and continued, "Don't get it twisted; he's far from perfect. However, he has been consistently growing alongside me in this brief time. He takes his relationship with God seriously and it's genuine."

Dem smiled, took my hand, and gently hugged me. "I appreciate you more than you know," he said.

"Well, now that you're all settled in, let's enjoy our time together before you two head out in a few," my mom said, her smile brightening the room. "Dem, I'd love to share a little about the Potters with you. Would you join us in the living room? I'm sure Narra has already told you a few things."

Sitting on the plush sofa beside Dem, across from my mom, I noticed her stealing glances at him. Her gaze was intense and contemplative, making the air between them crackle with unspoken emotions. "Before we dive deeper into this," she began, her voice steady yet soft, "I want to express how much I appreciate the seriousness of the relationship blossoming between you and Narra. It's truly beautiful to witness. However, I gently suggest that perhaps a little space might be beneficial for both of you." Her expression shifts to one of sincerity as she continues, "Your growing bond is something special, but with graduation approaching, maybe it would be wise to ease back on the time spent together. After all, we wouldn't want her to lose focus on what's ahead."

"You are correct, Mrs. Potter. I understand completely," Dem said seriously, trying to keep a straight face.

"And please, it's just Ms. Nicole or Nikki and Mr. John to you. We truly don't mind it at all.

"Also, don't you think you're a little too young to be talking about marriage? I think you both would make wonderful spouses one day, but I truly believe it's too early to get so serious. Enjoy your life."

"Mom, it's not like we are getting married tomorrow or anything. We're just in love and taking our time."

Dem narrowed his eyes at me then turned to my mom, feeling the urge to speak on behalf of both of us. "Uh, I want you to know just how profoundly I love your daughter. I see a beautiful future ahead for us. Though we're not rushing into anything, I have to be honest: I won't sit idly by while someone else tries to win her heart. Our love is real and deep and I dream of spending the rest of my life with her." My cheeks flushing, I smiled at Dem and my mom.

My mom's curious and warm voice broke the gentle atmosphere. "Has Narra spoken about her father, Landen, at all?"

"Oh, yes! Absolutely," I answered for him, feeling a flutter of anticipation. "He only knows a little bit, Mom, so please, share more!"

Dem's eyes flashed with earnest interest. "Yes, I'd love to hear more!"

As my stepfather, Levi, and Micah lingered back in the warmth of the dining area, my mom began recounting her short version of our family's story. With Dem now familiar with my family, I felt ready to unveil more details later today, to let him in on the love that shaped us.

My mom relaxed into the soft, velvety embrace of the forest-green sofa, her arms elegantly folded like a pretzel, with a warm smile gracing her face. "On a sunny Thursday during a college football game, we were invited by friends from various schools. It was there that I met Narra's father, Landen, and felt an unexpected flutter of excitement in the air, as if the day held the promise of new connections and shared stories. Our meeting ignited a beautiful journey and two years later, Narra arrived—cute, alert, and a bit fussy. Celebrating that joyful milestone filled my heart with vast hope. I had always dreamed of marrying the love of my life before turning thirty, yearning for that fairy-tale moment. However, life took a different turn." She paused.

"Narra came unexpectedly and Landen and I had to focus on parenting, so we weren't ready to commit to marriage vows. In a beautiful twist of destiny, he moved abroad and found love, building a wonderful family that thrived overseas. During this time, I maintained my faith and raised my daughter with the help of my family. In my late forties, I finally met the love my heart had been seeking—Mr. Handsome himself, John Potter." She swooned. "This journey serves as a poignant reminder that sometimes the sweetest moments come from the most unexpected paths. Perhaps this was God's divine plan all along, guiding us toward our true happiness."

"That's a beautiful testimony, Ms. Nicole."

"Thanks for listening, Dem." She grinned.

Hearing about Narra's parents' love stories only made me more excited about what Narra and I shared, but I couldn't help wondering if Narra's dad helped with any finances as she grew up. I kept my thoughts to myself for a later conversation with her.

Narra glanced at her watch and shot me a quick text: *It's getting a little late. Let's roll out of here.*

I looked over, smiling, and replied, *Yeah, we should go. I don't want my dinner to get cold. Lol.*

"Alright, family, we have to get out of here. It's been great catching up with you all," I said, standing up and stretching.

"Nice to finally meet you, brother-in-law," Levi chimed in.

I looked at Narra and noticed that she couldn't help but blush deeply, a playful smirk spreading across her face at Levi's teasing remark about me.

"Same here, bro. Safe travels back to Arizona!"

I gathered my things, excitement bubbling inside as we headed out together. Dem opened the car door for me and I swiftly secured my seat belt, the familiar click grounding me. As he moved gracefully around the vehicle, he lifted the trunk with purpose and retrieved something, a small act of mystery. My curiosity awakened and I followed his movements with attentive eyes, each motion adding a thread to the tapestry of the moment.

"Babe, I have something for you," he said with a playful smile as he slipped into the driver's seat. He pulled out a bag that appeared to have just come from a high-end store. I eagerly opened it to reveal a luxurious box and inside was a stunning small, baby-pink Chanel purse with a gold chain as the strap. My eyes lit up. *He knows me so well.* "And it's my favorite color!" I exclaimed, feeling overwhelmed with gratitude as I wrapped my arms around him in a tight hug.

"I knew you'd love it, Narr," he said, his eyes sparkling with joy.

"Of course, I love it, Dem. I paused, turned, and stared at him as he buckled his seatbelt. "But Dem, you know you don't need to buy me expensive gifts, babe."

"I know, Narr. But I really wanted to."

As we drove towards Dem's house, I stole a glance at him and said, "So, do you want all the juicy details?"

"Absolutely! We've got time and I'm sure there's much more to the story."

"It's a good one. This moment was often replayed in my childhood memories. I would feel the gentle warmth of my bed, drifting towards sleep while recalling my parents whispering about their dreams for the future. They shared a deep, loving bond and longed to be united in marriage someday. From my innocent, young perspective, I believed my mother's unwavering faith that she would marry my father. She poured her love into every action, carrying the role of a devoted wife long before vows were even considered. Each evening, her love filled the house with the fragrant aroma of dinner, a carefully crafted feast for him. Morning light often found him greeted by her lovingly prepared breakfast and sometimes she would surprise him with a lunch packed full of affection."

"So, she was already in wife mode, huh?" Dem asked, his eyebrows raised with curiosity.

"Exactly! My mom catered to my dad as if he were a king. Through observing their relationship, I've picked up many valuable lessons about what to do and what to avoid in a partnership. I can't share everything just yet, but I have a feeling more will come up later," I said, a hint of mystery in my voice.

"I'm intrigued; please tell me more! I'm just so happy that they both eventually found real love. Oh, and you turned out all right. Haha!"

I scanned Dem's eyes, feeling a flutter of affection amid his sarcasm and flashed him a playful grin. "Okay, so I heard my mom's heartfelt prayers and saw tears for my dad echoed with a love that deepened each day. Although I was only a kid, she often shared her dreams with me, expressing a desire to marry my dad without the fuss of a grand wedding. I like to think she imagined that he would embrace this simplicity, relieved from the pressures of elaborate planning or the burden of choosing an extravagant engagement ring. Her heart spoke of love's true nature—uncomplicated yet profound, shimmering quietly among life's chaos. But something changed in my dad and my mom's relationship —a shift occurred, and a shadow of unhappiness descended between them. My dad, a man deeply committed to the Lord, nevertheless stumbled through his share of human mistakes. Yet, my mother possessed a heart full of grace, always ready to forgive and embrace him anew. Despite her unwavering love, my father grew troubled, harboring the unsettling belief that he was unworthy of her, convinced a man better suited to be her husband existed.

"I still remember my mother trying to whisper to my father with a sigh, 'I sought God for nearly a year on this and counsel has not helped us. My heart hasn't felt the 'yes' I'm searching for. Something just feels off, Landen. I love you, but I don't believe you are my soulmate. I genuinely think you will make a wonderful husband for someone else someday.'

"They are completely unaware that I know all this about their early relationship. I have never mentioned it to them as I have taken the saying 'Stay in a child's place' to heart. You feel me?" I chuckle.

"I get it. You understood that it was not your place to interfere in their business, especially being so young."

"I'll never forget this one thing my dad told my mom before she truly recognized he wasn't the man meant for her. He shared that something crucial was absent—God's approval. In his heart, he felt he hadn't received a 'yes' from above and he realized he wasn't prepared to be her husband just yet. Though he was right, my mom couldn't see it then. For her, the thought of marrying anyone but my father was unfathomable. That was the future she envisioned, but God had a different, brighter plan for her. His designs are always better than our own.

"Sometimes we might endure painful seasons so that we can appreciate the divine moments that follow. We may not understand the heartbreaks we face, but my parents' journey was pivotal in guiding me toward my own path. My mom prayed that my love life would differ from hers, desiring to spare me the same heartaches she had endured."

"Narr, you are so wise beyond your years and I am truly amazed by it!"

"So, my mom often reminded herself that marrying someone, knowing it could likely lead to divorce, would have been even more painful. Yet, through it all, she continued to attend church and seek the Lord with unwavering faith, even after what she called her little breakdown."

"What breakdown?"

"It's a long story, babe, and I promise to share it with you at another time.

"As I wrap this up, I remember how my mother prayed for a godly husband, yearning to become the woman described in Proverbs 31—a woman who understands God and knows what a good man requires. She hoped for a divine connection, perfectly timed.

"In 2010, God smiled upon her as she met the most wonderful person—a man she had prayed for. They discovered in each other the divine partnership they had long sought."

"Wow, that is an amazing testimony, and I love all the lessons you learned from it. It's like you learned from some of your parents' mistakes."

I nodded in agreement. "I like to call it breaking generational curses and cycles!

I understand what it means to settle for less, and I have no intention of ever doing so.

"So, what was it you needed to talk to me about?" I asked, raising an eyebrow.

"Oh, yeah, that. We'll discuss it soon. Trust me, Narra, the atmosphere isn't quite right for the conversation we need to have."

"Is it about spending time apart and my grades? I truly apologize for that. I should have been more open with you. Sometimes, my mom treats me like I'm still a child, as if I don't know how to raise my grades. But I promise, I've got this; I can manage it."

Dem remained quiet, focusing on the road ahead. With approximately 20 minutes left according to the GPS, we continued our journey toward the Foxer residence. With the sunset painting the sky in warm apricot and rose pink, a profound silence filled the car, filled with unexpressed emotions that lingered in his heart.

Finally, he exhaled softly and said, "There are a few important things I want to share with you after we settle in." His voice was smooth and sincere, filled with the depth of his feelings and the sweet tension that surrounded the moment. He remained gentle with me.

I tuned into one of our favorite radio stations, enjoying the familiar music as I settled into the car's comfort. Dem kept his eyes on the road and I silently admired how he navigated the drive in silence. I kept myself busy with my phone, knowing this trip to his house was off-limits for anything we needed to discuss regarding school. It was easier to stay calm and let the moment be.

As we settled into the Foxer residence, Mrs. Foxer greeted me at the door, clearly thrilled to see me again. "Narra, I'm so happy to see you! It's been a while!" she exclaimed. We all shared a laugh. "I know you probably ate dinner already since it's getting late, but please take a plate or try a taste of my famous spaghetti!"

"Oh, Mom's spaghetti is the real deal. It's lit!" Dem chimed in.

"Sure, I'll take a small plate, please. Let me unpack my things and I'll be back for a taste," I replied, feeling the kitchen's warmth.

"Sounds good, Narra," she said with a smile and a hint of excitement.

As I began unpacking my overnight bag in one of the guest rooms on the second floor, down the hall from Dem's bedroom, he softly knocked and entered the room, his demeanor noticeably more serious than it had been earlier. He had changed into a pair of black sweatpants and a light blue RU T-shirt, appearing more comfortable than before.

"Hey, babe. You all good in here?"

"Yes, Demery. So, what'd you want to talk about?" I calmly asked, sensing the weight in his tone.

Dem sat down on the bed. "All the things your mom was saying… It's really starting to weigh on me," he admitted, though his voice remained gentle.

"I know, I know. She's correct. We both need to prioritize our studies," I reassured him, but something felt off.

"No, Narra, I'm serious. We need to take a little break to clear our heads," he urged, sincerity etched on his face.

"What's gotten into you, Dem?" I asked, my voice tinged with surprise at his sudden seriousness.

"Your slipping grades are a big deal and I genuinely care about you," he said softly, securing his gaze within mine. "Let's take some time apart. I just need some space to think this through."

In the air between us hung a tension that felt strangely intimate, a reminder of the bond we shared even in moments of uncertainty. I sat quietly on the bed, my feet tapping gently against the floor, then rose to my feet. "You're right, Demery."

"Don't stress too much, my love; you'll always be my girl. Let's just focus on making wiser choices and being more thoughtful in our actions together. We need to take a moment to breathe and slow down. There's so much more I want to share with you," he said, his voice softening.

I walked up to the desk, settled into the chair, resting my right hand thoughtfully on my chin as my eyes drifted into the distance, as if I were staring into space. He approached softly, standing before me with gentle purpose, and took my hands in his. "I love you, Narra," he whispered, his heart pouring forth in silent song.

I smiled, and it felt as if I had a quiet glow in my eyes from my tears. "I love you, too, Demery."

"I'm not going anywhere," he assured me. "I know you are my wife. I'm wildly in love with you. You are the best thing that has ever happened to me.

"Narra, you inspire me to love God and you even more," he added, his gaze steady on me. Every time Dem confessed his love for me, my heart fluttered with excitement, but in this moment, I had to stay composed.

In the gentle silence, he was asking for space, leaving me wandering in a maze of wonder. *Do his words hide secrets yet to be revealed? The weight of grades presses down on me, while his elusive gestures craft a tapestry of ambiguity: does his heartbeat echo mine? Does he genuinely feel the same? I don't want to be apart from him; in fact, I long for his presence more fiercely with each passing moment. If his love is true, why does he seek distance, despite the storm of my academic battles? Who cares for my mother's opinions when my heart beats solely for him?*

"Is that truly what you want, Dem?" I asked with tears forming in my eyes. I carefully tried to hide my emotions, determined not to let them show. Yet, despite my efforts, they betrayed me. I wondered why I couldn't simply remain emotionless, especially in moments that felt so delicate and profound. The tension in the air was palpable and tears began to fall from my eyes.

"No, I don't really want that," he replied, as if he were searching for the right words. "But it feels like the best decision for us at this moment."

With a heavy heart, I rose from my seat. "Alright, if that's what you truly wish." My voice was barely above a whisper, filled with unspoken affection that lingered between us. "I'll respect your decision."

"Narra, come here," Dem muttered softly, gently pulling my hand to stop me from walking away and out the door. He did not want his parents to know we had had a little disagreement and neither did I. I relaxed into Dem's embrace, our bodies aligning in a seamless harmony as we gazed outward together, our backs facing the door. He wrapped me in a warm bear hug then placed a soft kiss upon my cheek. I turned slightly, leaning in to steal a soft peck, just missing his lips. "I love you so much, Narra, and the thought of being apart is unbearable, but we have to for a short while."

"Dem, this will be so difficult," I whispered, slowly loosening his embrace and turning around to face him again.

"We've got this, Narra. We can do this. We'll still talk and text like normal; we just won't be in the same place as much."

"Alright, Dem," I replied, a hint of determination in my voice.

Just then, his mother's gentle knock echoed through the door as she inquired, "Are you all excited and ready for the games?"

Dem swung open the door, his eyes bright with excitement. "Yes!"

We both surged forward, eager to join the others in the dining area. I saw Connect Four, Trouble, Monopoly, and Uno spread out on the table. "Oh, this is going to be fun! I'm the best at Uno!" I boasted.

"This is about to be a battle," Dem replied with a grin, ready to take on the challenge.

Later that night, after all the fun and laughter, I snuggled into the cozy bed feeling refreshed from my warm shower. As I lay there, my mind began to wander, replaying moments of joy from the evening, and then suddenly worry started to overshadow my happiness. The joy I felt was like a gentle lullaby, soothing my heart; yet, my mind began to spiral into doubts and uncertainties that nagged from my earlier conversations with Dem, each word echoing in my thoughts and pulling me deeper into reflection.

Unexpectedly, my world had shifted and a flood of questions flooded my mind: *Is this it? Is this truly happening? Am I too young for real love? Could Dem be my husband? Is he prepared to embrace a godly love and relationship? I've never been the kind of girl who wanted to play hard to get; I believe in the beauty of genuine connection. My future husband will experience my heart and all of me in intimate ways that no one has ever experienced before. The uncertainty of my feelings leaves me flustered. Will he wait for me?* "I'm really starting to overthink everything," I whispered to myself, barely moving my lips.

Around midnight, Dem's message lit up my phone: *Hope you're still awake, babe. I meant to tell you, Benny, A Wess, and a few of the guys are having a get-together tomorrow and I would like you to meet some of those you haven't met yet if you're interested.*

I replied, *I think I'm good. I don't want them to sense anything wrong between us, plus I should head back to campus early. You need some time to hang out with your friends. I get it.*

I suggested, *Let's just create some extra space starting tomorrow.*

He replied, *You sure?*

I reassured him, *Yeah, I'll back off a little now, but I'll be looking forward to talking to you later tomorrow night after you get back.*

The last text of the night read, *Alright, my love. Sleep well, see you in the morning.*

Morning arrived, marking our last day at home for spring break. At around 10:00 a.m., I brought breakfast my mom had prepared for Narra, setting it down on the desk in front of the computer. To my surprise, she was already dressed beautifully. Her hair was styled in cute curls and her makeup was subtle yet elegant, completed with a touch of pink lip gloss. The sweet scent of cinnamon wafted through the air and I could hardly contain my admiration.

"Dang, girl!" I exclaimed, unable to hide my approval. She chuckled, wrapping her arms around my neck in a sincere hug. The familiar blend of vanilla and cinnamon from her perfume surrounded me. I pulled back to look at her, teasing. "Are you doing this on purpose? Haha, really funny, Narra.

"You look so beautiful," I added affectionately. "Remember, you're all mine; space doesn't mean anything when it comes to us." I glanced at her then turned my attention back to the task at hand. "Hold on, let me grab a to-go bag for your food. I'll make sure to collect all your bags too."

Narra and I stepped out of the house together. On the porch, my parents were enjoying the calm breeze when they spotted us. They stood up with warm smiles and embraced Narra and me in turn. My mom, with a heartfelt tone, said, "It was truly lovely to have you here, honey. We had such a wonderful time last night."

"Yes, I really enjoyed myself," Narra replied with a smile. "We have to do this again sometime."

"Absolutely, I'll plan something for us. I'll have Dem get in touch with you. Actually, take my number."

"That's a great idea," Narra said, nodding. "I'll keep in touch."

As Dem and I traveled toward my parents' home in Locakee, PA, our words flowed in gentle effects, a soft melody of light conversation beneath the warmth of morning. The sun's warm, calming light encased us like a beautiful layered scarf, comforting as he led me to my car, transferred my overnight bag and belongings to the back seat and gently eased my car door shut at the Potters' residence. The goodbye turned out to be less difficult than I had anticipated. As we reflected on our time together, it became clear that we genuinely needed some time apart. I expressed my deep appreciation for Dem and we shared heartfelt "I love yous" along with promises to see each other soon. We clarified that while we respected each other's space, our bond remained unbreakable. *He's my man, and I'm his lady.* It was all about love and understanding that space is essential. "A literal spring break"—that's all there was to say.

Later, at Benny's, the guys were hanging out when I walked in, instantly capturing everyone's attention.

"Ayeee, man! It's the lover boy, Demery! We're no longer calling you Dem; it's Demeryyy from now on," Aaron teased.

I moved around the room, shaking hands with everyone. "So, it seems everyone has something funny to say, huh? The food smells amazing! What's on the grill?"

"We've got everything! I've got my mom in the kitchen whipping up some sides for us," Benny said. "My dad helped a little with the grilling," he added.

I peeked into the kitchen and said, "Thanks, Ms. Lorraine!"

"You're welcome, Dem! I'm proud of you. Don't listen to those guys; they just aren't as mature as you yet," she stated.

"You got that right; I hear you!" I agreed with a smile.

"Real love is a beautiful thing!" she added.

"Aye, Dem, the guys and I are heading to Bendov's club tonight. Are you joining us?" Benny asked.

"Of course I'll do the pre-night out, but I don't know about the strip joint. Y'all know I usually don't go to strip clubs, no matter my relationship status. It's just not my thing. I'm trying to live right and avoid tempting situations, you know?"

"I get it, man, but you should have a little fun!"

It was a night out with the boys—just the six of us. We started at a lively sports bar, enjoying each other's company and shared laughs. As the night progressed, our friends planned to continue the adventure at a gentleman's club, but two of us stood firm in our decision not to join that scene. We wanted to stay true to ourselves and our values. Instead, we opted to relax a little longer at the sports bar, where the atmosphere was vibrant, filled with the clinking of glasses and cheerful banter. While others indulged in drinks I stuck with my choice of water on the rocks, but that didn't dampen my spirits. It was wonderful to catch up and reminisce with my friends, appreciating the bond we shared on this memorable night.

While spending time with my friends, my thoughts kept drifting to Narra. Despite my longing to text her, I decided to give her the space she needed. I desperately wanted to reach out, but I chose to wait for her to message me first. I guess I'm a sucker for love because I silently resolved that if I don't hear from her soon, I would text her myself. It'd been less than 24 hours and I was already acting like I hadn't seen her in a while. Narra had shared her desire to be married within the next couple of years and that thought occupied my mind relentlessly. I couldn't help but reminisce about the intimate, sweet moments we shared a few days ago, especially when we finally introduced each other to our families.

Sitting in the sports bar, my thoughts began to run wild for her. Her skin was like a soft layer of butter, and the scent? Pure, sweet honey. Her hair, oh man, it had that vanilla cinnamon vibe that just drew me in. I missed her fiercely, craving her spirit. How was it possible to feel so intensely in such a short time? This had to be God at work. I knew she was destined to be my wife.

Chapter Twelve

A Crazy Day at Kraze

*E*ach day, I crave to experience the sweetness of your loving and kind spirit, I read as I found another note tucked away in my gym bag that felt like treasure as I shifted from the gym to the rhythm of my workday. I was searching for my name tag when I spotted a sweet note from Narra that I had somehow overlooked. She certainly had a knack for keeping me cheerful, making me long for her presence.

Without hesitation, I texted her, letting her know that her note had brightened my day. *Dang girl, just found your note in my bag. I truly appreciate your thoughtfulness and I cannot wait to see you.* She replied with a heart emoji. Narra and I had been taking some time apart, but we hadn't missed a beat. We talked on the phone almost every other day and shared sweet texts daily. I never realized how hard it would be not seeing her in person; the space between us made my heart ache. I even tried inviting Narra to my dorm suite to study, but she gently declined. she was taking this little break to heart and I deeply respected her for that, even if I missed her dearly. We often prayed together over the phone, experiencing a deep connection.

Additionally, we partook in virtual worship, entwining our spirits in the shared resonance of the message. Afterward, we would converse, deepening our understanding. When time allowed, we united once more—selecting songs from the same playlist and harmonizing our hearts in song on a phone or video call. Sometimes, we would get so absorbed in the calming effect of worship songs that we dozed off during the call. Eventually, one of us would wake up, surprised to realize we had spent hours peacefully sleeping. Our connection was truly divine.

Her love for God enhanced my affection for her each day. I found myself enthusiastically sharing with my friends, family, and my pastor how much I loved her. I even shared my feelings toward Narra with one of my previous professors, expressing the beauty of our bond at every opportunity. Lost in daydreams of her, I craved her presence like a breath of fresh air. My deepest desire was to lead her in Christ, loving her as the Bible instructs a husband to love his wife.

I clocked in for my shift as one of my co-workers wrapped up hers. While she updated me on the day's events, I set up my cash register and organized my workspace. Just then, I heard a soft, familiar voice. "Oh, hey Dem! It feels like an eternity! How have you been?" It was Simone Wright, a girl I had once dated, entering the shop, her eyes glimmering with joy and surprise. Her gaze reminded me of the way she looked at me just a few weeks prior when I was driving Narra home—a moment that still lingered in my memory, stirring a mix of emotions within me.

I remembered the moment when I closed the passenger door after ushering Narra inside; Simone had caught a glimpse of me and called out, "Demery Robert Foxer!" Yet, amid the rush, my focus was only on Narra as she passed by.

Narra had leaned in curiously and asked, "Who was that? Wow, they know your middle name, huh?" I brushed it off, saying it was just an old friend from high school.

As I prepared today's flavors of vegan ice cream and frozen treats, I couldn't help but smile back at her. "Hey, Simone! I'm doing well, just working here part-time at Kraze to earn a little extra cash while I focus on school. Can you believe I'm already a junior at Rovane? It feels like forever since we last saw each other! The last time was just before you left for college for your freshman year. How have you been?"

"I'm doing well, thanks! Time really flies. I'm in my senior year now and I'm so ready to graduate!" she replied, a wistful smile lighting up her face.

"It truly does! What brings you back to this part of town?" I asked, genuinely intrigued. "Ah, just looking to see you and maybe grab some fresh ice cream from the best place around," she said playfully, giving me her best googly-eyed look.

"Is that right?" I asked, trying to conceal my nervousness.

"Actually, I'm visiting some family and handling a bit of business, but I've also been thinking about taking a job nearby," she responded, her cheerful tone layered with contemplation.

"Ah, I see. What can I get for you today?" Handing her a menu, I said, "Today's ice cream flavors are Blueberry Vanilla Icing, Triple Chocolate Crunch, Vanilla, Cherry, and Plain Jane Strawberry Jam." I intentionally left out the Narr Barr Delight. It would have been so awkward to mention to my ex. I was relieved when she didn't ask about it. I dived into explaining each flavor, highlighting the creativity behind the names. "We offer a variety of options, including cones, cups, and bowls in small, medium, large, and extra-large sizes. Additionally, we have other vegan sweet treats available."

"Wow, that all sounds so delicious!" she whispered. "I want to try the Plain Jane Strawberry Jam ice cream cone, please."

"And your desired size?"

"Medium, please!"

"That's a fantastic choice and a very popular one."

She leaned on the counter and said, "Dem, I've been thinking about us a lot lately. Have you ever considered how we used to be?" Her gaze was steady, as if she was searching my eyes for an answer.

I looked up from making her order, "Certainly, I've thought about us … before. Ugh, but not lately. Honestly, my heart belongs to someone else now," I admitted, feeling the weight of honesty.

"Really?" she asked, surprise evident in her voice.

"Very much so. I adore her; she fills my thoughts, even invades my dreams." My heart felt lighter as I said it.

"By the way, I sent you my number in your IG DM. Make sure you save it!" she said playfully.

I replied, "Yeah, I saw it. You sent some pretty wild pictures too. Keep them for your future husband's eyes only, young lady," I teased back, attempting to lighten the mood even with the hint of sentimentality lingering.

Curious, she asked why I hadn't responded sooner, her brow furrowed slightly. "I saw that you left me on read."

"Is this for here or to go?"

"It's to go, thank you!

"Are you not single and not married?" she teased playfully, her eyes glinting as she noted the absence of any romantic posts and the lack of a ring on my finger. "Your Facebook profile clearly states you're single, Dem!"

"I don't pay much attention to Facebook statuses and I've never shared my dating life online. You know how I am—I'm just not that kind of guy, Simone!" I shrugged, trying to keep the mood light. I preferred to keep my life private on Facebook, sharing only the occasional gym selfie or work update. I had deliberately chosen to keep my romantic life out of the spotlight, holding out for what I believed to be 'the one from God.'

I laughed playfully as I carefully drizzled strawberry jam syrup over the base of the cone, allowing it to flow over the ice cream area before dribbling a final touch of syrup on top to complete the presentation. "It's a bit strange for you to show up at my job. Are you stalking me or something, Simone?"

"Not at all!" She giggled, her eyes glinting mischievously. "But seriously, everyone knows where you work and which gym you go to. Your Facebook is overflowing with those adorable work and gym selfies you always post!"

"Oh, haha! Yeah, I guess that's just my thing. I need to keep up with my weekly work and workout posts."

"Here is your order!" I said, reaching over the glass counter and handing Simone her ice cream. "Would you like to add anything else?"

"That should be it! So, do you have time for a quick, friendly lunch on Friday at noon?"

"No, I'm busy working."

"All day? How about the evening then?" Simone asked, her anticipation clear.

I glanced at her and replied, "I've got plans with someone," feeling a rush of excitement in my voice. "We might not be Facebook or Instagram official just yet, but we are definitely exclusive. I told you, I'm really seeing someone. She's the most amazing girl. She's different, special, and I'm determined not to mess this up."

I caught Simone giving me a teasing side-eye, her eyebrow arched playfully. "Well, good for you!" she said. "She's a lucky lady!"

I stood behind the cash register, surrounded by a few customers enjoying their treats. The two tables were full and those customers had already been served, which gave me a moment to breathe. "That will be two dollars and eighty-three cents!" I announced, keeping my tone professional yet warm.

Simone handed me a five-dollar bill to pay for her ice cream cone, a small piece of paper tucked inside with her number, and a smile lingered on her lips as our playful banter continued.

"Here's your change." As I placed the change in her palm, she folded the bills and tossed them, along with the coins, into the tip jar next to the cash register —a lighthearted gesture of camaraderie.

"All yours!" she said and I couldn't help but smile a little as I watched her walk away.

Simone pulled out her cell phone and walked back, spinning around with a playful smile. She leaned back slightly toward the counter and told me to smile while boldly grabbing my chin.

"Demery, I never know when I'll see you again! Let's snap a quick selfie!" she said excitedly, leaning in as our shoulders brushed. She held her ice cream cone near her chin with a playful pout, serving up that classic duck face, while I tried to focus on assisting the new customers who just walked in.

"Simone, I'm sorry, but I have to take care of the next customers," I whispered back, a smile creeping onto my face despite her relentless snapping. With a few gentle clicks, she captured the moment on her cellphone. Turning just inches from my cheek, she pursed her lips for one photo, and in another, she revealed her tongue while licking the ice cream.

"I hope to see you later sometime, Dem!" she said, a slight smile warming her face as she walked toward the door, leaving the creamery shop behind.

"Have a great day and enjoy your ice cream… I'll take the next customer, please!" I called out, maintaining my professionalism as more customers filtered into the shop. The shop became busy and time began to slip away. Eventually, I took a well-deserved break from the cash register, thanks to a supportive co-worker who stepped in to cover for me. Recognizing the importance of honesty with Narra, I decided to text her about my conversation with Simone, making sure to assure her that it was completely innocent. My goal was to ensure that Narra could fully trust me. At first, I hadn't thought too much about it, but later, during my short lunch break, I walked to the back to grab my bag, phone, and smartwatch. As I dug out my phone, I saw a few notifications on the lock screen. I slid my phone into my back pocket, took a few bites of my lunch, then pulled my phone out and laid it on the table. I had a few missed calls, one voicemail, and I noticed that I was tagged in a post that had already gained close to ten thousand likes and over a hundred comments. I hadn't realized that Simone

A Crazy Day at Kraze

was somewhat of a social media beauty sensation with over 300k followers.

Suddenly, I heard a persistent ding from my watch and felt my phone buzzing nonstop in my pocket. I noticed a few unread text messages and DMs from my friends: Benny, A Wess, Chris, and a few other friends who used social media. I immediately checked my texts—"Fifteen unread messages? What is going on? What did I miss?" I whispered.

Benny had sent a few texts, one reading, *Ayo Dem, you're really living your life out there, huh? You could have let your best bud know!*

Chris also messaged me: *Dem, call me when you get off work, man.*

I even had a missed call from my mom. I ignored the texts for a moment to unpack what was happening. I returned to Facebook to see Simone's pictures, realizing I should have adjusted my tagging settings long ago. I checked the comments on the pictures and saw people saying things like:

"Y'all look good together."

"Y'all babies would be so cute."

"I always knew y'all would end up together."

"Relationship goals."

"When's the wedding?"

"She's gorgeous, Dem!"

"High School sweethearts!"

"Power Couple."

Heart eyes emojis

"The Perfect Couple!"

"Okay, Dem! I see you!"

"How long have y'all been together?"

"We ship this couple!"

"Happy for you both!"

"Y'all are fine together!"

I felt a wave of nervousness and worry flow over me as I realized Narra might have seen the tagged photos. I immediately texted her to explain.

Hey Narra, I wanted to hit you up earlier, but work's been wild busy. I've got to share what happened with a girl I dated back in high school. I want you to know that it wasn't anything serious; she flirted with me and I told her straight up that I'm seeing someone. But even after I said that, while I was on the clock at work helping customers, she kept snapping pics of me at the shop just a few hours ago.

What time did she share these pictures? I wondered as I reopened the Facebook app. "This is crazy!" I exclaimed, putting my hand on my head and letting out a deep sigh. A few hours ago, Simone had shared two photos and a short ten-second video. One photo captured her playful duck face as she posed with her ice cream cone, tilting her head slightly towards me. The second photo showed me beaming at the camera with her fingertips lightly brushing my chin, cone still in her hand, as if we were sharing the cone or she was trying to feed me. The short video clip featured her leaning in close, our shoulders touching, while she delicately licked the ice cream cone. Not one word was spoken in that clip; she must've edited it that way for sure.

And that caption! Just three heart emojis and an ice cream emoji—she left plenty of room for imagination, making everyone wonder. "How did she even capture that video clip?" I said aloud. A co-worker overheard me and shot a curious glance in my direction, but I excused myself and stepped outside for more privacy to finish my break. After seeing that post, I quickly scrambled to figure out how to untag myself from the photos and post, but then I realized it was probably too late. I started scrolling through the likes and comments and noticed several family members had liked it, including my grandmother, whom I hadn't seen in a few months. Among the comments, there was one from Aaron, which included the wide-eyed and big eyes emojis.

I considered making my page private, but I wasn't social media savvy enough to figure it out while my emotions were running wild. I couldn't even recall if Narra and I were friends on Facebook. Then it struck me—of course, we were connected on socials. I finally figured out how to set my profile to private by doing a quick search but soon realized that it wouldn't make a difference since Simone had already posted the pictures and video, which were over two hours old. I removed my name from the tagged post, but the pictures and video seemed to have already gone viral, even landing on one of those "cute couples" pages.

Benny couldn't resist sending me a screenshot in my DMs to keep me in the loop. I considered reaching out to Simone privately to ask her to take the pictures down, but ultimately I felt it would be better to close that door on any conversation. There was a reason I left her private message on "read" weeks ago. Simone was gorgeous and we dated for about a year at the end of high school and we even attempted a long-distance relationship for a short time. She was my first real girlfriend and we shared many "first" things. We had that youthful romance, but I wouldn't quite label her as my high school sweetheart. Others might feel differently, but I'd prefer to keep that under wraps around Narra, unless she brought it up. After taking a brisk walk for the last ten minutes of my break, I returned to the shop with my mind racing. Once the end of the work night came, I left a few minutes early to reflect during my drive to campus.

Despite Simone's eagerness to meet my parents, she never got the chance. Deep inside, I sensed she wasn't the one for me, so that was out of the question. My parents knew of her, but they had never spoken to her. She often questioned why she had not met my parents earlier. Back then, she was head over heels for me, and the recent photos she sent felt like a thirst trap. It was her posing in the photos; not going to lie, she looked good, but nothing compared to the beauty I saw in Narra. I could never even compare any other woman to my future wife. So, engaging with Simone? That thought was firmly off the table.

Five hours had slipped away since I had texted her, the evening deepening into night, yet Narra still hadn't replied. Usually, she was quick to respond; there had never been a moment when my messages went unanswered. As I settled into my dorm, I stood under the shower, letting the warm water pour over me. Each droplet reminded me of Narra and the love we shared. I savored the love I felt for her and the profound impact she had on my life. Yet, unease crept in as I worried about her well-being and pondered what thoughts might be consuming her mind.

These moments made me wish I had a roommate—someone I could hang out with and share my thoughts with, without the hassle of a phone call. Just a little while ago, I called my mom after leaving work to explain everything. I told her to keep it under wraps from my dad; he was not really into social media like that. I promised I'd fill him in soon. I felt like it was on me to have that talk with him. I didn't want him to jump to conclusions or get the wrong idea. My pops knew me, but if he saw those pictures Simone posted and caught wind that Narra and I were on an official break, I worried he might start thinking I was up to no good, like I was out here living wild or something. It would be better if I set him straight on what had transpired. What a crazy day! I still couldn't wrap my head around why Simone would share those pictures without checking with me first. It felt like I'd been living in a cave, unaware that people you know would act this way.

The more I dwelled on it and saw the comments piling up the more frustrated I became. I'm not usually the kind of guy who lets things get under my skin, but this situation had struck a different chord. I found myself genuinely angry. In that moment, I turned to prayer, realizing I had allowed this to drastically shift my mood. "God, please intervene and help Narra understand my feelings. Father, grant me the peace I desperately need after all this has happened. Let our hearts find ease, regardless of what lies ahead. In Jesus' name, Amen."

I decided to silence my phone, replying only to a few texts. I updated Benny and Chris on what happened with Simone and mentioned that I would catch up with them another day. I was sure someone would pass the information along to A Wess. Yet, nobody knew how Narra truly felt—not even me. All I could think about was the possibility of losing her. She might never speak to me again.

Chapter Thirteen

Unprepared Cries

fter my last class, I left promptly instead of lingering for small talk. This decision allowed me to drop off a classmate at her workplace so she could arrive on time. After dropping her off, I headed to my after-school tutoring session, where I was scheduled to teach. I arrived at the tutoring facility about 25 minutes early and parked outside. Taking advantage of the extra time, I decided to catch up on some emails and check one of my favorite social media apps. As I sat in my car, enjoying good music, I found myself mindlessly scrolling through my feed. I laughed at a few funny posts, losing track of time for a moment. But then I paused, scrolling slowly, when something caught my eye, making me do a double-take. My heart instantly sank as I saw some photos and a video of Dem with a stunning girl, one where they were close together and she was touching his chin. It seemed to be more than just a family connection. My heart felt as if it had shattered into countless pieces. He rarely posted pictures with anyone but his family, selfies from the Get Fit gym, or sometimes from work, but never with anyone else at work. I saw that the post had quickly generated a surge of likes, igniting a flicker of curiosity in me. My heart plummeted when I realized that the girl had posted it, tagged Dem, and shared their location just ten minutes ago.

Desperately clutching at hope that she was merely a distant cousin, I wandered into the comments, only to be crushed by a mountain of regret. The revelation that it was a fragment of his past—his high school sweetheart—made tears spill uncontrollably from my eyes without warning. In that sudden moment, my heart became a storm of emotions. Though Dem and I had paused our relationship temporarily, in my soul he was still my man and I was still his lady.

Doubt gnawed at me: *Was this pause a pretext for him to seek other relationships?* My mind unraveled with suspicion—*was he exploring intimacy elsewhere while we were caught in this fragile pause? Was Dem truly the person he had always portrayed himself to be? After all, why would he have introduced me to his parents and embraced mine if there wasn't something real between us?* The weight of those questions pressed on me like a heavy shroud, threatening to suffocate me, and I felt like I was slipping further from my grip on reality.

In a fit of desperation, I quickly exited the app and all my social media. I placed my phone gently on the plush passenger seat, screen facing downward, loosened my seatbelt, and paused to breathe, as if the earth itself slowed for a moment. I drew a breath then let it go, seeking to steady my spirit amidst the blizzard of emotion within. "I can't go in there and tutor those girls today," I whispered, my heart pounding like a distant drum.

Fumbling for my phone, I scrolled through my contacts, each tap a reluctant admission of my inability to guide those girls today. A staff member shared that only one of my students had arrived today and she could join her group for tutoring, lifting a weight from my shoulders. Relief flooded over me; since the start of the school year, I hadn't missed a single session, and that thought filled me with gratitude.

Before driving off, I contemplated reaching out to Sasha— calling or texting—yet a wave of embarrassment gripped me, waging a silent war within. I was left caught in a labyrinth of emotions. Driving back to campus took about 20 minutes and the ride was a peaceful escape. I rolled down the windows, letting the wind bathe me as I tried to push aside the unsettling images from my mind.

Back at our dorm suite, opening up to Sasha felt like a breath of fresh air; I shared my thoughts and allowed myself to be vulnerable with her, wrapped in the affability of our friendship. After my conversation with her, I experienced a rush of exhaustion compelling me to take a nap. A couple of hours later, I woke up to a text from Dem, who was eager to explain the details of his encounter with his ex. But by then it was too late; I had already seen the post hours earlier and felt a pang of longing as I remembered the moments they shared. Based on how I felt in that moment, I thought I might never want to enjoy a sweet ice cream cone again in this lifetime. I couldn't help but laugh to myself, but I was sick to my stomach.

I lost track of the countless calls from Dem, each ring a silent reminder of unspoken words. I hadn't answered his calls for some time and my longing grew to skip classes and even the gym, seeking relief. I was adrift, feeling unwell both physically and spiritually, caught between the weight of fatigue and the quiet ache of disconnection. Everything was just so overwhelming and I didn't know how to cope with it all. I had believed Dem was it—my future husband.

The pain cut through me with the force of a dagger; yet, strangely, it also mended the broken fragments of my heart. A strange sensation as the sweet echoes of the past lingered, allowing me to breathe easily. He had matched most of my prayers, but I still had so much to learn about him. Naturally, he wasn't perfect and I embraced this reality fully. I'd believed I had found my forever partner, and it felt even more special because he loved Jesus. In this heart-wrenching moment, I felt my emotions begin to overwhelm me. "I'm not a weak girl! I won't settle for being anyone's second choice or a leftover!

"Did he love-bomb me all this time?

"Who do Dem and that girl think they are?" I snapped, my voice filled with fiery indignation. "I can't believe this!" I buried my face in my hands, overwhelmed by a rush of embarrassment. "Thank goodness I didn't rush things with this guy and post about us on social media! Who does Dem think he is? Some playboy?"

I noticed a few more texts came through from him, yet I chose not to respond. The thought of blocking his number crossed my mind several times. I had already severed ties with him on all my social media accounts, but I couldn't help but return to the one lingering post still on Simone's public profile.

The late night flowed into the early morning and under my covers on this cool morning everything was fresh in my mind. I prayed and shed a few tears, desperately trying not to overthink everything. It was a struggle, yet I summoned the courage to prepare myself for whatever the day might hold. I considered whether I should go to my only class of the day, silently yearning for a chance to cross paths with Dem, even though a part of me hesitated at the very idea. I missed him deeply, with unanswered questions echoing within my mind. Usually, I handled surprises and mishaps with ease, but today everything felt different. An unfamiliar blush of embarrassment warmed my cheeks.

After showering, I spoke with Sasha for a bit. She urged me to go to class, emphasizing its importance. I slipped into a pair of RU black sweatpants, their fabric whispering comfort against my skin, paired effortlessly with a matching top. A pearl-colored hoodie shielded me, adding an extra layer of warmth, while a low navy-blue cap rested gently on my head. My chocolate-brown slides showcased freshly pedicured toenails as I didn't want to ruin my fresh nail polish. Oh, and I remembered to grab my sunglasses. I sat down to gather some items for the day.

"Narr, everything will get better. I know you're hurting and need those answers, but you have to go to class today. You've worked too hard for your grades and I don't want a guy to distract you," Sasha said with conviction.

"You're right, Sash! I can do this, but honestly, I need more time to process everything that has happened. I need to calm my mind and not dwell so much on it all," I admitted.

"Can I pray with you?" she asked.

My eyes widened in shock and I abruptly stood up from the sofa. "You're speaking my language! Girl, yes!"

We grabbed hands and Sasha began to pray. "Dear Father God, please help Narra through these challenging times. Give her peace and settle her mind and heart. Work this situation out between Narra and Dem if it's your will. In Jesus' name, Amen!"

"Amen!" I responded. "Sash, I appreciate you so much."

As we hugged, she said, "I understand, Narra. You didn't deserve what's happening. I'm here for you, girl. Just let me know if you need anything and I'll be there for you." Her support felt like a comforting anchor amidst the turmoil.

As I walked to class, it felt like the longest journey of my life. I hoped to see my girl Lena there, eager to share the latest news, although I couldn't shake the feeling that she might already be informed. The campus buzzed with life around me; vibrant green leaves danced alongside some deep purples, enhancing the beauty I had come to cherish. Nature wrapped itself around me—birds chirping melodiously, the sun shining brightly through a patchwork of playful clouds—and, somehow, this perfect setting lifted my spirits just a little. "Thank you, God!" I whispered to myself.

Yet, despite my efforts, I struggled to focus in class. My thoughts battled with my peace, but I was managing to make it through. *No Lena today, and, surprisingly, no Michael either.* The class felt lighter than usual, which brought me a small measure of happiness. During a brief 10-minute break, I seized the opportunity to reach out to my therapist. It had been far too long since our last session. Unfortunately, she was fully booked for the next month but kindly offered me a note to excuse my future absence. Before class resumed, I approached my language and literature professor, Mr. Govan, to discuss my need for a mental health break.

"Hi Mr. Govan, I wanted to let you know that I've emailed a letter of excusal from my therapist. I'm currently dealing with some personal issues and I'm finding it really challenging today. I plan to take a few days off, but I will still submit my assignments online," I explained.

"Oh, Narra, I noticed you weren't your usual bubbly self. Take all the time you need. Just remember to submit your assignments on time," he responded with understanding. I couldn't fully disclose my reasons but shared just enough to convey my feelings as it was ultimately a personal matter that didn't concern anyone else. I had decided to take the rest of the week off and possibly miss the following two classes, assuring him I would still submit my assignments on time. I even emailed my Eng lit professor to keep them updated.

In an attempt to blend in, I had dressed differently from my usual style, not wanting anyone who knew about Dem and me to recognize me. This change felt like a protective shield against the prying eyes surrounding me, allowing me to navigate my emotions as discreetly as possible. I made my rounds via text and email, informing the two young ladies I tutored that there would be no English lit after-school tutoring sessions that week.

As I headed back to my dorm, I made it more than halfway to my building, walking quickly as if someone were chasing me. I decided to grab something to eat from the small convenience store, Tea and Treats, located in a nearby building. As I approached the walk thru window, I placed my order: "Can I get a peach iced tea and a bagel with egg whites, please?"

Suddenly, as I stood there, lost in the flurry of sounds around me, a familiar voice called out, "Narra! Hold up! I'll take care of that for you." I was quite perplexed as to how anyone could identify me while I was wearing shades and a cap. "What's the price, sir?"

Turning, I met Michael's warm smile, his eyes flashing with gratitude. "Thank you so much!" Before I could react, he wrapped me in a tight embrace that caught me off guard.

"What was that for, Mike?" I asked, a blush creeping to my cheeks, surprised by the sudden display of affection.

"Narra, because of you, I have a relationship with Jesus Christ and I've found someone special. I've found a girl who truly loves the Lord. She's incredible, Narra!" He couldn't stop smiling.

"We even attend church together whenever we can. I owe you so much for planting those seeds of faith in my life."

As I processed his words, I couldn't help but smile.

"That will be three dollars and twenty-four cents." Michael reached for his wallet, his eyes softening as he paid for my items.

"Thank you, Mike, but you really didn't have to do that."

He paused for a brief moment, a glimmer of joy illuminating his face. "It's no problem at all, Narra. And I promise to invite you to our wedding in a few years."

As I embraced Mike, joy bubbled up inside me. "Jesus and a future wife?" I exclaimed, laughter hopping between us. "I am so happy for you, Mike!"

Yet, beneath my excitement, a hint of jealousy tried to creep in. I couldn't help but question whether I should have been more patient with him, admiring the God within him.

No, Narra. It's just your emotions, I reminded myself. I felt neither anger nor resentment—no, I recognized this was God's plan. Michael was a genuinely great guy; kind and safe in a world where those qualities are rare. He was exactly the type of man that many women dreamed of. Honestly, he demonstrated everything I desired in a husband, but he was clearly not the one destined for me. The man I envisioned as my husband was someone whose presence transformed each passing year into a richer, more profound harmony, making our lifelong love story ever more enchanting with time. Even after countless nights when he might get on my nerves, I would steal glances at him while he slept, whispering my gratitude to God for bringing him into my life. *Just because someone is nice and kind to you doesn't mean they're your spouse.*

A purposeful marriage was calling to my heart, a union from Heaven that felt at home within me. As I walked towards my building, I thought, *Wow, I see what you did there, God. Michael entered my life so I could plant those seeds that only God Himself could nurture. Your will for him is being fulfilled. I helped him find Jesus and his wife by remaining obedient and not settling for less.* I made my way back to my dorm with Michael accompanying me halfway until he had to make a turn to head to class.

Another day passed and the image had garnered over 20,000 likes, even landing a spot on another huge blog dedicated to showcasing adorable couples. I watched Dem and Simone's photos and video go viral across Facebook, Instagram, and TikTok, drawing attention from everywhere. As I delved deeper into Simone's profile, a rush of nostalgia flooded my thoughts—I vaguely remembered subscribing to her beauty blog back in high school. Though I was familiar with Simone from a distance, we had never interacted or crossed paths personally. Memories of countless tutorials on skin and hair care twirled in my mind, each one a testament to Simone's creative flair. A mixture of emotions stirred within me, my heart whispering that perhaps Dem and Simone were now an item. I could hardly believe what I was seeing. "There's no way Dem would do this; he's not that type of guy," I said quietly to myself, but deep inside, something felt off.

The next few days, I remained in my dorm, submitting my assignments online. I knew I had to keep Sasha informed; after all, she was my closest friend now and I couldn't hide my pain from her. She was always there, a supportive listening ear, ready to help me navigate this tough time. I avoided making phone calls, choosing instead to text my friends and family to assure them I was okay. Everything felt so raw in my mind and I wanted to gather my thoughts before diving into any detailed conversations. Typically, I spoke with my mother daily and my distant cousin Andie once a week, despite having only met Andie twice. However, this time I hesitated. If I called my mom, I feared she might detect the worry in my voice. Andie had always been easy to talk to and supportive, always just a phone call away for the past six years. I was concerned about what my family and friends would think. I didn't want them to see me as foolish for falling for another 'college guy' again. To my knowledge, they hadn't seen or heard about Dem since they weren't connected with him on social media. Known for my intelligence and ambition as a dedicated young woman of God, I worried that others might think I had lost my way if they discovered the situation from the past few days. I was particularly anxious that my mom would dislike Dem and despise him altogether.

Sasha checked in with me and then continued with her usual activities for the day, since she would be away for the remainder of it. Overwhelmed by everything that had transpired, I found myself on my knees, whispering a heartfelt, intimate prayer for my mental and emotional well-being. The weight of anxiety clung to me, and in that vulnerable moment, I recalled the scripture, "Be anxious for nothing." Yet, even with this gentle reminder, my heart ached and I couldn't suppress the words that slipped from my lips, "God, why does this hurt so much?" I found myself sobbing on my knees.

After about five minutes, I managed to gather myself and sat down on the mini sofa. I began to pray, first for me, then for Dem. It was clear that I was deeply hurt, yet I was the type of person who even prayed for my enemies. I was madly in love with Dem, and despite my emotional turmoil, I cherished our shared moments of prayer. I reflected on some of our most powerful and beautiful experiences together, which brought a sense of passion to my heart amidst the pain. "Dear Heavenly Father, I ask for your protection over my mental state, spirit, and heart. Help me find ease and focus on You, myself, and my studies. Allow me to rest in Your presence tonight. Holy Spirit, comfort me and grant me the wisdom to release those things and people not meant for me, knowing that whatever is truly meant for me will remain.

"Lord, I acknowledge that I am connected to You first and this is preparation rather than punishment. I trust that all these experiences are shaping me for the challenges to come.

"I pray for Dem, asking that he sees You as his everything and leader. Help him to know You truly so he can appreciate me spiritually as his wife, who has the qualities of a Proverbs 31 woman. If he is hurting, please bring healing to his heart, and if his intentions are sincere, let me recognize that truth. In Jesus' name, Amen."

As the chaos of the day enveloped me, I sank into my cozy dorm. Just as my heart began to calm, a rush of frustration hit me when my phone's battery died. I realized, with a sigh, that I had misplaced my phone charger; the other rested in my car, just out of reach. Yet, stepping outside felt like a daunting task as the comfort of my space held me close—its inviting corners whispered sweet promises of solace and dreams.

After nearly half an hour of searching, my fingers finally brushed against the familiar shape of my charger, hidden beneath a pile of items on my pink plush mini sofa. Plugging my phone in, I felt a gust of anticipation as I rechecked my missed calls and notifications. Only one voicemail caught my eye, dated from the previous day. It had to be from Sasha or my mom, I thought, my heart quickening. But to my surprise, it turned out to be from Dem—an unusual occurrence as he rarely left voicemails. The unexpected message made my mind wander, pondering what thoughts could have prompted him to leave a voice message. "Voicemail?" I whispered to myself, intrigue flickering in my chest. I listened intently, my heart fluttering with anticipation. It wasn't just about wanting to hear him out; it was the sound of his voice that I craved. I felt a profound emptiness without him.

As I pressed play on Dem's voicemail, the warmth and concern in his voice felt like a comforting hug. He said, "Hey Narr, I love you and miss you so much and I need to talk to you in person. I was wrong for not protecting your feelings more. Trust me, I didn't do anything to hurt you or jeopardize us. I need to see you and explain everything. I mentioned that girl, but I know now it was too late to bring it up. However, it's not too late for us. I'm going to fight for what we have. I can't let go of someone as beautiful and sweet as you. Narra, you're unlike any woman I've encountered. I see beyond your breathtaking outer beauty; it's your spirit and soul that truly captivate me. God lives within you and the light you radiate reflects His presence. It's a light I want to bask in forever."

I couldn't help but ponder, remarking with a hint of sarcasm, "Ah, he desires to see me, eager to dazzle me with his enchanting presence and awaken my heart. He knows my soft feelings for him well and his beautiful words resonate with my soul in such an exquisite way."

In that brief moment, I found myself swept away in daydreams of him. His words, "I love you and miss you so much," resonated deeply in my heart. I played the voicemail four times; each time I heard his voice, it sent my heart into a flutter and made me melt, causing passion to spread through my entire being. I then recalled Dem's last few text messages. One message read, *What do I have to do to prove that I am who God says I am and what God clearly told you about me? Come on, girl, just reply! It's me. Stop playing around and call me back. This is tough for me and it hurts, Narra. But I'm not giving up on us.*

After gathering my resolve, I entered the warm, misty cocoon of the shower, where gentle waters whispered serenity over my skin for fifteen tranquil minutes. Just as I had surrendered to a flood of peacefulness, a gentle knock at the door shattered my peace. My heart raced with curiosity, wondering who it might be. I took a deep breath, dried myself with a large, soft, light pink towel that wrapped around my body and donned a red, short, twisted microfiber towel to cover my damp hair. Peering through the peephole, I gasped in wonder, "Flowers?" *Surely, these must be from Sasha,* I mused, feeling a flutter of excitement.

I eagerly opened the door to reveal a breathtaking bouquet of white and lavender tulips, elegant in a vibrant hot-pink vase and decorated with a delicate white bow. I gently grasped the bouquet, feeling a surge of joy, and hurriedly closed the door to avoid being seen in my towel by anyone on our hall floor. As I placed them on the small dining table, I was wholly captivated by their delightful fragrance when my eyes caught a glimpse of a note peeking from the blossoms, inviting me to explore its message further. The note read:

My Dearest Narra,

Let's create boundaries, not barriers.

With all my love, your future husband.

A few minutes later, my phone buzzed with an unexpected call from Rya, my childhood friend. Rya, who was friends with both me and Dem on social media, had seen the recent photos that stirred up emotions within me. Concerned for me, she had reached out multiple times in the past few days, eager to check on how I was handling everything. I felt an immediate warmth at the sound of her voice, a comforting reminder of our bond. As we spoke, I unloaded my thoughts, sharing my mental struggles and the spiritual turmoil that clouded my mind. Always the empathetic listener, Rya covered me in words of comfort, praying for my peace while offering heartfelt advice steeped in faith. In that moment, I listened to my friend and embraced her godly advice. As I listened to her, my heart raced at the thought of him—his infectious laugh, the joy that sparkled in his eyes, and the way he treated me not only as someone to love but also as a dear friend.

"How could I miss him this much, Rya?" I whispered, my voice barely breaking the serenity. "Why does he keep reaching out to me? I want to move on, but my heart hesitates." My thoughts swirled, a chaotic dance of hope and doubt.

"What about the times you and that man prayed together and in his prayer room with nobody else around, just the two of you? And he hasn't pressured you into sex or anything! Whew, Narra, that sounds like a true godly man to me. I'm sorry for referring to him as 'that man,' but wow. I need you to seek God on this."

"How can I be sure his parents haven't met other girls? What if he's not being honest?"

"Narra, I think Dem is an honest man. I see something special in him, and yes, I'm saying this without having met or spoken to him myself. You know I'm here for you. I've been listening to everything you've shared these past few days and now I feel compelled to tell you what God has been laying on my heart.

"My dear friend, you must seek the Lord to discern what is truly from Him and what isn't. I may not have met Dem, but you have. Talk to him. I know he's hurting. Please try not to add to his pain. Lift yourself up and return to in-person classes.

Yes, the few people who know might give you side-eyes, but honestly, it's because they have not seen you as well.

"Narra, it's clear that this man truly loves you. It's been almost two weeks and you should consider listening to him. He has sent you flowers, your favorite tea, and even a breakfast sandwich—he's making an effort for you! Even though you've been ignoring him, he continues trying to connect with you." I hadn't mentioned one crucial detail to Sasha yet: food was delivered here shortly after the flowers, courtesy of Dem.

"Don't let one of your greatest blessings pass by unnoticed."

"Rya, I truly thank you for being a true friend. You've made me feel so much better; I needed to hear everything you said."

Rya continued, "Narra, can I pray for you before we hang up?"

"Please do."

"Dear Heavenly Father, in the precious name of Jesus Christ, I come before You with a heart full of humility, seeking Your divine wisdom, strength, and discernment for Narra. Please wrap them both in your loving arms as they face this challenge together. If she is truly his wife and he her husband, I earnestly pray that every circumstance in their lives works together for their ultimate good and aligns with Your perfect plan. Lord, may Your will unfold in their lives—even when we struggle to comprehend it. We choose to place our complete trust in You, dear Father, leaning not on our limited understanding but resting in Your unfailing guidance. In the sacred name of Jesus, we pray together. Amen."

"Amen!"

♥♥♥

I felt utterly heartbroken. The girl whom God revealed to me as my wife was now avoiding me, leaving me to wonder if she ever wanted to see or speak to me again. Just moments ago, I had been trying to explain the girl in the picture—a message meant to be honest and open—but it now felt like a barrier. The unexpected viral photos and video of us had irrevocably shifted the dynamics of my relationship with Narra. I couldn't shake the nagging feeling that our once-intimate connection had changed forever. Upon realizing the pictures and video had been posted, I quickly untagged myself, but it was too late; the images had gone viral and remained public for all to see. I knew that Narra must be feeling humiliated. Most people were unaware of the depth of our relationship as we had planned to reveal this private information to the world together, sharing it only with our closest friends and family.

Desperate to mend the rift, I began praying fervently each day, hoping that Narra would embrace grace and understanding in such a challenging time. I silently pleaded that we could navigate this storm without jeopardizing God's plan for our lives. Yet, Narra's silence was deafening; she wouldn't answer my calls or respond to any text messages, leaving me feeling more isolated than ever.

Several days passed without a word from Narra, leaving me in a state of unease. This week, I only had two classes, and as I exited my physics class, I spotted Benny on his way to art history. I looked at him as he exclaimed, "What's up, playa playa? I've been waiting to see you. Where have you been?" He chuckled and pulled me into a tight hug, followed by a firm handshake.

"Hey, my guy! I missed you big time," I replied with a grin.

He continued, "You really have been ghosting us ever since that girl posted those photos at Kraze, you know, with her licking that ice cream off your face. Plus, I haven't seen you at the gym in a few days!"

"Yeah, Benny, I've just been hanging out in my dorm, concentrating on my assignments and my faith. I'm really trying to get my mind and spirit right, you know? And she unquestionably did not lick my face! Don't start any rumors and make things worse than they already are."

"Dude, that's just one of the rumors floating around and it did not start from me."

I threw my hands up in the air feeling distraught.

"My bad, it seems like you're really hurting, huh?" Benny said in a concerned tone. "Aaron, Chris, and I are heading to the new local coffee shop that just opened up about twenty-five minutes from campus. You should come by and join us!"

"Not today, my guy. Soon, though."

"I sense that you're not quite ready to open up, but I have to get to my next class, Dem."

"Yeah, I'm off to my last class of the day too." We both started walking toward the northern part of campus, eager to avoid being late.

"Dem, you can absolutely talk to me about what's troubling you." With a playful grin, Benny added, "I'm just dying to know what's up with Narra and when Simone re-entered the picture."

"I'm definitely not seeing Simone." My frown transformed into a serious expression and then a light smile.

"Dem, I heard she was a girl you dated back in high school. If only I'd attended your school because the girls must have been stunning. Simone is beautiful! Oh my gosh! Dem, I had no idea you had such gorgeous girls around. I would have assumed she was way out of your league."

"Yeah, no, I'm definitely out of her league. She was just a high school fling—puppy love at best. Narra is my only match and I'm the only one in her league."

Benny glanced up. "Ayo, is that Narra with some guy?"

"Yikes, bro, looks like it," I replied, nervous and shocked.

"This drama is just getting sweeter." Benny chuckled.

"Narra is not like that." I peeked, trying to watch her every move.

"I hope she's not like that because you are wildly in love with her and I don't want you to get hurt."

"I know the dude she's with. That's Mike; he's in one of her classes and I know him a little."

"Oh, right, pretty boy Mike! He's a decent guy," Benny said. "She's smiling and that hug looks more than friendly. Oh man, Dem, that was not an ordinary hug."

"I'm sure it's nothing."

"Then why is your girl dressed like she's sneaking into our campus? Haha."

"That's what I'm trying to figure out."

"Wait, you haven't spoken to her since the whole Simone Kraze thing?"

"Not yet. I tried calling, but she's been ignoring me pretty seriously. Alright, let me head to class, Ben. I'll catch you later."

"I'm here for you if you need me, Dem."

"Thanks, bro; I appreciate you."

Later, back in my dorm, I paced restlessly, stealing glances at my cell phone every three minutes, yearning for my favorite notification—a text or a call that would light up my screen with Narra's picture.

There's no way Narra moved on this fast. I know that girl's soul, I thought.

I sat on the edge of my bed, scrolling through my recent calls. I tapped on Narra's name and hesitated for a moment before starting to text her again, a mix of concern and longing twisting in my chest. *Narra, I need to know you're okay. I've seen you around campus when you've been out, so trust me, I'm making sure my future wife is alright. And oh, I saw you hugging Michael—what's the deal with that?*

I sent the message, hoping for a response from Narra. A few hours passed, but still no reply. Suddenly, my phone lit up. It wasn't Narra; it was my dad. "Dad, I don't know what to do! I've made a mistake and I really need your help. What should I do?" I rushed my response, cutting him off before he could even say, "Hello."

"Hold on, Dem, slow down. What are you talking about?" His stern tone added weight to his words, making me uneasy. "Dad, it's been almost a week since I've heard from Narra and I'm devastated. Do you think it's over? I know she's okay because I've had a few people check on her for me and I've seen her from a distance," I assured him.

"Dem, what did you do wrong?"

"I can explain what happened. Have you seen or heard about the picture of me that went viral on my social media?"

"Oh yes, Dem! I've been meaning to ask you about that. At first, I was completely lost. Your mom was so confused, and even Aunt Mary and cousin Lauren called, all asking when the wedding was and commenting on how cute you two looked together. I had to dig deeper to understand what was happening. I know it's innocent because I know you, but do you realize the trouble you're in, young man?"

"Dad, that was never my intention. Especially since Narra and I are on a break. Seeing those pictures crushed me."

"What do you mean crushed you? You were in those pictures, Demery." His tone was stern, but there was a hint of laughter in it.

I chuckled. "Dad, you know what I meant. I haven't heard from her in a few days, and honestly, Dad, I feel like this might be the end. I feel defeated. You know how deeply I care about Narra from our previous conversations and I've shared with you how God led me to believe she is my future wife.

"Dad, this is serious. I need to know that we are okay as a unit. I can't imagine life without Narra. Please agree in prayer with Mom and me. It has been five days since I last heard from her and I was filled with anxiety this entire time. I need to know she is mentally okay!" I exclaimed, desperation pouring out of me.

"Wow, I can hear your urgency loud and clear," my dad said. "Your mom and I will be adding you both to our prayer list. But Son, you need prayer right now too.

"One essential thing to keep in mind about our connection with God is that He is always available to listen, never sleeping or slumbering."

"Dad, I really appreciate you recognizing how important my connection with Narra is to me. I understand her worth as a woman of God—someone created for me."

"It feels impressive to see you fighting for her, even this early on. Let me tell you something vital: Remember this moment. Remember how you feel right now. That pain and urgency you feel to ensure Narra's safety? Never forget it. Always maintain this mindset and heart about your marriage. Cultivate an urgency to ensure your wife feels safe—mentally, spiritually, physically, and emotionally. Always put her before yourself, Son. That is the core of strength and submission—both to God and to each other in your marriage. I know Narra will do the same. God is within you, Dem. When the time is right, you will know exactly what to say and God will guide your words. Let it flow from your heart, from your spirit.

"Father, in the mighty name of Jesus Christ our Savior, You have been my son's answer to everything. Please heal my son's heart. I ask that he may breathe in Your Word right now as a source of comfort, correction, and reassurance that You are with him and Narra. As it says in 2 Corinthians 1:3–4 'All praise to God, the Father of our Lord Jesus Christ. God is our merciful Father and the source of all comfort. He comforts us in all our troubles so that we can comfort others.'

"Grant Dem the confidence that You possess, Father. Help him to be the husband that Narra needs, even if she does not yet know what that entails. May he be kind, caring, loving, compassionate, and faithful. Enable Dem to lead and to be an even better husband and father than I ever was. Lord, raise a patient husband that Narra needs by her side. Bless their union with the support and strength necessary to overcome any challenges they may face. As You remind us in Ecclesiastes 4:12, 'A person standing alone can be attacked and defeated, but two can stand back-to-back and conquer. A threefold cord is not easily broken.'

"With You, Heavenly Father, their bond will not be easily shattered. Their marriage is secure in Your hands. Let the love they share be gentle and kind. May every lie from the enemy be cast back to the pit of hell. Let Narra and Dem continue to seek You first, prioritizing their relationship with You above all else, even their marriage. In this way, they will always have a divine source of strength to connect to—You, Heavenly Father."

I sensed in my father's voice a heartfelt plea to God, a sincere cry for me and Narra.

"May Dem and Narra find safety in mind, spirit, and body. May this little mishap draw them closer together and bring them closer to You. Heal Narra's heart from any pain she may be experiencing and guide them back to one another if it is Your divine plan for them. We pray for all of this for Your glory. In Jesus' name we say Amen."

"Amen." As my eyes brimmed with tears, I felt the Holy Spirit comfort me through my dad's prayer. Sitting there, I couldn't help but wonder to myself, *Why am I feeling so emotional?*

"This girl has an inexplicable hold over me, Dad." I chuckled softly, realizing how deep my feelings ran.

"Dem, you make me proud," my father said, a genuine smile across his face. "You've observed your mother and me for many years now. While our marriage has faced its challenges, what's always been easy is knowing that we have never, ever given up on each other. In the journey of marriage, it is essential to fight side by side against the challenges that life presents, rather than opposing one another.

"I believe in you, Dem. I know you'll find a way to mend things with Narra.

"God's timing is perfect. There's no need to worry; she won't give up. That girl loves you beyond your imagination. Your love for one another is deeper than you know. Just offer her a little more time."

I cried, but I would never admit it to my father. "It's okay to cry, Son," he reassured me, his voice sincere with concern. I hadn't shed a tear since yesterday, but as I spoke, my eyes overflowed with emotion once more. I couldn't hold back; I began to sob, releasing a flood of feelings I had kept bottled up inside.

"Son, I wish I could hug you right now," he continued, his voice thick with a hint of worry. "I want you to come home this weekend. I need to know my boy is okay, you understand?"

"Understood, Dad!"

Chapter Fourteen

♥

Waves of Deep Love and

Safe Boundaries

$\mathcal{A}$ nother week passed and I felt the weight of anticipation pressing down on me. I finally decided I could no longer resist the pull towards Narra. With the help of Sasha, Narra's suitemate and a mutual friend, I orchestrated a plan to meet her. Sasha, already aware of the unspoken bond between Narra and me, had helped me deliver food and flowers a few days ago. She came up with a clever idea to help me slip into their residence hall without raising any suspicion. She believed that I was a genuinely wonderful person, someone who would be perfect for Narra.

At around 11:45 a.m., I met Sasha and Cooper on campus near Delfo Hall. To keep the situation casual and inconspicuous, we dressed smartly, resembling a trio heading out for brunch. Cooper waited outside while Sasha and I engaged in low-key conversation.

"Just act natural, Dem. Seriously," Sasha urged, her eyes sparkling with amusement. "Laugh a little, look ahead, and keep the conversation flowing."

We headed back outside, "I feel like a smooth criminal," Cooper said playfully, eliciting snickers from Sasha and me.

Sasha whispered, "Everything will be fine. I'm really glad to see you here. You're a wonderful guy and your girl truly deserves someone like you."

"Thank you; that means a great deal to me," I replied, appreciating the support.

"I appreciate you, Coop!" I murmured with a bit of excitement, looking at Cooper. "You don't even know me that well, so I really appreciate you reaching out to Sasha and helping a guy out." I offered him a firm handshake, a smile spreading across my face, as joy engulfed my heart, realizing the bonds of friendship were deepening in that moment.

"You are familiar with this school, and not long ago, you spent a lot of time exploring these halls," Sasha stated as we all walked together, attempting to appear composed. "Your face is quite recognizable around here, so this shouldn't be a big deal. But if Narra takes her time opening the door, and if anyone asks what you're doing here, though they probably won't—show them your campus ID and give a good knock." I nodded at everything Sasha told me. "You could also hang out in the lounge or the community kitchen area. Just text her and let her know you're waiting in the lounge."

Sasha used her key fob to enter the SV hall building, it seemed like her pulse had quickened as she exchanged a swift fist bump with me. With a smile, she dashed down the hallway outside their dorm, eager to remove herself from the scene. I stood hesitantly outside Narra's dorm suite, my knuckles rapping lightly against the door with a firm but gentle knock. I had considered retreating to the kitchen area to send her a text instead, my nerves twisting in my stomach. Thoughts darted through my mind. *What if she keeps ignoring me?* But today, I decided, would be different. Today, I would be bold. With resolved determination, I knocked three times, each tap echoing in the silence. Knock. Knock. Knock.

Sasha headed to class, leaving me alone in our dorm once again. Not long after, I heard a knock at the door and wondered if she had left her fob to get back in. I peeked through the peephole on the door and gasped before taking another deep breath. As my heart sank, I froze like a deer in headlights while I watched him turn his face, seemingly checking his surroundings, and then I quickly tiptoed in a hurry to grab some clothes. I reached into my drawer and pulled out a pair of clean navy-blue sweatpants with "RU" written in white letters on the right pocket, letting them drape comfortably beneath my long-sleeved, fitted light pink shirt. Now fully dressed, my heart raced as I peeked through the peephole again. This time, as his back was turned, I could only see the words "Rovane University" on the back of his black T-shirt while he was carrying a navy-blue hoodie over his shoulder. At first, I couldn't see his face, but he must've heard me slightly rattle the doorknob or breathing hard as he began to turn around slowly. Now, gazing at the side of his face, I noticed how his charm grew with the soft sprouting of his beard.

Lord, who is this man at my door, looking like a biblical figure from ancient days, BC times? I thought, a grin spreading across my face. *But he looks so good, he's so handsome.* Tears were already resting on my eyelashes. He knocked again, almost identical to the previous one. This time, I swiftly freed the latch and held the door slightly ajar, permitting him to slip through. "Hey," he said in a low voice, meeting my eyes directly, but I looked away as soon as our gazes united, my hand still resting on the doorknob. As I slowly shut the door, leaving it just a whisper ajar, our eyes rested in each other's for a brief moment, a full flame heating up between us.

We embraced, our bodies melting into one another in a dance of intimacy. His hands found the gentle curve of my waist while my arms softly curled around his neck, holding on with peaceful support. The hug was a lingering embrace, each moment deepening our connection as our hearts beat in harmony, echoing love, calmness, and patience. As we finally pulled away, I felt my eyes crinkle with joy, a big smile revealing my happiness. I gazed at Dem for a moment then quietly closed and locked the door behind us, sealing in the warmth of our divine connection.

Now standing in front of the closed door, I gently took Narra's hands, our fingers intertwining and swaying. My deep stare was fixed on her sweet, inviting honey eyes, capturing the moment for a couple of heart-stopping seconds. "I've missed you so much," I whispered softly into her ear. Leaning in closer, I tilted my body forward, brushing her hair aside. I cradled her face in my hands, my fingertips whispering against her cheeks as I softly pressed a gentle kiss to the curve of her cheek, just below her ear.

I immediately went in for a kiss on her lips as I delicately slid my lips from beneath her ear to her lips, my lips never parting from her face and leaving all our cares behind. She seemed to yearn, her lips parting ever so slightly, yet she restrained herself.

I was momentarily taken aback, but I would never have dreamed of stopping a kiss from the love of my life. It was a kiss filled with unspoken words: "I miss you; I love you; I need you; you're my everything." And I'd never needed it more than I did just at that moment.

That kiss consumed me like a ripple of reassurance, affirming that I was safe and that Dem loved me without reservation. Honestly, it stirred all the emotions within me, making my heart swell. As I rested in his arms, feeling my back and shoulders softly brush against his abs and chest, I couldn't help but joke, "What took you so long?

"Are you ready to explain everything?" I inquired, my voice thick with longing. I desired nothing more than for him to embrace me completely, every part of me. Yet, deep down, I understood that we had to wait. So, I chose to savor the passion of our embrace, cherishing the intimacy we shared in that brief moment.

"Are you ready to listen and hear me out?" Dem asked, pushing up against me again, planting another kiss on me, this time on the side of my forehead as he leaned to the right while still behind me, feeling a deep, natural yet spiritual connection.

"You don't trust me, do you, Narra?" Our eyes were still locked as I narrowed mine at him. "Do you know that I am in love with you and I would never intentionally hurt you?"

After slipping into his hoodie, he grabbed my hand to calmly twirl me around as if we were in the middle of a dance, so he could work his eyes within mine, knowing our genuine eyes could speak so much to one another's spirit.

"Well, before all of that, you had my complete trust!" I said, maintaining a gentle tone. "It was all too much and I needed time to process everything. I've been thinking a lot." I paused, my eyes falling upon a hoodie draped on a nearby chair. As I extended my hand, he was quicker, taking hold of it as well. He was kind enough to help me shimmy into my soft pink Rovane University hooded sweatshirt. My head still beneath the hood, I muttered, "I know you're different, Dem. But..."

"But what? Thinking about what?" Dem asked with concern in his voice and eyes as he took my hand and led me to the mini sofa to sit. "Narr, you could have just texted me that you needed some time and that we were good, you know?" he said, sitting next to me with his arm resting around my shoulder. "Did you receive the flowers I sent you? What about the note with them? And unblock me from all social media!"

"Gosh, slow down," I teased, my eyes glancing away momentarily before spiritually and physically locking onto his gaze again. "I did receive them, but they died a few days ago. I looked at them every day and thought of you. Even on the day I threw them in the trash, I thought of you, as if that was a sign." I chuckled, looking away and then back at him.

"But I missed you so much," I continued, my voice thick with emotion. "I love you, Demery. However, you're not off the hook just yet. I'm no pushover and there are certain things I simply won't tolerate in my life or our relationship. We need to set some boundaries."

"Did you read the note?"

"I have the note. And yes, I did read it. I am not going to lie; it probably saved at least a friendship between us." I grasped Dem's right hand, turning to meet his eyes as I locked mine with his. I leaned in, kissing his lips softly, then pulled away just as quickly. Undeterred, I edged closer, a playful smile twirling on my lips, yearning for another taste of affection. Teasingly, he retreated slightly, yet with my eyes softly closed, I embraced the moment, capturing another kiss. This time, he lingered a bit longer on my lower lip with his top lip, savoring the gentle closeness before parting.

"We've never kissed this much before," I whispered.

In a serious tone, Dem said, "Narra, we need to get married very soon because this is a lot on me. Whew, I need to keep my hands to myself!"

"You sure do, sir." I nodded with a wide smile, showing all of my silver braces.

Dem sat quietly, taking in every detail of me as he lovingly inspected me from head to toe. I sensed an undeniable warmth in his eyes, a reflection of the love we shared. Leaning in, he pressed a gentle kiss to my forehead, cradling me in his arms as we shared a soothing moment.

"Moments like these feel endless," I whispered softly, my voice barely above a hush, yet filled with profound meaning. We cuddled intermittently as the sun settled deep, ushering in the night, the deepness reminding us of our love. I nestled against Dem, my head resting on his chest, sinking into the plush comfort of our loveseat. In this intimate embrace, our conversations flowed effortlessly as we explored our past, present, and dreams for the future. We shared our thoughts on love, marriage, children, education, careers, business, books, ventures, ministry, and our unwavering faith in Jesus.

The atmosphere felt surreal, as if the moment were a beautiful dream—but it was undeniably real. For me, this was a long-awaited dream come true. I felt covered in a nest of safety, shielded spiritually, mentally, emotionally, and physically. I was able to express my feelings and profess my love freely. "I love you so much, Demery. Please forgive me for the pain I may have caused you by ignoring you."

"I'm in love with you, Narra. Actually, I feel that I am 'LOVE' when I'm with you," he voiced. He could hardly contain himself. "You have brought me closer to God," he murmured. I could feel his heart racing as I leaned against his chest. "I cannot bear the thought of being apart from you ever again. You are my greatest need, the light of my life. You are truly Heaven-sent, and in my heart, I know that you are my wife, Mrs. Narra Foxer. Nothing will stand in the way of God's plan for our love."

I blushed at his declaration, the sincerity of his words floating over me like a gentle wave in the ocean. "The way you love God is the most beautiful part of you," he continued, his voice softening. "It draws me nearer to you every day. My love for you runs deep, fueled by your passion for Jesus. You're going to be the mother of my children one day. I don't see it any other way. I'm going to show you that I'm sure about you and us through my actions."

I lifted my head slowly, re-engaging Dem's eyes again. He gently cupped my chin, drawing me closer as he kissed me softly on the lips, maintaining our eye contact throughout our shared moment. In that cuddle, he whispered, "I heard God's gentle whisper while the night was still. 'Love has arrived right on time.' It always belonged to us. It just hadn't arrived yet."

As I looked deeply into his eyes, I felt at ease; I felt God's purpose for my heart brighten within my soul. He continuously planted sweet kisses on my lips, forehead, and cheeks, which blossomed into a spiritual garden of love as he gently held my face with both of his hands. There was kindness and gentleness in the soft kisses he placed on my lips. Then holiness and peace with the next few kisses on my forehead. There was joy, faithfulness, and patience with the kisses on the sides of my face. It felt as if divine love and God's goodness were wrapped in that instant, culminating in a profound sense of self-control and divine grace.

I didn't want the moment to end, so I gently lifted my chin, inviting him for another kiss with my eyes. "Come here right now," my eyes said. This time, he softly pressed his slightly parted lips against my chin, just beneath my lower lip, and then smoothed his lips from my chin back to my lips, sending a warm thrill through me.

When our lips finally separated, I spoke. "Dem, from the very first moment my heart encountered yours, my spirit felt a stirring of relief. When our hearts beat closely together, my beauty flourishes. It's as if the light of our perfect God fills us, filling us with His beauty and eternal love.

"Demery, do you really know? Did you hear from God about me being your wife?

Also, you have to stop kissing me!" I exclaimed, my tone firm, yet my heart betrayed me. Despite my words, deep inside, my heart was a tempest of longing. "Kiss me everywhere. Kiss me softly. Kiss me endlessly," it pleaded with each quickened heartbeat, even as my mind protested. "Seriously, you cannot kiss me like I'm your wife when I'm not yet," I insisted, trying to regain control. "I know you missed me and I missed you too. But we must not let this lead us into temptation. We have to be mindful of our physical touch." Each word weighed heavily, the sincerity in my voice echoing my internal battle.

In that moment, it felt like love had found us. My spirit was in a state of joy because this was home. "Okay, I understand. The boundaries are clear and set," Dem replied, his voice steady yet tinged with underlying tension, reflecting the struggle between desire and discipline. "I'm not begging for your love, Narr, but I won't give up without a fight for us. For our destiny and our purpose together," he added passionately.

"Will you forgive me? Everything was unexpected for me, but I see your perspective on it all," he continued, not claiming he was right. Of course I forgave him. My spirit had already established forgiveness before he showed up at my door. "I didn't even smile in those pictures," Dem said, awkwardly chuckling at the realization. I narrowed my eyes at him.

"I can tell you forgive me by the way you kissed me," he said. I forced a smile. "Okay, maybe I should have set some boundaries, even without us being 'official' to the world."

"Our love is official," I asserted. "God finalized our relationship long ago." In that moment, our love story began to wrap in the warmth of God's presence softly.

"I wholeheartedly take responsibility for my actions and any shortcomings in our relationship; I realize I should have protected your feelings and our relationship even more," Dem said with a smile. "I won't entertain anyone else, not even for a moment. I'm learning and growing, Narr. I will shut everyone

down if necessary. None of you girls better look my way!"
Dem assured me playfully, yet with heartfelt sincerity.

I smirked. "Dem, I honestly don't find anything funny in this
moment." I tried to keep my voice calm. "Why did you allow her
to take those photos of you? Also, I saw you slightly smiling in
one of them, which made it seem like you were okay with it."

"There were customers in the store and I didn't want to create
a scene. I aimed to keep it professional."

"I think you could have still said no, or at least covered your
face. You're too nice, Dem."

"Narr, you're right. I should have been firmer. But you need
to trust me, to hear my side before jumping to conclusions."

The smile on my face said, "He gets it."

"Just because there are pictures doesn't define my character.
For heaven's sake, I took you to meet my parents. All I ask is
that you hear me out and never, ever ignore me."

"But I haven't known you for that long. We are still getting to
know each other, Dem."

"Narra, you don't need to know me that long to know my true
character. I am exactly who I claim to be and you know it," he
replied, the passion in his tone revealing true honesty in his
voice. As he added a hint of seriousness to his voice, I felt an
electrifying thrill surge through me. I reveled in his intensity,
sensing that he could easily match my playful sass. It was a
beautiful sight to see a man stand his ground, exuding strength

while maintaining a gentle and loving tone. In that moment, I envisioned him not just as my man but as a loving and godly husband, a protector of my heart.

"I'm truly sorry for that, Dem. I should have called you first. But can you understand why I reacted the way I did? Seeing those comments and discovering that you two had been high school sweethearts only deepened my insecurities. The remarks like 'When's the wedding?' pierced me to my very core. And then, reflecting on that day, I realized she may have been the same girl who called out your full government name as she drove past. You insisted she was 'no one.'"

"Okay, you're right. I take full responsibility for that. It would have been uncomfortable to disclose her identity at that moment. I understand that our break and everything leading up to this has influenced how everything has unfolded. I genuinely apologize for not being more upfront with you. I would never purposely deceive you or lead you on; my commitment is to be honest with you."

"I hear you, that all sounds great, and now I understand. I need to know, though: are you absolutely certain that I'm your wife? Did you seek God for guidance on this?" I asked, my voice steady yet filled with emotion. "When we get married, it's until death do us part. That's it."

Dem stared at me, his expression serious. After a moment, he nodded slowly, breaking the silence. "Yes, I heard from the Lord. Come on, Narr, you sound like a broken record at this point!"

"Demmm!"

Dem was a structured, high-value young Christian man, brought up with positive examples of godly individuals. However, I was resolute in my intent to hold him accountable.

He was still young, just a junior in college, and I often wondered how he could be so sure and ready for a young godly woman as mature as I was. A person who knew what she wanted in life and desired a godly husband. *Could Dem handle my heart with the care it deserves?* I thought.

"Dem, I'm a lot. I know who I am and I have a godly purpose. Whoever is my husband must meet me in the spirit and match my purpose as both a wife and a woman of God.

"I need a leader who follows Jesus Christ," I continued, my gaze unwavering. "I desire a husband who possesses integrity and respect," I emphasized, my commitment evident. "A man of great character, called by God Himself to be my husband.

"We are not about to play house or games," I said, my tone reflecting slight irritation.

"Do you want this for real?" I asked, catching him off guard as I stood up abruptly. He then stood up, towering over me at about 6'2". It was thrilling to look up at him, getting lost in his beautiful brown eyes before glancing at his chest.

He embraced me playfully from behind, a sweet gesture that made my heart flutter. After releasing me, he took hold of both of my hands and secured his gaze on mine. I experienced a thrilling mix of affection and slight frustration; his every move had that irresistible power over me. Dem looked at me with tears in his eyes, which I understood as signs of joy and relief. He was honest and gentle, making this moment breathtaking for me. *Is this man truly real?* I wondered. *Not perfect, of course, but do men like him still exist?* I thought. Witnessing my future husband unveil his vulnerability was a beautiful moment. I couldn't help but reflect that true strength often resides in those tears.

"Dem, you're strong and I admire your strength," I said. Tears began to flow from both of us. He quickly reached for a tissue from the nearby table, my touch gentle as I wrapped my arms around the back of his neck. With a playful laugh escaping my lips, I whispered, "Keep your hands off," even as tears continued to stream down my cheeks. He softly brushed my tears away with his fingers then gently dried my cheeks with the soft tissue. The weight of emotion was overwhelming and tears continued to flow despite his comforting touch.

Dem took my hands and then slowly pulled me close, hugging me. "Narr, take a moment to truly hear my heart," he whispered, his eyes shimmering with vulnerability. He took a deep breath, his voice steady yet earnest. "I may be young, but my heart is wide open for you, Narra Jones. Yes, I'm in my very early twenties, but I firmly believe that God is guiding my path. I might not be perfect, but I am a man of intention and readiness. In just a few years, I'll be prepared for even more meaningful adventures with you and I'll be better equipped to commit to a loving marriage with you. My desire for our relationship is deep and genuine. I promise to show my love through my actions—just give us the time we need to grow together."

"How can you be so sure, Demery?" I asked, my eyes searching his eyes for answers.

"How can you not be sure?" he replied quickly, his voice laced with a mix of confidence and vulnerability. "I'm certain, truly. I need to know that you're connecting with me on a deeper level, spiritually, and receiving the same divine message I am. Just so that you are aware, I believe wholeheartedly that all my dreams will come true and my prayers will be answered.

"Narra, I understand what you might be thinking; men often say such things, but I assure you, I'm genuinely different. It feels as if God has brought you into my life for a profound reason. Together, we have an incredible legacy to build.

"Sure, I'm still on a journey of learning and growing, but my heart knows what it needs. And you, my dear, are the woman God has chosen and prepared for me. In my moments of quiet prayer and seeking God's face, it becomes ever clearer."

In a moment charged with emotion, we stood together, our presence surrounded by an atmosphere heavy with spoken promises. A bright future beckoned, illuminated by our mutual hope, as if the very needle and thread of God conspired to weave our souls together. "I know I'll make mistakes, and I'm thankful for God's tender grace that guides me through life's ups and downs. But one thing I'm absolutely sure of is that I want to get it right when it comes to who I marry, and that person is you, Narra."

Narra's eyes widened as I confessed, "You know, I even thought about changing my number just so I could call you, just to hear your voice … and maybe find the chance to explain everything."

In a burst of laughter, Narra threw her head back, the sound echoing through the quiet space. "Really?" she exclaimed, still laughing and crying at the same time. "You're crazy, Dem!" I leaned in and kissed what was left of her drying tears.

"Dem, you are a dream," she said, still resting in my embrace.

"No, Narr, I'm real. I'm your answered prayer and you are mine," I said as I kissed the fresh tears resting on her face, attempting to dry them with my lips.

Narra gently released her grip from me and stuck out her hand with a playful smile. "Babe, just hand me a tissue," she said. We both chuckled, enjoying the moment.

We spent the evening talking, wrapped in each other's warmth. Every word served as a promise; we comforted one another, assuring that neither of us would ever give up on the other. In that precious moment, surrounded by laughter and understanding, our bond grew stronger, deepening into something beautiful and profound. I said, "We both are mature enough and understand that challenging times do happen."

As the clock struck 9:23 p.m., I glanced at my watch and realized how the evening had flown by. My thoughts drifted to Sasha and I quickly texted her, *Hey Sasha, Dem is here. Could you give us about an hour?*

Sasha replied with playful enthusiasm, *Girl, I'll see you two lovebirds tomorrow. I'm hanging out at my cousin Jazzy's place tonight. P.S. I knew you two would figure it out. Y'all are meant to be together!*

A flutter of excitement filled me. I responded to Sasha with a heart emoji and eagerly turned to Dem to share Sasha's message. "Do you want to stay over tonight since Sasha isn't coming back until tomorrow?" I asked, my heart racing at the thought.

"Girl, you know we can't do that! You've already got me all worked up. I'm a man, your man to be exact. We need to pace ourselves. We both want each other, but we also want to wait and take our time." His tone was playful yet serious.

"You're right. I'm just getting ahead of myself, aren't I?" I said with a grin as I now sat next to him, my head on his chest.

"That would be like bait for me, and I'll gladly let you reel me in like a fish out of water, baby!" he said, adopting a teasing country accent and raising his eyebrows.

"Haha, so you'll stay as late as you can?"

"Yeah, let's vibe to some love songs. I made a new playlist filled with songs just for you because, of course, I've been picturing you in my mind a lot lately," he said while lifting his head off the couch and staring at me as we both shared a laugh. "Have you eaten dinner yet, Narr?" he asked.

"Yeah, I just ate before you showed up at my door like a charming stalker or the Incredible Hulk trying to break in.

Haha, it's the first time I've eaten a complete meal in, like, a week."

"Staaalker?" he laughed.

"Wait … how did you even get into our hall, Dem?"

"I reached out to my old buddy, Cooper. He acted as the middleman, helping Sasha and me coordinate a time for me to come in while they went off to class."

"Oh, so you all had this planned out, huh?" I chuckled, my heart light with joy.

Inwardly, I wished for the night to stretch infinitely, wanting to cuddle with him, to bask in every possible moment together. The thought of him becoming my husband—well, he was going to be—sent my heart racing. Just the idea of it made me crave to pounce on him. I thought, *Goodness, he is so attractive, so easy to look at. He is not just eye candy; my man is an eye buffet—all you can eat style.* I wanted to savor every bit of him, including the dessert.

His curly hair had grown a bit longer and I found myself imagining how it would feel to run my fingers through those soft, luscious curls. *But Lord, let me stop 'demdreaming',* I thought. My mind began to race again. *Whew, I thank you for making him so incredibly handsome in my eyes, Lord. I am organically loved and I feel so thankful!*

"Narra," he said in a sternly sarcastic voice, "girl, you were starving yourself over me? You're cray cray! I know you love me, but come on—please stay healthy! We have our whole lives ahead of us. And why haven't you been attending your classes?"

"I've been in class! Online classes, Demery. What else do you want to know? I have a note from my therapist saying I needed a few days to catch up via online work. All my assignments have been submitted on time, Mr. Foxer," I shot back, a confident sneer on my lips. "Are you my professor now?" I said with a slight grin.

"I can be if you'd like," he whispered, a playful wink in his eye. "I'll teach you all the sounds of the English alphabet."

I just sat there, avoiding eye contact with a big grin on my face. "What?" he asked.

"Oh, nothing," I replied, my cheeks flushing slightly. We both chuckled softly, stealing glances at each other as I gently adjusted the throw blanket around us.

In that moment, our friendly playfulness filled the air, blending concerns for each other with the warmth of our connection. Despite the tension, a thread of romance was woven through our playful words; it reminded us both of our shared journey, filled with ups and downs, yet always together. Dem cared for me deeply and it was that care that fueled our playful exchanges, no matter how serious things sometimes felt. I needed to know I was not alone in this life—Dem was right there beside me, every step of the way.

"While we were joking earlier, something important occurred to me that I'd like to share," I said with a serious tone. He lifted his head from the comfy sofa and paused the song from his phone's playlist. "My life and childhood haven't been perfect and they remind me of my mom's experience after her breakup with my dad when I was a kid. I wasn't intentionally trying to starve myself during those past few days; it was an unimaginably difficult time for me. I witnessed my mom endure a mental breakdown, facing numerous challenges, including the inability to eat. She lost a significant amount of weight, yet through it all, God carried her and all of our family. We continued to pray for her and alongside her when we visited.

"She had to stay in a mental health facility for a few months when I was around eight or nine years old. During that time, I stayed with Rya and her family, occasionally visiting my aunt on my father's side. It was a challenging period for both my mom and me, which might explain why I sometimes feel anxious and ask so many questions. I sincerely apologize if I seem a bit tough; my heart's goal is to remain soft for myself, for you, for our future children, and the people I'm connected to, babe."

"Oh, I understand now, Narra. I apologize for what I said and my delivery."

"Yeah, my mom prefers not to share that part of her story. I understand, but I wanted you to know a little more about our testimony. To be loved softly and safely is incredible. Thank you for showing me such love and kindness, Demery."

"Narra, loving you has been one of the easiest things I have ever had to do," Dem said.

"I want you to know that a few days ago, I did eat, although it was very little. Today was the first time I had normal portions, but please don't worry, I'm okay. That bloodline curse is broken; I decree and declare it so."

"Amen, Narra! I agree." Dem shouted.

"I am incredibly grateful for my stepdad, John, and the beautiful blended family we share. Witnessing my mom radiate joy and love has filled my heart with hope, particularly when I reflect on her past and see how far she has come. My mom's love story is truly beautiful; she found her true love in her late forties and their happiness together is palpable! They serendipitously met at a church event, thanks to a mutual friend's invitation, which I believe was a sign of God's work. Their marriage is a true blessing from the Lord and what they both prayed for!

"God is good! I've learned that when your own pleasures begin to falter and life gets tough, stand firm in God's divine plan while gently letting go of your personal goals and what you once saw as essential. God may have something, or someone, more beautiful and meaningful waiting for you.

"No matter how old you get, never let your dreams fade. We are here to love and be loved, deeply and authentically. Always keep dreaming; embrace God's perfect way, new dreams, and passions that set your heart aflame, filling your spirit with warmth and enchantment.

"Now that you have a better understanding of the Joneses and Potters, Dem, what's happening with us? What are we doing?"

"Girl, why do you think I'm here? You're mine. You're my beautiful wife-to-be. I want to do this right." He paused for a moment. "Narra, can you be my sweet, loving, caring girlfriend?"

"Well, of course, babe," I said, embracing Dem once again. He opened the Spotify app, turned the volume up a notch, and the sweet songs of his new playlist began to fill the air again.

Setting his phone on the armrest of the cozy mini sofa, he turned to me with a playful smile. "Do you want to dance?" he asked, his eyes sparkling with love. I couldn't help but giggle uncontrollably as we stood up. I took his hands and gently guided them to my waist, my fingers finding a gentle spot on his back. To my surprise, he was an excellent dancer, more skilled than I had realized, as if he had taken dance lessons since the last time we moved gracefully to some good music. He pulled me near, yet maintained a respectful distance, like a true gentleman, as he struck a balance between closeness and decorum. I soaked in the kindness that radiated from his grip as we moved in coordination with the rhythm.

"I love you, Narra," he professed for maybe the 25th time that day, always heartfelt and genuine. When he took my right hand and spun me gracefully, our eyes met once more, igniting a joyful flurry in my chest; I cherished that electric connection that eye contact brought.

"I love you, babe," I responded softly.

Narra squinted playfully. "Oh, my goodness, are you tearing up again?" A glimmer of comfort danced in her eyes as she noticed the sheen of emotion in mine. "Oh, you're serious, Dem?" she teased, unable to suppress her smile while handing me another tissue.

I took a deep breath, my voice steady but laced with vulnerability. "Yes, Narra, you scared me. I can't imagine losing my wife; I need you by my side. Please promise me you won't disappear on me again—it was a heart-wrenching experience. Just promise that you will show me grace when you may have to remind me what you need from me, both as a man and as your man."

With sincerity in her gaze, Narra nodded. "I will, and I won't do that again. It hurt me deeply—I've never experienced such pain and I never want to endure that again."

In that moment, we were enclosed in a bubble of shared emotions, crying, praying, and laughing together. "Look at us!" she cried, as if her heart was swelling with love and gratitude. Narra said, "We're in love and it's all because of God."

"Lord, you deserve all the glory for this beautiful love story," I added.

That feeling of victory, freedom, and joy when you know it was God who created your unique union.

As we settled down, we had just finished up our third love song out of ten. Relaxing on the couch, we sipped cool bottled spring water, feeling cozy and drowsy. Both of us were fully clothed and comfortable. As we relaxed further, we decided to slip off our hoodies. I gently laid them on the couch's arm while she reached for the blanket again, swaddling us in an intimate cuddle that deepened the moment between us.

Dem stretched out languidly, his long legs exceeding the petite dimensions of the sofa. I placed my head against his warm, muscular chest, surrendering myself as my upper body melted into his embrace. We drifted off to sleep, protected in each other's presence, only to awaken around 1:00 a.m. Dem softly brushed his hands along my back, a gentle nudge to rouse me from sleep. "Hey Narra, it's about time for me to head out. I have class at 9:00 a.m.," he murmured, his voice tinged with reluctant sweetness. It seemed as if part of him longed to hold on to that transcendent moment forever. "This feels safe, like home. You make me feel like a king and I truly need that."

I didn't want him to leave, but he began gathering his things. I handed him his hoodie, our fingers brushing softly, igniting another flame that lingered between us. He grabbed his keys, campus ID card, and wallet, slipping them into his kangaroo pocket on his hoodie with a reluctant sigh. As he moved toward the door, I could see the indecision in his eyes. He knew that if he didn't leave now, he'd end up staying the entire night and the thought of him in my space—maybe even in my bed—made my heart race. But he hadn't brought a change of clothes and that heavy reality loomed over us. We both understood the risk. If anyone found out he had stayed overnight, it could lead to trouble we weren't ready to face. But still, that unspoken connection hung in the room, a tantalizing possibility that neither of us wanted to let go of. As Dem paused at the door, I felt that familiar ache in my chest, wishing he could stay just a little longer, hoping for another moment that could last forever.

"Girl, stop it. I can't stay! I don't even have a toothbrush or deodorant!" he exclaimed with a teasing smile.

"Be safe and text me when you're inside and let me know if everything's okay."

"I'll be alright. Campus security is available twenty-four hours a day, so you have no worries. I'll pick you up on Friday. I'm taking you out and then to church on Sunday?"

My eyes sparkled with excitement. "Church? Are you really saying you want to go to church with me in person finally? That's a big deal!"

"We are a big deal, Narra. We're doing this. It's real. Yes, I'm going to your church with you and that won't be the last time! I know you'll be teaching Bible lessons or something. I'll let my parents know I have to ditch my church this Sunday."

I chuckled, "Actually, I don't have to teach this Sunday, but our twenty-minute sessions are designed for kids aged twelve to sixteen and are highly engaging! You could even be a guest at one of our sessions someday. The whole session is a rapid-fire Q&A where we are required to be honest and keep our answers concise without dwelling too long on any question. We have a strict time limit. My mom and stepdad attend on the days

I'm leading the sessions. It's just for twenty minutes, and after that, I look forward to seeing you around in service!"

"Oh yes, I would really like that! I know I'd learn so much from you. Speaking of which, we need to decide on a time and day of the week for our own couple's Bible study—just the two of us for now—"

As Dem spoke, I felt an exhilarating surge of courage and interrupted him mid-sentence with the most extended, most passionate kiss I had ever shared. Unlike the brief pecks that defined our previous encounters, this kiss was a beautiful fusion of anticipation and tenderness. I allowed my lips to linger against his, savoring the sweet moment with slightly parted lips, yet kept it uncomplicated, mindful to stop before venturing too far. It was just enough to deepen our connection while respecting unspoken boundaries, consciously refraining from using my hands, even as his rested gently on my lower back. "Okay, you have to go. Now, Dem."

And just like that, the door swung open, closed, and finally locked again. I leaned my back against the door, my head lifted towards the ceiling, releasing a soft sigh, overwhelmed by the intensity of what had just transpired. "God, I need to marry that man tomorrow!"

At times, God's timing may seem distant and His voice quiet, but when we listen tentatively, we can hear the wisdom whispers of God's loving voice saying, "Long ago, I lovingly painted both of you in one portrait yet with divine timing in mind."

Chapter Fifteen

❤

Treasure Discovered at Golden Leaf

I stood before my father, the weight of emotion palpable in the air. "I'm still trying to make it up to her, Dad, and I'm doing everything I can to surprise her and make her feel special. But I also want to be a better man for her, someone she can rely on. What do you think I should do?"

My dad leaned back in his chair, a knowing smile curling at the corners of his lips. "Being a better man isn't about grand gestures, Son. It's the small, consistent actions that matter. Listen to her, respect her needs, and always be honest." He sat up. "Show her your commitment, not just in words but through your everyday choices. That's how trust is built. Keep that in mind and you'll both be just fine."

Something I discovered and loved about Narra early on was her ability to let go of past grievances, which filled me with relief. However, it also served as a touching reminder of her generous spirit, fueling my determination to show her how much she truly meant to me.

"You know her well, Son. You know what she likes. Do something thoughtful for her and be a consistent man in her life," my dad advised, his voice imbued with encouragement.

As I left the room, a renewed sense of purpose filled me. I was ready to put my heart into making her feel cherished, one little step at a time, and prove to her that I was truly worthy of her love.

We made our way to the enchanting Golden Leaf Book Vault, a hidden bookstore nestled 22 ft. up in a tree house, deep within a secluded wooded area that took an hour and 20 minutes to reach. Surrounded by towering trees, the place offered about six private library tree bungalows for rent, each cozy space accommodating only two people. Here, one could listen to the birds, breathe in the fresh air, and read in blissful serenity. The warm and inviting atmosphere was illuminated by a soft radiance that emitted a charming light throughout the space, making it feel dreamlike. Narra could hardly believe her eyes; it was as if she had stepped into a dream. Inside, an eclectic array of colorful furniture filled the few rooms, bringing the place to life. The front of the store resembled a majestic, ancient tree, but stepping inside revealed a vast interior that expanded further back with two levels: a cozy basement and an engaging entry room. In this enchanted hideaway, it was easy to forget it was a tree house, especially in the corners where the stillness of the wood remained undisturbed by the windows.

I reveled in the artistry of the wooden structure—it was skillfully crafted, glowing with warmth and charm. It was everything Narra adored: books, a space of stories scattered everywhere! Despite being a self-proclaimed book hoarder, I was convinced that Narra had yet to discover this hidden gem, known only to a select few. People traveled from great distances just to experience its beauty. I had learned about it from a former professor, who was part of a secret book club, and he revealed this treasure when I visited his room and asked if he knew of any amazing places for book lovers.

As we settled into one of the library bungalows, a sense of intimacy surrounded us. Narra grabbed a book from the shelf while I leaned in, catching the soft scent of her hair mixed with the fresh pages. Time felt suspended as we exchanged glances that lingered a little longer than necessary. The world outside faded as laughter and soft whispers filled the space between us. Lost in our own little world, surrounded by the rustle of leaves and the distant sound of birds, we began to share tales of our favorite stories, our passion for literature weaving a deeper connection.

As the golden afternoon light streamed through the windows, it cast soft patterns on the wooden floors, merging our hearts with the enchanting peacefulness of the Golden Leaf Book Vault. The small entry fee seemed insignificant compared to the treasure within as the books were free—an almost unbelievable privilege! Though there was a limit of five free books per visit, exceeding that came at a price, making it a book lover's paradise. Patrons could linger all day in the main lobby area, creating their perfect reading nest, though that was accompanied by an additional fee. But that day, I had a secret plan. We agreed on a strategy: to choose between three books and then stay for only two hours, savoring the experience without overstaying our welcome and embodying an adventurous spirit as we basked in the joy of shared discovery.

As part of a surprise, we agreed to each select a book for the other, with the unveiling set for later, but we could not wait. Narra chose a pristine new Bible for me, reflecting her deep respect and love for me and knowing I needed a new physical bible. In turn, I picked out a profound book titled *A Husband and Wife's Love Letter to God* by John and Ronette Johnson, which perfectly encapsulated our shared journey and aspirations. After the big reveal, we dove into our new treasures, reading, praying, and starting a light Bible study together right then and there. It was a radiant dawn of renewal for us as we immersed ourselves in the Bible together, each page a testament to our new beginning.

The very next day marked the start of our new chapter in faith, love, and consistent Bible study together as a couple united in purpose and affection. Narra penned a sweet note of love and carefully tucked it away in my new Bible, unaware of when I might discover it. It read, "I cannot wait for that 'You can tell God is with them' kind of marriage."

Chapter Sixteen

Heightened Love and Enlightenment

People gathered at the altar—young and old, from every race and nationality—while soft worship music flowed from the piano, interspersed with wholehearted hallelujahs and moments of profound silence. It was a scene of indescribable beauty.

It was 10:55 a.m. on a beautiful Sunday morning. Narra and I walked in hand in hand, stepping into the welcoming atmosphere of Living Word Ministries, arriving just before my parents, who would soon join us. A gripping excitement surged within me as I introduced Narra to a few friendly faces, just before the service began. "My church occupies a unique space—caught between the grandeur of a megachurch and the intimacy of a small gathering, whatever term fits best," I said softly to Narra. "Hi, Pastor Jack! I would love for you to meet Narra," I said, my heart racing just a little as her warm smile lit up the pastor's face.

"Is this the young lady you were telling us all about?" His eyes glowed with genuine enthusiasm. I nodded, a smile breaking across my face, feeling proud.

"It's so wonderful to meet you, Narra, finally!" Pastor Jack exclaimed, warmly shaking her hand.

"Great to meet you too, Pastor Jack," she replied, her voice soft yet confident. "I've heard so much about you and I can't wait to hear your thoughts on today's sermon after the service." Pastor Jack's eyes shifted to the altar, ready to prepare for praise and worship.

We took our seats next to my parents, who had quietly slipped in without us noticing. We greeted them with a warm hug and exchanged hellos with those around us as the vibrant energy filled the room. At precisely 11:15 a.m., the church service began. I rose to join in the worship, reaching for Narra's right hand, my fingertips brushing against hers in an electrifying moment.

She responded by taking my left hand, allowing me to hold it gently. Our eyes remained closed, lost in the sanctity of the moment. We raised our hands towards Heaven, entranced in our devotion, but it felt as if our souls connected on a deeper level—beyond sight, beyond words. In this intimate moment, all that mattered was our shared love for Jesus. I cherished the freedom we felt, unburdened and embraced by our faith. As I took a peek, I was captivated by how Narra lifted her hands in worship. The way she poured herself into her connection with God moved me profoundly; her spirit resonated with my own.

As we worshipped, our fingers interlocked tightly, every slight squeeze echoing our unspoken bond, lifting each other's spirits higher and immersing us in the joy of our divine connection In this moment, it was all about Jesus, yet I couldn't help but feel that it was also about our godly union. I fell in love with the way Narra gracefully lifted her hands as she worshipped. The passion in her heart for God showed and drew me closer and moved me spiritually. It was both magnetic and freeing After a few moments, I gently released her hand to take a breath and gather myself. I glanced at Narra, completely lost in her worship; it was the most beautiful and authentic thing I had ever seen. Watching her in this state of reverence was liberating, like observing a breathtaking spectacle of genuine love and devotion.

Look at my imperfect woman, lost in worship for our perfect God, I thought, overwhelmed with gratitude. I whispered, "Jesus, thank you for all that you mean to me and everything you're creating between us." I had learned that we don't have to be perfect to fit into each other's story. Only God could create a love story so beautiful.

The following Sunday arrived, bringing with it the calmness of shared faith at Trinity Worship Center. This was special for us as it marked our first service together at my church.

Dem and I had made our own plans for the day: I took my usual role guiding the pre-teens and teens in a separate area, while Dem opted to enjoy a cozy moment with my parents.

I arrived early and introduced Dem to several members, excited to connect with the youth. After a rewarding Q&A session, I moved to the row where my parents and Dem were seated. As I joined them in worship quietly, my heart filled with joy. My hands were raised high, and while I tried to focus deeply on the moment, I couldn't help but steal glances at Dem, who was wholeheartedly praising God. The sight was enchanting, effortlessly drawing me deeper into my own worship. In that sacred space, the harmony of voices, both near and far, intertwined, creating a sense of divine connection that filled the air with love and reverence. I wanted Dem to be close to flawless, but I realized that he embodied everything I had ever prayed for, yet he was far from perfect. He was someone who wholeheartedly served our perfect God beside me, someone who understood that seeking God was the first step, not a last resort. When we prayed, we prayed with a fervor that caused mountains to move. I didn't need someone desperate for me; I needed someone who was passionately committed to serving God alongside me, someone who shared in the divine love and didn't conform but strived to live by God's beautiful definition of love. It was a day bathed in beauty, carrying a profound message waiting to be unraveled later. Today's message was titled: "Made in God's Image to Mirror What Love Looks Like."

I'd been saving my heart just as I saved my money, each dollar I tucked away echoing a dream of a love story filled with passion and laughter. Late at night, after honest conversations with my parents, I found myself daydreaming about the woman who had captured my heart, imagining a future where romance filled every moment.

One evening, as I joined Narra for our usual virtual church service, I felt a flicker of something more ignite within me— every shared prayer and laugh felt electric. Each interaction became a delicate dance of unspoken feelings, my faith seamlessly intertwining with a growing affection. As we consistently connected in worship, it was not just a spiritual journey; it grew into something more profound. With every glance and every word, I felt God nudging me closer to Narra, whispering that this was it—no more precious time should be wasted.

On a Friday night, with a mixture of excitement and nervousness, I called my mom. "Mom, it's time. We are heading to Randi's Jewelry Store tomorrow."

"What? Seriously, tomorrow?" came her surprised reply.

"Yes, Mom. I heard from God again and just had another conversation with Dad the other night."

"Let's do it, Son. I'll be ready, just let me know a time."

I felt a surge of joy. "We are doing it!"

"Son, God's will is being done and He knows that you are ready."

The bold, dazzling beam of light filled the space, accentuating the charm of its unique design. And that itself set the tone for the rest of the day. My mom had mentioned weeks earlier that we would embark on a ring shopping adventure when I was ready and now that long-awaited day had finally arrived. My heart fluttered with nerves, acutely aware of how much I valued my mother's opinion, and I hoped every detail would be just right. Each exquisite light fixture harmonized beautifully with the shimmering facets of the architecture, projecting a dreamlike atmosphere. "Lights, camera, action!" I exclaimed with a sense of anticipation.

The pristine, glass-like brilliance of the structure was utterly mesmerizing, drawing gasps of admiration from those in the shop around us. It bathed the entire area in a dazzling, gentle glow, wrapping us all in an adoring speckle of light. "Mom, what do you think?" I asked, my eyes likely sparkling with excitement and hope.

"Son, this is the moment you've been praying and preparing for and saying I'm proud is such an understatement! God has taught you well! I have only been a wise vessel, guided by God to support and nurture you as you've grown. Narra is worth more than any material possession. She will soar beyond the stars."

I looked at my mother with sincerity and said, "Mom, sometimes I wonder if I truly deserve such a miracle as Narra."

She responded in a soothing voice, "That means she is everything you need and more than you ever imagined.

"Dem, as you prepare to be a husband, remember that you'll make mistakes, honey. It won't always be perfect. It's natural to feel how you are feeling, Son. You both deserve this beautiful, divine love story.

"God's blessings will often make you feel as if He has given you more than you deserve. He provides us with gifts that exceed our imagination, far greater than we could ever merit. This blessing is a sign that it comes directly from Him, that she is your favor bestowed by Him.

"Blessings from God are extraordinary, almost inexplicable. Your marriage will be beautiful and graceful, a testament of God's assurance that it was created through His love.

"Shall I continue, Dem?" she asked. We exchanged a gentle smile. "I am speaking of beauty found in grace, forgiveness, sacrifice, peace, safety, and oneness. These are gifts bestowed only by our Heavenly Father.

"Your dad and I have a beautiful marriage because we choose to forgive each other daily and extend grace. You won't always get it right on the first try. You have to put your trust in God, honey. Continue to work on yourselves and your marriage and never give up on each other. Choose to love and forgive, always—even when it's tough.

"I see it already. God has already saturated your marriage with His perfect love, Dem. God is getting the glory."

"I see it too, Mom!" I chuckled as we finished paying for the jewelry.

"Always remember Matthew 19:6. So then, they are no longer two but one flesh. Therefore, what God has joined together, let not man separate. Your father and I have no doubts that you and Narra have a true relationship built on God's definition of marriage and romance."

"I understand, Mother!" I replied, my tone laced with respect.

My mom and I agreed that she should keep the ring for the time being, securely stored in a safe at the Foxer residence. I didn't want to risk losing it and it was too expensive for me to carry it around or even leave it in my dorm.

I found myself reflecting on the bittersweet moments that were about to come. The thought of returning to Locakee, Pennsylvania, to my parents' house, filled me with a strange mix of excitement and nostalgia. In the midst of this, I decided to take one last tour of the area, soaking in every memory I could. As the school year drew to a close for everyone, my anticipation for graduation in a week bubbled over; each day felt like a new beginning, yet I held on to the past.

Just the day before, I had my braces removed—a change I had eagerly awaited. My smile felt different, more confident, like it was ready for new adventures. Riding that wave of excitement, I planned to surprise Dem during our workout meetup. I knew he might be suspicious since I hadn't been to the gym in weeks, especially with him, but I couldn't resist the thrill of seeing the look on his face after my reveal. As I waited for him, I started my workout, feeling the rush of endorphins coursing through me. Just then, out of the blue, a guy approached me. My heart raced, and for an exhilarating moment, I thought it was Dem sneaking up behind me, ready to tease me about my unexpected visit. The atmosphere was charged, every second stretching with anticipation as I turned around, eager to see the face that might change everything in that passing moment.

"Hey, beautiful!"

I had my headphones in, so I initially ignored him, pretending I didn't hear anything. But the music was low enough for me to catch his words.

"Hi, gorgeous!"

I took out my left earbud and replied, "Hi, do I know you?"

"No, but I just wanted to tell you that you have a beautiful smile. You're gorgeous!"

Out of the corner of my eye, I spotted Dem walking in and relief splashed over me.

"Thanks so much. My husband is meeting me here," I said, half nodding towards the door while keeping my hands on the exercise machine.

Dem walked over and I paused my music. "Saved you a spot, babe," I said as he took the machine right next to mine.

"What did that guy want?" he asked, a hint of concern in his voice.

"Oh, you saw that? He was giving me a compliment."

"A compliment about what?" I had never seen him so worked up before. "He tried to flirt with you?"

"Not really. He said something about me being pretty and I told him my husband was meeting me here," I replied, a playful smirk on my face.

"Good." He leaned in to give me a quick peck on the lips, and I thought, *You better know what you have when you have it*, trying not to burst into laughter.

"So, babe, all set with credits and stuff?"

"Yes, I am! What a relief. I'm so glad it's over, Narr. I'm burnt out and here to unwind from the stress." It took him at least five minutes to notice the change. "Narr! Wait, what?" He did a triple-take, his eyes widening in surprise. "Why didn't you tell me you were getting your braces removed?"

"I wanted to surprise you in a big way!"

"Well, I'm definitely surprised!" I couldn't help but beam at him, my smile wider than ever. He stepped off the elliptical, his smile mirroring mine. With a tender gesture, he turned off my machine. My heart raced as he leaned in and the air between us ignited with a sweet kiss on my lips. I swiftly said, "I love you, Demery."

As we both pulled away, smiling, I remembered something important. "I wanted to let you know that I don't have many tickets for graduation, but I'll check with Sasha to see if she has an extra."

"No worries, Narr. I'm not thrilled to hear that, but I'll be outside waiting for you if I can't snag a ticket." His calm, supportive demeanor made my heart flap even more, knowing he would be there for me regardless.

"But girl, you're looking even more beautiful today!" he exclaimed, genuine admiration in his tone as he narrowed his eyes, examining me from my toes to my hair, as if appreciating every detail in reverent silence.

"Thanks, babe. I even put in a little extra effort to look cute for our workout."

"Oh, I've noticed. Your hair is all done and looks good."

"School's almost done for you, too, huh?"

"Yeah, it's finals week, I'll be finishing up soon and then my junior year will be over," he replied, an excited lilt in his voice.

"I've already started looking for a job and an apartment. You know, the usual stressors for college grads. But I'm doing my best not to let it overwhelm me." Knowing he was part of my future and that changes awaited us both, I could only think positively.

"Like I told you before, don't worry, Narr. Things will work out. I'll help you in any way I can until you find a job."

"I appreciate you, Dem, but I think I can handle this."

"I hear you, Narr."

As I walked Narra to her car, I reminded her, "Don't forget we have another Bible study at my parents' house coming up."

Narra replied, "I'll be there for sure!"

"You know I love couples' Bible study!"

"I know; it should be fun."

"See you in a few days, my college graduate!"

She said, "I love you!" as I opened her car door and watched her slide inside.

I couldn't help but repeat, "I love you!"

"Call me when you get home!" she said before driving off.

The long-anticipated day had finally arrived—May 25th, a date filled with promise, purpose, and dreams. Graduation was here, marking the beginning of a new and exciting chapter.

Hey Narr, meet me in Crepe's lower-level restroom. Sasha's text buzzed on my phone. Ten minutes later, we found each other in the quiet sanctuary of the bathroom near the lobby at Crepe auditorium, close to Rovane's south entrance. Tears welled up and blurred my vision, streaking down my cheeks and smudging my makeup. But Sasha was there, gentle and caring, dabbing under my eyes with her soft makeup brush, her presence soothing me. In that moment, I realized how much we had grown together, how strong our bond was. "Sasha, I'm going to miss you so much," I whispered, my voice trembling with emotion. We embraced tightly, swaying in a quiet dance of farewell, as if the world outside had momentarily paused, holding on to these fleeting seconds of closeness and friendship.

"Narra, girl, we have to meet up at least once a month! Spa dates, church, workouts—anything!"

"Church? Really?" I couldn't believe it.

"Yes! I'm totally in for that!" Sasha beamed, her excitement contagious. "But before anything, can I be a bridesmaid or what?"

I blushed and laughed. "You absolutely can!"

We shared one last squeeze before reluctantly heading back to our seats, realizing the ceremony would start any moment now.

"I did it!" I sat just a few feet away from my best friend, bursting with pride over all we had overcome to reach this milestone. The excitement was electric as we both prepared to graduate together.

"We did it!" Sasha whispered, a grin spreading across her face.

"We sure did!" I replied with glee. Dressed in our stunning navy-blue caps and gowns, we represented Rovane University Class of 2018 with pride—nearly 5,926 strong! And both of us graduating with honors only made it sweeter. The Potter family was deep. My parents and stepbrothers were in town to watch me walk across the stage and an overwhelming mix of emotions swept over me, joy taking the lead as I fought back tears.

As I heard the announcer call out, "Narra Anne Jones!" a ripple of applause filled the air as I made my way across the stage. Suddenly, screams erupted amidst the applause—it had to be my family. Though I couldn't see them at the moment, I knew they were somewhere inside the building. As I scanned the audience, searching for my best friend Rya, my granny, or even my mom and dad, I hoped that maybe the twins might stand out as well. The vast room buzzed with excitement as the names of other graduates echoed in the background. About five minutes later, I looked around again to see if I could spot my family. There he was—Demery Foxer! Looking handsome as ever. I waited for him to spot me, knowing it might be a challenge in the crowd. Yet, as the ceremony continued, I found myself searching for his familiar and striking face and it was easy to recognize him, remembering the outfit he wore. My heart raced at the thought of seeing him again, every moment amplifying the anticipation.

I could spot that fine man from a spaceship in outer space, I thought, smiling at the sight of him. Somehow, he had managed to sneak in or get a ticket, even though the hall was completely sold out and each graduate was limited to five tickets and Sasha had set aside one for my granny.

There he was, my man, standing proudly among the crowd, holding a beautiful bouquet and a few colorful balloons. The only reason he was standing was that all the seats were taken. *This man is a dream,* I thought as I shook my head in disbelief and smiled, displaying every front tooth I had. The Holy Spirit then corrected me, saying, "He's more than a dream, Dem is real, an answered prayer." I quickly pulled my cell phone from my small pink clutch. *Dem! How did you get a ticket?* He replied with a grin emoji. *I know a few people who know a few people who were able to pull some strings! Lol.* I sent him a laughing emoji and a heart.

After the ceremony, I hugged my family, met some of Sasha's family for the first time, and then caught a glimpse of my stunning man again from afar. "Hold these cards and balloons for me, Rya, and take them to the car for me, please!" As I maneuvered through the crowd, it felt like being in a bustling airport. People were streaming in and out of the large auditorium. I spotted a few of my balloons, including one huge bright rose-gold balloon that read, "Congrats NAJ!" in royal-blue letters, swaying in the air each time a door swung open. Dem seemed a bit distracted as I noticed him scanning the crowd for me, reminiscent of a "Where's Waldo?" moment, with every grad dressed in the same navy-blue cap and gown.

Just as I reached him, our eyes met instantly and I could feel an electric connection. We embraced tightly, sharing an intimate moment, though we refrained from kissing for the time being. His cell phone was in his hand as he quietly recorded me and snapped pictures. "Congrats, Narr! You did it! How does it feel?"

"Hi, baby! I'm soooo happy you are here!" I said with a sweet, surprised, and soft tone as we held each other close. He handed me my balloons, a card, and the flowers, saying, "Narr, Lord willing, I will always move mountains for you." In that moment, my heart, slightly parched from missing his face, as I hadn't seen him in a few days, was full and refreshed. There's just something about a man who shows good, godly intentions—it's different, romantic in a pure, genuine way.

I smiled then glanced up to see one of his good friends, Chris Plemming, approaching with a few other grads. My eyes lit up. "Oh, Chris! That's right! How'd I forget?" I tapped him on the shoulder, adding, "Congratulations, Chris and thank you so much!"

"Nah, it wasn't me," Chris said as he resumed hugging and taking pictures with other graduates. I beamed at Dem, narrowing my eyes in wonder.

I turned around to Chris, thinking he was telling a fib, when I heard, "Congrats, Narra!" in a deep familiar voice as he gave Dem a hug and a handshake.

It's Michael Needan!

"Mike! Congratulations!"

"Was it Mike?" I muttered, raising one eyebrow at Dem.

Dem nodded. "Thanks again, man!" he said to Mike with a firm handshake.

"Oh, my goodness! Thank you so much, Mike!"

Mike gestured with his praying hands. "My pleasure, Narra. Congrats! We did it!" We shared a kind embrace. I took out my phone to ask Chris to take a few pictures of Dem and me, as well as some with my classmates. I did the same for Chris and Mike, snapping perfect photos of them in their caps and gowns. I also got to meet Michael's girlfriend, Mandi, and made sure to take the cutest photos of them.

"Where are your parents and granny, Narr?" Dem asked.

I replied, "Oh, they are around here somewhere, talking with Sasha and her family. My granny was a little tired, so she's probably sitting down somewhere or in the car with Rya and the others. You'll meet them all later at our home for a graduation dinner party."

Dem leaned in, whispering. "Oh, Narr, Mike and I had a quick chat a few days ago. He mentioned your little fling y'all had going on. Haha." I couldn't help but feel a flicker of nervousness at Dem's discovery.

"Oh, I should have mentioned that," I said softly, a gentle smile appearing on my lips as I revealed only the top row of my teeth.

"Relax, Narr. I know you guys haven't done anything too serious. It's fine, babe. There's nothing to be worried about. I'm just glad he had a spare ticket for today."

"Yeah, me too, babe."

"Mike cautiously avoided specifics, but I could tell how serious it was. He's basically your ex, huh?" Dem teased lightly.

I smiled softly, the awkwardness of the moment lingering. "I wouldn't quite call him that, but I appreciate you knowing a bit more now."

"Yeah, Narr. I'm sure glad he messed up too."

"Me too." We both chuckled.

I continued to weave through the crowd, allowing Dem to hold my flowers and balloons while I clutched the card, hugging several more people. I texted my mom, saying, *I'll be riding home with Dem. Be there in a few for dinner.*

I had a feeling that was Dem earlier; tell him I said "Hi." That man loves you, Narr! You better not take too long or we all will eat all your cake!

Chapter Seventeen

A Promise in Progress

As November drew near, it marked six months since I graduated. Dem, who had started his senior year a few months back, decided to commute this year—a choice many believed I influenced, although he would never admit it. His parents were undoubtedly thrilled to have him around more often, relishing the warmth of their family's closeness once again. This new arrangement allowed Dem to reconnect with his family and focus more intently on his assignments while he also attended church services in person more regularly. His frequent presence at Living Word Ministries meant he was introducing me to more members of the congregation. I felt an increasing desire to stand by his side as he wholeheartedly embraced this new commitment, infusing our lives with a sense of assurance.

Throughout the summer, I immersed myself in a whirlwind of job hunting, juggling interviews, church summer activities with the youth, and nurturing my family, all while deepening my connection with Dem and his relatives. I had already rejected two job offers, feeling the salaries were insufficient even for an entry-level role. With every shared moment, my belief in Dem as my future husband grew stronger. Yet, as our relationship developed, we encountered the complexities of intimacy. Our interactions evolved beyond playful kisses into very affectionate embraces, but we understood the necessity of pausing to resist the allure of going further. To uphold our mutual boundaries, we agreed to avoid solitary moments together in our homes. Despite this, we continued to cherish our dates and the simple pleasure of each other's company, completely focused on our purposeful romance.

I could tell he was wildly in love with me and I had fallen hard for him too. Sometimes, I had to pinch myself to believe this kind of love was real. He was incredibly patient with me, uncomplainingly guiding me through the chaos of apartment and job hunting. Despite my efforts not to overwhelm him, he insisted on helping me with my search for a place to live.

I appreciated the beauty of this season, with cooler yet still warm days, where leaves shift from bright green to shades of red, yellow, and brown, resembling a natural tie-dye masterpiece. It reminded me of the winter chill approaching, making me look forward to more intimate and cozy dates together. Amidst our shared dreams, we begin to discuss the prospect of marriage, envisioning a beautiful timeline that lay ahead of us. I felt full of patience and unwavering faith, finding comfort in my trust in God and Dem because they both held my heart. As I considered a new job opportunity that looked promising, I also felt a warm longing for my own home, which prompted me to think of the cozy comfort of my parents' house as I hoped to have a similarly comfortable space.

With excitement fluttering in my chest, I heard my phone ring. It was Narra calling and I could almost feel her energy through the line. "Hi, Demery!" she sang, her voice brightening my day. "How have you been? It's been a few days since we last saw each other and I miss you so much, my honey!" she added.

"How are you? Ready to see me?" I calmly asked.

"Yes. I. Am," she said with a brief pause between each short, sweet word. I could hear her enthusiasm bubbling through our conversation and it made me smile. "Babe, I've been doing well! I'm hoping we can continue apartment hunting this week. I came across some interesting listings near my hometown since I know you mentioned considering a move closer to Whisby." I could sense her excitement as she replied, ready to embark on this adventure together. My spirit was energetic and I could feel the pull to seize new opportunities as I considered launching my career. As I chatted with her, I also thought about how I was currently only working at Kraze twice a month. But truthfully, I found comfort in my architectural internship.

At that job, I assisted in preparing design models for a prestigious company in Philadelphia and it felt like I was paving the way for my future in a field I was passionate about. This internship wasn't just about gaining experience for me; it was a stepping stone towards my dream, a dream I hoped to build alongside Narra as we shared our lives together.

A few days later, after touring several apartments together and considering Dem's insights on each one, we took advantage of the last few warm days of the year. We were also looking forward to our scheduled Bible study with his parents that evening. Sharing the scriptures with them had become one of our favorite new traditions. This was our fourth Bible study with the Foxers and with each session we had deepened our bond, enriching our relationship through every shared moment and insight. In past gatherings, we would often select one individual or couple to lead the study, taking turns in this intimate exploration of faith. Tonight, Dem's father, Mr. Robert, would guide our discussion, and we anticipated the insights he would bring.

As the clock ticked closer to the hour of 7:30 p.m. on that captivating Thursday evening, Dem and I gracefully arrived at the welcoming doors of the Foxer household; the soft amber glow of streetlights had guided our way after a delightful stroll through Center City. We rolled into the driveway in my stepdad's sleek midnight-black two-seater Beamer, my car temporarily sidelined at the shop and Dem's car already parked in the garage where he left it earlier today.

The tone between us was filled with power, both from our cozy clothing and the subtle electricity of the moment. I wore a light blue denim jacket that rested casually over a snug black sweatshirt, emblazoned with the striking phrase, "Living In My Love Story," in bright hot pink from prayedforpraywithapparel.com. Complementing this ensemble were my comfortable black jogging pants and light blue block-heeled ankle boots, which mirrored the rich hue of the denim, grounding my look with an air of effortless style.

Still seated in the driver's seat, I took off my light pink-lensed, black-framed sunglasses and turned to look at Dem with a soft smile. "Have I mentioned today how amazingly handsome you look?" I whispered, my heart pulsating at the sight of him. A rush of affection flooded me as we prepared to engage with his family, fondly sharing one of our most cherished traditions.

"For the fifth time, haha. Thanks, Narr Barr! And babe, you know you look flawless. You are stunning!"

"You're very welcome, Demmer!"

Dem was donned in black slacks that perfectly complemented a long-sleeved button-up shirt in a playful mix of red, black, and white plaid, the top two buttons casually undone to reveal just a hint of his collarbone. His stylish black winter boots added a touch of sophistication to his look. The shirt hung untucked, giving off an effortlessly relaxed feel that made him even more enthralling. I found myself captivated by him every day, reminding myself how handsome he appeared, whether he wore a simple graphic T-shirt paired with denim jeans or dressed up in a suit. To me, he was absolutely attractive and I made it a point to express my admiration often, ensuring he never doubted just how remarkable he truly was.

As we made our way inside the house, the burning fire crackled in the fireplace, its glow projecting a bold, golden, burnt-orange light throughout the room, creating an atmosphere thick with intimacy. The gentle hum of the TV made for a comforting setting as I took in the beauty around me. The living and dining areas exuded elegance, adorned with delicate white Christmas lights and fragrant white flowers that surrounded the flickering flames. From the corner of my eye, I caught a glimpse of the dining area, stunningly arranged with twinkling lights, white blooms, and shimmering silver ornaments.

"Ms. Foxer, it looks absolutely fascinating in here! I love the way you've transformed the Christmas décor. Did you create all this alone?" I asked, my voice filled with genuine admiration.

Her eyes sparkled with delight. "Oh, Narra, you flatter me! I'm skilled, but I had a little help from one of my good friends in the neighborhood. I was yearning for a shift from the traditional green and red colors that dominate each Christmas. As much as I adore those hues, this year felt like the perfect moment for a change," she responded, her grin radiating friendliness and joy. Dem and I settled onto a cozy nearby sofa, our voices soft as we shared our excitement for the night's exploration of the Book of John, Chapter 15. Earlier, we had skimmed through the chapter in preparation for our gathering and the anticipation in the air felt electric, much like the twinkling fairy lights that decorated our surroundings.

As the evening unfolded, we exchanged heartfelt confessions of our love for Jesus and the joy spread between us, especially with Dem's upcoming graduation shining a light over the night. With a playful smile, he stated, "My shirt is a bit sweaty; do you mind if I dash to my room for a quick change?"

"Of course not, babe. Take your time."

In an earnest gesture, I made a quick call to Narra's mom and stepdad, nervously asking for her hand in marriage. Excitement bubbled within me as I shared my plans, having obtained her stepdad's number during Narra's graduation dinner. "It's happening, Mr. and Mrs. Potter—no, I mean Ms. Nikki and Mr. John." I corrected myself with a chuckle, remembering their desired names.

"Alright, Dem, be sure to send us a picture later!" Ms. Nikki exclaimed from the background, her voice brimming with excitement.

"We believe in you, Dem," Mr. John added, his supportive tone electrifying the moment further.

After a brief moment, I returned, now clad in a crisp white dress shirt that framed me perfectly. As I reentered the living room I said, "This was the only shirt I could find in a hurry. I really need to do laundry." I gave a casual shrug, the flicker of awkwardness I felt most likely evident in my eyes.

"You look so good, babe! It's the fresh shirt, haircut, and curls for me."

"I'll get dinner out of the oven for us," Mrs. Foxer said, swiftly walking toward the kitchen.

"I'll give you a hand with that, honey!" Mr. Foxer added.

♥♥♥

I rose from our cozy spot in front of the fireplace with Dem and made my way toward the dining area. Dem grabbed the remote, turned off the TV, and quickly pulled out a seat for me at the dining table. I reached for a Bible from the stack of three standing upright in the center of the table. "Narr, can you grab the other Bible there?" He pointed to one.

"Sure! Oh, are we using this Bible tonight?"

Narra had no inkling of what was about to unfold, her demeanor perfectly casual. But inside, my heart ran a 5k marathon; I could feel a tremor take hold of me as nerves bubbled up and a bead of sweat trickled down the side of my face. It was the Bible Narra had surprised me with at Golden Leaf. This precious keepsake usually remained tucked away in a safe place, outside the usual basket of study materials. A handmade wooden bookmark, designed exclusively for this purpose, was tucked away in the Bible, with only the ribbon peeking out from the top. The delicate and charming light pink ribbon dangled enticingly, inviting her to take a closer look. "Oh, how neat is this. Is this a new bookmark?" She opened the Bible to the marked page, revealing Proverbs 31, with verses 10 through 31 vividly highlighted in lime green. Her gaze flitted between me and the page, a swirl of curiosity and anticipation sparkling in her eyes. There it lay—a stunning diamond engagement ring, resting flat on its side, poised to change everything.

Narra gasped and covered her mouth with one of her hands, in shock, and then her eyes darted to mine. My mother had placed the wooden bookmark, intricately carved with the words of the "Sweet Narra" poem I had written for her back at Rovane. It was the perfect size; the ring cushioned perfectly into the space I crafted to keep it secure.

"Dem, what is happening? Is this a promise ring?" Narra exclaimed, her voice bubbling with excitement. She looked around, her gaze sweeping toward the kitchen area, from where my mom and dad peeked out. My mom captured every moment with her digital camera while my dad lit up the scene with his cell phone's bright video light.

"I wanted this moment to be pure and intimate, which is why my parents decided to leave us alone and observe from a distance." I calmly walked over to stand directly in front of her, giving her enough space. "I don't have time to play games," I said, my voice steady but vulnerable. I looked at Narra, my eyes secured within hers, feeling an indescribable connection that transcended words.

"You're truly worthy of this, Narra," I whispered, my voice thick with emotion as tears began to fill my eyes. I gently took both of her hands in mine, our fingers entwining naturally. I then carefully released her hands, placing mine just below her shoulders, gradually sliding both of my hands down her arms to gently hold her again. With a light touch, I pulled her into a soft, warm hug. "Dem! Is this really happening?" she asked as she slightly pulled away from our embrace, looking softly at me, the Bible, the ring, and my parents simultaneously with tears in her eyes.

I nodded and said, "Yes, Narra."

"Dem!" Narra muttered, covering her mouth and giggling.

"Yes, it's real," I whispered, the weight of the moment settling around us. "Yes, this is happening," I said as a tear rolled down my face. I turned my gaze towards my mother; there were tears streaming down her cheeks, while my father beamed with a proud smile that reminded me of the Grinch. "This is not a promise ring; it's one of God's promises," I declared with unwavering confidence. "This is God's promise to both of us.

"Just a moment, Narra," I said, gently picking up the ring and cradling it in an open fist. I stood tall, took both of Narra's hands into my own, and began to hold and caress them gently.

As I stood there, holding Narra's hands, I could feel the warmth of her skin, sending oceans of nervous excitement through me. My palms were clammy, revealing my anxious heart, but I couldn't let go. Instead, I gently dropped to one knee, fixing my eyes on hers, making sure she knew my intentions. Tears flooded Narra's eyes as laughter bubbled up in a delightful mix of emotions. Just then, my mom dashed over, sliding a box of tissues toward Narra from the side of the table before stepping back to capture the moment in a photograph. Meanwhile, my dad stood tall filming this milestone that would forever be etched in our hearts. Amid our laughter, I grabbed a tissue to dab my hands, offering another to Narra, our chuckles punctuating the air with lightness.

As I began to speak, a bold confidence surged through me, even though my voice had a slight tremor. With a hopeful inflection,

I looked up at Narra and said, "Tonight, during our Bible study, I come to let you know that I've been studying you for long enough. In my exploration of Proverbs 31:10–31, reflecting on the virtues of a wife of noble character, it dawns on me how profoundly you embody those beautiful qualities.

"Narra, your patience encompasses me every single day," I continued, a smile softening the moment's seriousness. Laughter mingled with my words as we embraced this intimate connection, the air thick with passion.

"Your kindness radiates not only towards me but towards everyone blessed enough to cross your path. You exemplify the very spirit of beauty and grace. You are nurturing and we have a mature love wrapped in a fun, playful relationship where we can be our authentic selves without pretense.

"And the way you love, worship, and dedicate yourself to God is simply beyond words—it's a deep love that transcends the ordinary and elevates us both."

As I spoke, I could see the recognition in her eyes and with every word, I hoped to bridge the space between hope and promise. "Narr, I held this ring long before your graduation—patience steered me to wait for the perfect moment."

"Take your time, babe," Narra said softly, her voice a soothing balm that eased my nerves. As she spoke, my heart surged with warmth and confidence, igniting a lively spark within me and awakening a long-buried passion of my own.

"You and I both know that you work on yourself every day, carrying yourself with the grace and dignity of a wife of noble character." Her gaze was steady, full of faith. "I can't wait to witness how God moves through you, how He brings your light to shine in the world.

"I've been preparing myself to be your husband—a godly man, the partner you truly deserve," I declared, the intensity in my voice reflecting my firm and unwavering resolve as I met her eyes, the weight of my promise infused with love.

"Narr, what if I told you that I saw you as my wife from the very first day we met and that I recognized your worth in that moment? Would you believe me?" I asked, my heart yearning to reveal the truth that hung in the air between us, ready to be claimed.

As tears glistened in her eyes, she responded softly, "I would. I believe you and I love you, Dem."

This moment marked the beginning of a beautiful journey intertwined with faith, love, and the discovery of each other's true selves. I followed up with an honest promise. "You deserve everything that money could never buy. Baby, I love you and I'm giving you my heart and soul.

Whatever else you need, I'm here for you."

Then, taking a deep breath, I asked, "Narra Anne Jones, will you marry me?"

With infectious joy in her voice, Narra replied, "Yes, of course I will!" We shared a kiss, and this time it felt completely intimate as though we were the only two people in the room.

There was no hesitation; it was breathtaking. I poured every ounce of what she had dreamed of into that moment, entirely unbothered by my parents, who were watching us closely. In the midst of our gentle kiss, she smiled and giggled, whispering, "Dem, oh, Dem. You are so amazing," just as I parted from her lips. I leaned in again to kiss her softly; her eyes fluttered shut and we embraced delicately, completely wrapped in that precious moment.

My parents erupted in applause, the sound echoing as my mom dashed into the kitchen. "I got all of that on camera!" my dad exclaimed, a proud smile on his face. "That's my boy and his bride-to-be!"

"We've got dinnerrr!" my mom sang, her tone bubbling with excitement.

Mr. and Mrs. Foxer walked gracefully towards the dining table, each carrying a plate heaped with delicious food. "We have lemon butter wild caught lobster, organic green beans, and sliced roasted red potatoes on the menu!" Mr. Robert announced, gently placing his plate down with a satisfied grin.

"And a surprise for dessert later," Ms. Demi said as she gently placed her plate down.

Mr. Robert gently cleared the dining table, gracefully arranging two elegant candlesticks from a nearby box. He set them perfectly on the table and lit their flickering flames, creating a beautiful, well-lit room. "Here comes Mom with the champagne glasses and cider. Woohoo!"

Dem's parents had surprised us with a candlelight dinner and a movie of our choice at the cozy Foxer residence.

"Wow, Dem, you cannot top this! This is the sweetest thing anyone has ever done for me."

"Nah, I had nothing to do with dinner or the movie. I just thought we'd have something light to eat, like fries and a couple of sandwiches."

"I see where you get your charm from, Demery," I say, a bright smile lighting up my face.

"Well, I try my best, you know!" He chuckled as he rubbed his hands together, nodding enthusiastically with a grin.

"You thought this decor was merely for our Christmas display? It was meant for you two, but I think we should leave it as is!" Ms. Foxer exclaimed.

I looked at Dem with a mix of admiration and disbelief swirling inside me, tears forming again in my eyes. "I honestly didn't expect this to happen so soon! I'm utterly amazed! I loved how you went out of your way to show me just how much you've been learning about me. You truly understand me because you take the time to observe every little detail of my life every day.

"You are such a deep thinker, pouring your heart and effort into everything you do for us. Your ability to think outside the box, to be both clever and practical about saving, astounds me.

I know you've mentioned before how your parents can be a bit too involved in your love life, wanting them to take a step back sometimes, but we can also see how their investment has shaped you. The way you just proposed was nothing short of perfect—a surprise that took my breath away. You genuinely understand the depths of my heart. To me, pure and true intimacy is essential and you capture that essence effortlessly."

Ding! Ding! The soft sounds of text messages chimed from my cell phone, briefly interrupting our perfect moment. Narra and I exchanged glances, eyebrows raised, silently hoping our parents hadn't divulged our engagement news yet, just as we requested.

"Whew!" I exhaled in relief. "It's just a text from Mom with the pictures."

"Oh, thank goodness!" Narra whispered, her breath escaping with a big sigh of relief.

We decided to keep our engagement under wraps for a few weeks, sharing our special moment only with close relatives. In the spirit of excitement, we sent photos and a short clip to the Potters, who quickly video-called us to offer their congratulations.

"Dessert is on the table when you're ready!" my mom called out.

On the table lay a generous slice of lemon cake topped with vanilla icing—the perfect treat, as it was Narra's favorite. I had ordered an extra-large Narr Barr Delight from Kraze earlier that day and we eagerly shared our desserts, feeding each other while my parents quietly excused themselves for the night.

"Now, we know y'all are engaged and all, but separate rooms, please," my dad said with a knowing smile as he walked away.

"Of course," Narra responded lightheartedly.

Staying at the dining table, I slid closer to Narra, offering her spoonfuls of creamy ice cream between our shared kisses. With each bite, I pressed gentle kisses to her lips, forehead, cheeks, and fingertips, creating a soft, loving rhythm that echoed our laughter. Strawberry syrup clung to her lips and I playfully licked it away, tasting the sweetness and savoring the intimate moment we shared.

"Narr, can we go to City Hall tomorrow?" I suggested, a hopeful glint in my eye.

Narra glanced at me and replied, "If you insist, we can."

"Nah, we can't." I chuckled, shaking my head. "But I like that you're down for it, babe. We're equally yoked for real."

After we finished our dessert, we returned to the living room area. We found a cute romantic comedy to watch and I grabbed a throw blanket, with Narra comfortably resting on my chest. "The best way to end the night," she declared, a smirk of approval lighting up her face.

A Wife of Noble Character

10 Who can find a virtuous and capable wife? She is more precious than rubies.

11 Her husband can trust her, and she will greatly enrich his life.

12 She brings him good, not harm, all the days of her life.

13 She finds wool and flax and busily spins it.

14 She is like a merchant's ship, bringing her food from afar.

15 She gets up before dawn to prepare breakfast for her household and plan the day's work for her servant girls.

16 She goes to inspect a field and buys it; with her earnings she plants a vineyard.

17 She is energetic and strong, a hard worker.

18 She makes sure her dealings are profitable; her lamp burns late into the night.

19 Her hands are busy spinning thread, her fingers twisting fiber.

20 She extends a helping hand to the poor and opens her arms to the needy.

21 She has no fear of winter for her household, for everyone has warm clothes.

22 She makes her own bedspreads. She dresses in fine linen and purple gowns.

23 Her husband is well known at the city gates, where he sits with the other civic leaders.

24 She makes belted linen garments and sashes to sell to the merchants.

25 She is clothed with strength and dignity, and she laughs without fear of the future.

26 When she speaks, her words are wise, and she gives instructions with kindness.

27 She carefully watches everything in her household and suffers nothing from laziness.

28 Her children stand and bless her. Her husband praises her:

29 "There are many virtuous and capable women in the world, but you surpass them all!"

30 Charm is deceptive, and beauty does not last; but a woman who fears the Lord will be greatly praised.

31 Reward her for all she has done. Let her deeds publicly declare her praise.

He recognized her worth the moment he first saw her. - Ronette J

Chapter Eighteen

Bold Moves

"Do it!" Dem said with a stern tone. I hesitated—not because I wanted to keep our relationship a secret, but because I had cherished the privacy we'd had thus far, with only a select few in the know. Finally, I tapped the button. "There it is, babe. I did it!"

I posted our engagement pictures: one of Dem on one knee, placing the ring on my finger, and another of us sharing a cute hug. Though only the side of Dem was visible in both shots, I had no intention of hiding my handsome soon-to-be husband. I captioned it, *He loved her like she was a once-in-a-lifetime kind of woman. Because she was.* That was all we wanted to share for now; we preferred to keep things a little private. Half of our friends on Facebook had no idea we were dating seriously—only those closest to us were aware of our relationship, while others assumed they knew.

I deliberately did not tag Dem in the post. He commented, *Narra, you're powerful by yourself, but imagine the husband God promised you beside you*, accompanied by a heart emoji.

I simply replied to his comment, *I love you.*

The next day, I received a Facebook message from someone named Landen Jones.

Hello, Dem. Narra is my daughter. I have not spoken to her in close to a year, not because I didn't want to, but because of my unanswered text messages and social media attempts. I heard about your engagement from someone who saw it on social media. I would love to chat with you. I'm living in London with my family, but I hope to receive an invitation to the wedding. Above all, I want to rebuild a closer relationship with my daughter. She's only met her brother once. I started typing a response but paused to check with Narra first.

My phone rang and it was Dem.

"Hey, my future hubby!" I said excitedly, a flutter of joy dancing in my chest.

"Hey, babe, why didn't you tell me more about your complicated relationship with your father?" Dem's voice was smooth but a little probing, not giving me a chance to respond right away. "He reached out to me on Facebook and mentioned he'd like to talk." I could sense that Dem's heart was racing as the words spilled out.

"Dem, wait, what? Oh, my goodness! Landen contacted you?" My pulse quickened at the thought.

"Yes, Narr. He said he's been blocked for a long time and has been trying to connect with you."

"Wait, I can't believe he sent you a message. Have you replied?" My mind raced with a mix of disbelief and anticipation.

"No, that's why I'm calling for your permission. He was really nice to me and wants to talk."

"I'm sorry for not sharing more about our current father-daughter dynamics." I bit my lip, feeling exposed.

"I'll send you a screenshot of what he sent."

"Just got it. Why am I feeling anxious and nervous just reading this?" A rush of emotions engulfed me. "Well Dem, I've prayed for my father all these years, but it wasn't the right time for us to reconnect yet. How did he find out about our engagement? Who told him?"

I don't know exactly who, but he mentioned someone on social media, and I'd like to talk to him. Is that okay?" Dem's sincerity was palpable, stirring something profound within me.

"Ugh, I suppose so. I wonder what his motives are. Hmm."

"Narr, I might not know everything that has happened between you two over the years, but he seems genuine. I'm curious to know more about him and I wish I already knew more."

You should start sharing more with me about the not-so-great things and I'll do the same. I believe we can help each other grow and heal in those areas. You never know what could happen if you try to be open about certain subjects."

In that moment, the weight of our conversation hung between us, yet I felt a growing bond, a promise to share and explore together, making our connection even deeper.

I wasn't sure if I wanted my father at our wedding or if I would want him to walk me down the aisle, especially since he had not been part of my life during my formative years. After discussing it with Dem and hearing the perspectives of his parents and my parents, I reconsidered. God's grace was woven into each of us, waiting until I met Dem, now my fiancé, when everything started to shift in my relationship with my father. Truly, God's power is as limitless as love itself.

The next day arrived and I had just come home from a long day filled with interviews and apartment viewings. There he was—Dem—waiting for me, parked outside my parents' house. "What are you doing in Locakee already? I wasn't expecting you this early, babe!" I exclaimed, surprised as he opened my car door. He greeted me with a soft hug, a bouquet of light pink roses, and a small bowl of fruit. "Yesss, pineapples! You get me. Thank you, babe." As we got comfortable in my cozy bedroom and took off our outerwear, I carefully placed my pineapples in the mini fridge and arranged my roses in an elegant transparent vase on the dresser.

Kicking off my flat dress shoes, I draped my purse and scarf over a rack before settling onto the bed with Dem. He sat at one end, turned toward me while tapping his feet on the floor, while I curled up in the middle, my legs tucked in like a pretzel. The familiar comfort of my family residence wrapped around us. It had been nearly two weeks since I'd last seen him in person; our only connection had been through the glowing screens of our video calls. Now, with him so close, the tension between us crackled like electricity, filling the air with the promise of beautiful moments and divine love.

"I really missed you, Dem," I whispered, my eyes tracing his gaze as he observed me while I untied my hair from a ponytail holder, letting my curls drop softly onto my shoulders. I grabbed a small gift I had saved just for him from the nightstand next to my bed and handed it to him, eager to see the smile on his face.

"This is dope, Narr," he said, his eyes lighting up as he opened the small black box. It was a solid gold cross with our initials, D and N, elegantly engraved on the back. It was more than just a piece of jewelry; it was a symbol of our interlaced destinies. He reached out, brushing his fingers against the cool metal, and in that intimate moment, the weight of our divine love hung in the air. "This is perfect," he whispered, his eyes linking with mine.

"So glad you like it; twenty-four karats, baby!" We laughed.

"I appreciate you, Narr."

As we both stood up, the air around us felt electric with anticipation. We embraced tightly and I looked up to meet his gaze, absorbing the moment as our lips brushed in a light kiss.

In that moment, I desired to stay hooked in his beautiful brown eyes, never wanting to leave. He playfully teased by sticking out his tongue, lightly grazing my bottom teeth.

"Oh, you're feeling a bit extra playful today," I teased back, noting how his hand lingered against my lower back longer than usual.

"What, can't I kiss my wife?" he asked, a mischievous glint in his eye.

"No, not like that, Dem. And it's 'wife to be!'" I reminded him with a grin.

"This is getting tricky, Narra. I've been eagerly awaiting the day those braces were taken off," he said, peering into my eyes, making me glance away as I flicked through the pages of a yellow sticky notepad, my fingers revealing a hint of nervousness. I wanted him so badly, but thank God I was so good at self-discipline.

Initially, I had regrets about sharing my engagement on social media, but I eventually changed my mind. Now I was grateful that I did. I believe that God is capable of fixing anything; we need to be willing to address our issues. I found it within myself to forgive my father and I gave Dem my approval to reach out. He exchanged numbers with Landen and they had a conversation for an hour that day. During their talk, Landen presented his perspective, which surprisingly aligned with mine, although he added some further details.

"Okay, Narr, so Landen explained that he left when you were about eight and moved to another country. He stayed in touch by sending money occasionally, but he was rarely physically present. He told me that you have a half-brother and mentioned that he got married. He also informed me that before leaving, when you were a kid, he gifted you a Bible."

"Yes, I read it whenever I could and adored it; those pages were filled with stories that sparked my imagination and reassured me that all things were working for my good. I became attached to the scripture 'love is patient and kind' found in 1 Corinthians 13:4–8, which was the first long passage I learned as a child."

As I had a flashback to my childhood, I began to recite it: "First Corinthians, thirteen, Four through Eight!

"*Four* says: Love is patient and kind. Love is not jealous, boastful, proud, *Five*, or rude. It does not demand its own way. It is not irritable, and it keeps no record of being wronged. *Six*, it does not rejoice about injustice but rejoices whenever the truth wins out. *Seven*, love never gives up, never loses faith, is always hopeful, and endures through every circumstance. *Eight*, prophecy and speaking in unknown languages and special knowledge will become useless. But love will last forever!"

We both laughed. "What's so funny?"

"Nothing, you're just so cute, Narr!"

"Babe, I used to wonder why my dad had given up on my mom. But as I matured, my understanding of the Bible deepened. I realized that my mom and dad loved each other, yet they weren't meant to be spouses. My respect for them grew because they didn't force a marriage that wasn't part of God's plan. They understood that marriage is a serious commitment."

"Amen! That's good, Narr!"

Dem knew this moment would be etched in his heart forever. With a mixture of excitement and nervous anticipation, he took a deep breath and called my father back to ask for his blessing. During the call, his voice trembled with sincerity as he said, "Hi Landen, I'm here with Narra. I know it's late, but may I have the honor of asking for your daughter's hand in marriage? She is truly one of a kind and means everything to me." The weight of his words hung in the air, filled with the promise of love. His gratitude flowed freely as he continued, "I want to thank you for being a part of bringing her into this world and for all the efforts you made to nurture her. Gifting her that Bible when she was just a child was especially significant. Even though you weren't always there physically, that one gesture made a profound impact on her life."

You could hear the sniffles over the phone as if tears welled in my father's eyes as he poured out his heart over the phone. "Because of you and your leadership as a young man of God, who has been such a great influence on my daughter, I feel like I have my daughter back."

My father's response radiated warmth and acceptance: "Of course, you have my blessing. See you around wedding time, son." The joy of this moment brought a smile to all of our faces, solidifying the beginning of their beautiful relationship as in-laws. "My daughter feels safe with you; she's the most comfortable around you. That's beautiful, Dem."

"Talk to you later, Dad!" I said, excusing myself to the bathroom, a subtle signal to Dem that I need to step away for a moment. I knew this was a special bonding moment happening between my dad and Dem and I wanted to give them the space they needed.

I lathered my hands with soap then rinsed them with warm water and turned off the tap. While drying my hands, faint sounds drifted to my ears. I stepped out of the bathroom and the melody of prayer was emerging from the phone's speaker, a harmonious agreement between Dem and my father.

I observed Dem with the phone resting on the bed, speaker active, his hands raised high to the ceiling as he walked swiftly around the room, praying and worshipping. His voice echoed, "God is able. God is able, Landen. He's doing it now. Lord, You are worthy."

Tears threatened to flow as I softly whispered, "God is so good." I settled into a nearby desk chair, mindful of Dem, not wanting to interrupt. Minutes passed quietly; my hands raised and eyes closed, inviting God's presence.

My dad said, "Thank you, Dem, you have no idea how much I needed that prayer."

"Love you, Dad!" I shouted.

"You're very welcome. We will see you soon," Dem said.

Now sitting back on the bed softly, I said, "Wow, babe, I heard the last of your prayer for my dad." I marveled. "Dem, this is a side of you I've never seen or heard before."

"Yeah, I sensed that he needed it. I had to be obedient and follow the lead and instructions of the Holy Spirit. I've never prayed for anyone like I just did. I am overwhelmed by God's presence." I looked at Dem with a gentle smile. "My apologies if I was too loud," he said.

"No, you were fine. These walls are mostly soundproof." I grabbed a book to fan Dem, realizing he was all worked up; then I turned on the ceiling fan and grabbed him a hand towel to dry his sweat.

"Baby, I'm so proud of you." I kissed him on the lips.

"Narr, could you grab me a bottle of water, please?"

"Absolutely, babe!" I said as I opened the mini fridge to hand him an ice-cold bottle of water. *God knew all along of the power in this young man. Whew!* I thought.

He knew what I needed! Thank you, Lord. A man filled with God's love and the Holy Spirit. I started whispering, "Thank you, Jesus" over and over.

Dem stated with a smile, "Something just came over me. Narra, I want to tell you that Landen was facing some health issues a few months ago, but he's doing better now. I prayed for his complete healing, for his wife and your brother, and for other things as well."

"Wow. I'll make sure I follow up with my dad tomorrow. I want him to know that I care."

"Narr, your dad is so thrilled about the wedding and just us all spending some time together! I like him!"

"He's alright!" I said with a smirk.

Chapter Nineteen

Divine Beginnings

"Mm, these pineapples are so fresh and delicious!" I grabbed some tasty pineapples from the fridge, my fork finding a cool, ripe piece, and settled back on the edge of the bed, cradling the bowl in my lap as I savored each juicy bite. "So, how was class today?" I asked, plopping back a little on the bed and sitting up. He paused, looked at me, and sank onto my light pink plush double-loaf sofa across from my bed, grabbing a pillow and squeezing it tightly while holding it in front of him. "What's wrong, babe? Class was good, right?" I sensed something was muddled because he had arrived in Locakee way too early.

"I submitted some assignments online."

"Dem Foxer!" I narrowed my eyes at him as he looked away.

"Narra Jones-Foxer!" he said softly, a smile revealing all his teeth as he peered at me.

"It's not funny, Dem. How are your grades looking?"

"They're fine, Narr." He sat up, let out a sigh, and then sank back into the plush sofa chair.

"Oh no, Dem. You will not do this. You are so close. I was where you are now last year. You can do this. I can help you in whatever way I can."

"You did not have all these responsibilities, though, Narr. I know I can do it, but I've been so flustered lately. I've been thinking about our upcoming wedding and want to ensure you're settled into your new job and that everything else is going smoothly."

"But, Dem, we can wait a little longer for wedding stuff. It's not that serious. Let's take our time."

"Not serious? Have you seen me? I need you. I'm exhausted from being apart, Narr."

I narrowed my eyes at him, a grimace pulling at my lips. "I'm trying to make sense of this. We can pause on the initial wedding plans for now. Or I could start on a few details without bothering you about it."

He said in a calm voice, "I don't want you to halt the wedding plans, Narr. I'm ready to be your husband."

"Demery! What is wrong with you?" I stood up from the bed, pineapple juice dripping on my shirt and splashing onto the carpet as I inched closer to him as he sat on the sofa.

He stood as well, sliding his hands down both of my arms then swinging my hands side to side with his. "Narr, trust me, I've got this under control."

"You will not let the naysayers win, Dem." I loosened my left hand from his embrace and slowly placed it over his right hand, gently lifting his grip off my other arm.

"I'll still graduate … eventually."

"We are not doing this, Dem. You are going to graduate on time. No, no, and no." I raised my voice slightly with each "no" and folded my arms defiantly.

Dem remained calm, wiping my tears and wrapping me in a hug. But I didn't want to hug; I was angry. "Dem, how long have you been thinking about all of this?" I asked, my head down, still in his embrace.

"I've been having a hard time focusing for weeks now," he admitted, his gaze moving away as he thought about the challenging moments of his life. "Between juggling an internship, closing shifts at Kraze, and being there for you during wedding planning and apartment hunting, it felt like everything was pulling me in different directions."

"See, Dem, your parents will blame me."

"No, they won't. I already talked to my mom a little. She's very understanding and knows I need a break. I'm so stressed." His voice cracked slightly, revealing the weight of his worries.

"Babe, you never mentioned any of this," I replied softly, concern fixed on my face. "Dem, commuting isn't helpful, is it?"

"Yes, it is a little. I only need to drive to campus twice a week for class. But good Lord, I'm exhausted from driving so much," he confessed, the fatigue evident in his tone. "I miss you so much, Narra. All I want is to be with my family. I want to marry you and help you find your new apartment. School can wait; I can graduate next year." He took my hands again, swinging them in and outward playfully in the air, locking eyes with me during this vulnerable moment.

"Babe, I'm really sorry you're dealing with so much stress. This isn't what I wanted for you. Let's take a break from some things. Dem, please concentrate on graduating and refocus on your goals.

"I'll visit you whenever possible to help minimize your travel. I can also arrange a session with a therapist from a trusted source, which could help alleviate your stress," I reassured him, my voice steady.

"Narr, that's not what I want at this time."

"What do you mean?"

"I want you. I am ready and prepared and I believe you are too. Together, let's nurture our marriage and grow our family once I graduate."

"But after marriage, will you move into my new apartment with me?" I asked, biting my lip, hopeful.

"Whatever works, but we won't worry about that just yet. All I want is you. I want to attend church with you, work at my dream job, and come home to my dream woman and family. I'm tired of everything else weighing me down."

"Like, is schoolwork the problem? Is that what you're saying?"

"Exactly." He sighed in relief, feeling seen for the first time.

"I'm sorry, Narr, for seeming weak. I know I could graduate this year, but that's not what I want. School will still be there, right? I'd rather have a few therapy sessions than school right now. Sign me up," he said in a serious tone.

"Dem, you are not weak, please don't say that." The moment hung in silence between us.

"What will your friends think? Or your pastor? Or your dad? You know he's big on education!" I pressed.

"I don't care anymore about anyone else's opinions. It's my life, soon to be our life together. My dad will understand, sooner or later. I'm no longer trying to please people anymore."

Lost in emotion, Dem watched as tears crowded my eyes. The thought of our love, mixed with the challenges ahead, overwhelmed us both. I couldn't help but chuckle in disbelief as I started to cry, with both of us giggling between my sobs. "Dem, why do you want to do these crazy things? But maybe they're smart too…" I managed through my tears.

"I know, I know. I'm sorry, Narra." He approached me and hugged me, but I kept my hands at my sides. I was taken aback and didn't want a hug at that moment.

"I love you so much and I'm ready to be your husband. I was designed to be your husband, Narr."

"Alright then, Dem, call up the pastor and schedule our premarital counseling sessions!" I exclaimed, my spirit lifting but still in shock at what had transpired.

"Let's prepare for all the judgment and backlash we'll get," I said with a teasing grin, knowing we would face it together.

"I'll protect you forever. Don't worry. I've got you!" Dem said reassuringly with comforting eyes.

"When will you be done with classes?"

"I'll talk to my dad tonight or tomorrow and then handle everything the following day."

"Alright, babe."

As we sat hand in hand at the edge of Narra's bed, we prayed for one another's peace, protection, divine guidance, and mental health. After prayer, in that calm moment, I softly cupped Narra's chin, leaning in for a deep, intimate kiss. She initially kept her mouth closed along with her eyes, but then she surrendered just a little, allowing her lips to part slightly. Caught in the enchantment of our connection, she returned a hint of my passion with a gentle touch of her tongue. My gaze remained steady on her, watching intently as she gradually opened her eyes, her eyelashes fluttering slowly, cheeks flushed with warmth as I went in for more and again even more. "This feels amazing," she softly whispered; but then, realizing the intensity, she pulled back. I moved in closer, feeling more confident, and she allowed me a gentle, hesitant step forward.

Our first genuine, smooth kiss, free from the restrictions of braces on her teeth, blossomed into a moment of pure intimacy. It was calm and full of anticipation. As we continued, the air grew warmer, and I took her left hand softly, twirling her sparkling diamond engagement ring with my fingers for a moment. She slowly opened her eyes, a soft smile blooming across her face as our kiss deepened, while I held my lips there in the middle of her smile; then, again, she gently pulled back. With a delicate gesture, she used her thumb to wipe away the pink gloss from my lips, the intimate moment lingering between us, thick with unspoken desire. With her eyes closed again and leaning into my warm embrace, Narra softly declared, "Demery Foxer, I love you. I love everything about you and I trust you to lead me." Her voice was a sweet blend of affection and hope.

"You're speaking my language, Narr," I replied, my heart puffed lightly with joy.

"We're getting married!" I shouted.

Because of God's love, Narra allowed trust to settle within her spirit. She could think more clearly and love more deeply than ever before.

The following day, at the Foxer residence, Narra arrived shortly after I did, both of us ready for the family dinner with my parents. It felt like a spontaneous gathering and I couldn't help but think my parents might pick up on the underlying tension. Did they have any idea of what was happening? Earlier, I had prayed with Narra over the phone, hoping my parents would approach the situation with the gentle understanding it required. There was a palpable mix of anticipation and anxiety in the air as our hearts intertwined amidst the complexities of family dynamics.

Narra and I had decided to place our complete trust in God regarding this matter. Although she couldn't agree with my choice about school, and she genuinely believed I should continue school that year—often saying, "But you're so close to graduating!"—she understood the importance of learning to trust my decisions as her future husband. Our love guided us through this journey and I sincerely appreciated her support even when we disagreed.

"And it's your career, it's your life. And your mind is already made up," Narra stated as we entered my house.

As the evening unfolded, I could feel the warmth of family surrounding us, a subtle reminder of the bond we shared. The anticipation in the air was thick with unspoken words and hidden feelings and I knew that this dinner would change everything for us. Every glance, every shared smile felt laden with meaning, whispering promises of love and understanding amidst the uncertainty. I inhaled deeply, trying to savor the moment before stepping into the unknown of my parents' response.

"Mmm, by the aroma in the air, it seems baked ziti is on the menu tonight," I said as I walked into the living room area holding Narra's hand.

"That's correct!" my mom voiced from the kitchen.

After washing our hands, Narra and I sat at the dining room table. "Mom, Dad, I've decided to trade my college classes for therapy sessions." They didn't even appear bothered.

"I've been feeling a bit stressed and I need to center myself. I plan to graduate next year, but right now, my focus is on building a deeper connection with my wife, focusing on my internship, and starting a family in a few years." I let it all out immediately, not wanting to hold back any longer.

"Is that truly what you want, Son?" my father asked, his voice a mixture of concern and kindness.

I took a deep breath, feeling the warmth of Narra's hand in mine, grounding me. I looked at my dad and then at Narra. "Yes, Dad. She's my everything and I want to make sure we're ready for what comes next. We are being prepared for the marriage of our prayers."

The love in the room swirled around us, binding me to both my family and the future I longed to create with my wife.

"This is what I want, Dad!"

My father put both of his hands on the table with a gentle slap and said, "Then that's what it is, Son! This is your life. You'll graduate next year then."

My mom wore a gentle smile as she and Narra walked into the kitchen, collecting our plates. They soon returned to the dining room table.

"I'm delighted for you both, my sweet son. Narra has brought so much joy to the Foxer family; she's everything I've ever dreamt of in a daughter. I couldn't be happier. You both deserve this joy and why hesitate when you've sought the Lord? He is answering your prayers in the most beautiful way."

"Mom, thank you from the bottom of our hearts."

Narra said, "Thank you," placing her hands over her heart as her gaze shifted between my mom and dad, gratitude spilling from her eyes.

"God is having his way, Dem," my dad chimed in, his voice warm and reassuring.

"I've been patiently waiting for Dem to take the lead on this," my mom added with a teasing smirk, playfully nudging our conversation in a lighter direction.

Narra's eyes widened in surprise at my mom's comment as they placed our plates on the table. The aroma of my mom's famous baked ziti filled the air—crafted with vegan cheese and soft walnuts in place of meat, it was a delicious, comforting choice.

"He's been ready all along. That young man absolutely adores you, Narra. Just look at him; he's captivated by every moment spent with you, entranced by every little thing you do."

I smiled and kissed Narra on the forehead before settling into my chair right beside her, sitting across from my parents.

"Don't worry about those who will have opinions. We have your back, Dem."

"Well, let's get wedding planning, why don't we!" my dad stated.

My mom felt the need to protect me by preparing her responses for anyone who might say something negative. "Dem values education and the woman God placed in his life. He's not perfect, but he's not foolish either." She added, in a playful yet stern tone, "It's all about God's timing and he chose Narra first after God."

We all shared a laugh, but as Narra faced my parents, it was as if she felt a lump in her throat and said, "I just want you to know that your son chose me, us, despite my begging him not to make any tough decisions yet. What is he thinking? I asked him not to go through with this. I never wanted this kind of pressure on either of us. I made it clear that this situation was not normal."

My dad responded, "The man knows 'his good thing,' and that's you, Narra."

"But I promised him I'd be here waiting for him after graduation."

"Yeah, Narr, but that's too long. It's been long enough!" I said aloud.

As we were finishing up eating dinner, Narra stated, "He is a bit eccentric, you see. A blend of sweetness and stubbornness—his quirky nature always puts a smile on my face. I fondly call him 'swubborn,' the w sound on purpose because he's a sweet yet stubborn soul and wields his heart with such fierce determination. It's this combination that sweeps me off my feet, even when the world around us seems to be spinning too fast."

"That's my boy!" my dad said.

"Every moment we share is filled with the promise of something beautiful, even amid the anxiety of looming choices," Narra said with a smile. "Dem recognized that he was overwhelmed managing school, work, his internship, and our relationship, even though he wanted to excel in all areas. But is pausing graduation the answer? Ultimately, he made his own choice and must face the consequences of that decision."

"No need to explain, Narra. This is Demery. You're finally getting to know the stubborn—I mean, 'swubborn'— kid we love," my dad chimed in, offering a chuckle.

"But I plan to finish school. I understand how important it is, but right now, this is what I truly want," I asserted, reflecting on my desire to pursue my gift from God. "I want to chase my personal and spiritual dreams as well."

"Mr. and Mrs. Foxer, I have learned to accept that he will make mistakes and I cannot control every situation. He will grow from his experiences."

"Exactly, Narra. I'll learn." I smiled, my heart steady, confidence shining through. "Those who truly know us see our readiness. We've built this relationship on faith, with God as our foundation. We're not rushing; we're simply navigating this journey at God's pace.

"Mom and Dad, we cannot tell you enough how amazing it is to have parents who still care about their children even as we are adults in our early twenties; your guidance and support have been a key factor in our success."

♥♥♥

As we shared the news with a few close relatives, financing became a recurring topic in conversations with both sets of parents as well as our friends and pastors. They were all curious about how we were managing everything and our plans during premarital counseling sessions. It was challenging and sometimes stressful. Narra and I had to have a difficult conversation and concluded that it would make sense for us to get married in a year. With Narra preparing to move out and me pausing my schooling, my internship had turned into a full-time job. We planned to move in together, but I found myself busier than ever with my internship responsibilities.

A week went by and as I listened to Narra softly speaking on a three-way call, my heart raced with excitement. I tried to focus on her words, yet my mind kept wandering to how beautiful this moment would be for us on our wedding day. The venue owner exuded happiness, their voice filled with warmth. "As this beautiful land hosts its very first wedding, we are overjoyed to present you with this venue as a warm gift—entirely free of charge." Those words hung in the air, carrying a sense of possibility and romance, making me feel as though our dreams were beginning to take root in this captivating setting.

"Our parents are going to be thrilled!" I remarked.

"Thank you so much! I'm so relieved. You have no idea how you just made our dreams come true!" Narra's voice overflowed with joy.

"Ha, ha, ha! It's our pleasure! Just remember to tag us in your social media pictures! Please expect another call from Kindalle Brute, our in-house wedding planner, whom you briefly met on the phone. While she has fifteen years of experience, she is new to our company and her services are complimentary only for small, intimate weddings. We truly believe in both of you and we could probably accommodate you within a few months if the timing works out for you."

Things were beginning to fall into place, easing much of the earlier financial and mental stress, although some tension still remained. Kindalle had been extremely kind and supportive; she mentioned that we were her very first customers at Brimmer Fields, which meant we were guaranteed a discount for her services and they would possibly be free if our wedding was small enough. "Feel free to stop by tomorrow or any time before the end of the week for a complete tour. It would be wonderful if you could bring your fiancé along, so you both can enjoy the experience together!"

As the sun hung low in the sky, I rushed through the final hours of the school day, my mind preoccupied with thoughts of our wedding venue. My last day at school was approaching and the anticipation of seeing where we would begin our lives together consumed me. The next available tour was on Sunday morning, but church commitments made that impossible, so she hadn't even suggested it. Feeling overwhelmed, I pulled over to the side of the road on my way home. I quickly video-called

Divine Beginnings

Narra, eager to see the venue and offer my approval. We had both envisioned a simple, intimate wedding—a romantic scene unlike any other.

Inspired by whispers of a charming locale, Brimmer Fields, which couples favored for date nights, proposals, and Valentine's Day dinners, we had long dreamed of experiencing a date there. During the virtual tour, I learned that this enchanting place offered a hidden gem: 160 acres of land bursting with lush plants, vibrant flowers, cozy fire pits, and serene streams flowing from a mountaintop. Although I had never heard of weddings hosted there, the thought of holding our wedding in this fairy-tale setting had never crossed my mind until recently. A garden surrounded by greenery, adorned with blooming flowers, and a giant glasshouse serving as the centerpiece. The glass structure, shaped like a quaint little house, was completely transparent, offering an unobstructed view of the spacious hall from the outside, illuminated by the sun's golden rays. A graceful waterfall enhanced the environment, surrounded by patches of French marigolds, daisies, and pink butterfly orchids. Parlor palm plants punctuated the scene while butterflies danced in the air.

"God is good, Narr!" I shouted, sharing in the excitement of this pivotal moment.

Later that evening, we gathered at her parents' house for our own little Bible study, reflecting on our faith. I led her in prayer, reminding her of all the times God had intervened in our lives. "He never fails us," I assured her, knowing that even in the most challenging moments, He was always moving on our behalf.

It was a beautiful reminder of the strength we found in our relationship and faith, even as we navigated the challenges ahead.

A few days later, after a wonderful Christmas holiday spent with my family—the Potters and the Foxers united—I met up with Benny, Chris, and Aaron off campus at Beanies Cool Café, a cozy coffee shop nearby. They had already dived into the fun, playing card games and testing their knowledge with some sports trivia. As I walked in, I instantly noticed Simone, but she was with a guy and I chose to ignore her. "Hey, Dem, is that not Simone? I see she keeps looking at you like she wants to say something."

"Yeah, I saw her, but I have nothing to say to her."

"Dem, where have you been? We haven't seen you around campus or at any of the parties," A Wess inquired.

"Chris, thanks for taking the drive to join us," I said as I shook his hand. "How's everything with you? How's the grown-up life since graduating?"

"It's coming along. Life is not bad," Chris answered.

"Dem has been missing in action!" Aaron remarked.

"Man, I'm getting married in a few months. I'm really here to ask y'all if you all would be my groomsmen. Chris, my best man?"

"What? I know you just got engaged, but getting married so soon? So, you just quit school?"

"What the heck!" A Wess voiced.

"Aye. Chill out with all of that, Wessy Wess!" Benny said.

"No, just taking a break."

"Bro, we literally graduate soon. What the heck, Dem? So, when are you going back? Next semester?"

"Nope, next year."

"Dem!" Benny shouted in shock, his eyes wide with disbelief as he took a step back, struggling to comprehend the sudden commotion surrounding him.

"There's no way this is for real! No way," A Wess chimed in again.

"Bro is really in love for real," Chris remarked, his excitement palpable.

"I want to be like you when I grow up," Benny shouted, his eyes wide with admiration.

"Simone is walking over here, Dem. And she's by herself," Benny pointed out, drawing attention to the approaching figure.

"And that red dress she's wearing hugs her body perfectly," A Wess remarked, his gaze lingering appreciatively. I kept my head straight but stole a glance in her direction, curious to see if she was truly coming over.

"Demery Foxer," she said, her tone sardonic yet playful.

"Simone Wright," I replied, keeping my voice neutral and avoiding eye contact, only glancing in her direction.

"Hi Dem, can I talk to you for a moment?" she asked, a hint of urgency in her voice.

"Hey Simone, what's up?" I replied, surprised by her sudden approach.

"I mean in private," she said, gesturing toward a nearby booth where we could converse without interruption.

"You can say whatever you need to say in front of my friends; besides, we're kind of having a meeting here," I insisted, wanting to include my boys in the conversation.

"Congratulations on your engagement! I'm really happy for you," she said kindly before walking away.

"Thank you," I said calmly but loud enough for her to hear me.

A Wess nudged me, saying, "Man, Dem. You've changed and I like it!"

"You and Narra's relationship gives me hope and makes me want to settle down, maybe in the next couple of years, and hang up my player's card!" Benny added, laughter filling the air as we shared the moment.

"Yeah, I truly adore Narra. She means more than the world to me. This girl holds my heart for eternity."

A Wess responded, "You literally saw the girl you wanted and got the girl."

"Dem got the Gem," the three of them chimed in unison, making us all laugh.

"Nah, I first prayed for a Proverbs 31 wife. I prayed for Narra for quite a long time."

"Those prayers really work, huh?" Chris inquired, already knowing the answer.

"Yeah, bro. God is good!"

"Then you saw her and went and got what you wanted," Aaron said slyly.

"God presented her to me. I recognized a godly wife within her. I thought about her, saw her around, approached her, made her laugh, and prayed for her without even knowing her personally. Now I'm making her my wife."

"Okay, Dem!" Benny said, chuckling with the others at our table for four.

"Do you ever think you're too young or not ready, Dem?" Chris asked.

"Nope! My grandma thinks I am, but no one else has said it to my face."

"What about all those other girls out there? I've seen them eyeing you and you eyeing them at parties; they love you," Aaron teased.

"One of my friends who was at our BBQ get-together even asked about you, Dem," Benny added.

Aaron chimed in with a laugh, saying, "Yeah, we're all too young for something as serious as marriage. The only vows I'll be saying are the letters—as in vowels. Ayy ... Eee ... I..." Chris couldn't contain himself and sprayed water out of his mouth all over the table as laughter erupted around us.

"Chill out, Aaron WessWood!" I said with a chuckle.

"Could we get a few extra napkins over here?" Benny called out.

"You all are going to get us kicked out, especially A Wess!" I remarked.

Aaron said, "I'm just saying it's not for me. I want to enjoy my entire twenties and maybe even my early thirties, have fun, and not be tied down to anyone, and do what I want whenever I want."

"No disrespect. The girls might love me, but I don't love them— at least, not like that."

We all laughed.

"I have not laughed this hard in a long while. I missed hanging out with y'all. We have to all stay in touch. I know we will have a blast at the wedding too. It will be small and intimate, so if you get an invite, you're pretty important.

"I'm ready. I know I am. And Aaron, I still get to do what I want.

"I want to be married. I want to be a loving, godly husband and a great father. I want to continue growing in Christ alongside my wife. I want a peaceful home. I want a divine love story. I want God's promises, even if they come with responsibility, discipline, and some hardships at times. God has changed my wants. My desires are divine."

Benny stood up from his seat and shouted, "Say it again, Dem!"

"I'm not for the streets; I'm for the Kingdom," I stated. "No disrespect intended though," I added.

They all laughed loudly and started high-fiving me one by one. "Ohhhh, I like that, I want to be like you when I grow up!" Chris said.

"I have a purpose with the one woman of my dreams and prayers. Narr and I have gone through some tough times, one of which was this decision about school that I made all on my own because she truly tried her best to talk me out of it. However, she eventually understood my seriousness and that she had to trust me on this one. I'm still going to finish school. I've come too far not to."

"Exactly, Dem. Bro, you should be walking with Aaron and me across that stage," Benny said.

"I've made up my mind. I will walk that stage next year," I declared confidently. "I'm living in God's divine timing, not mine. And it's the best thing that has ever happened to me."

Chris responded, "You're about to step into one of the greatest chapters of your life, Dem."

I grinned and asked, "And you know the best part, Chris?"

In unison, we both said, "God is the Author."

"Love you, Chris! That's why you're my best man!" I stood up to give him a handshake, followed by a hug.

"Love you all and I'll see you soon!" Chris added, smiling as we all hugged and parted ways.

♥♥♥

Four months later, on a stunning day, April 24th, the charming town of Whisby—Dem's cherished hometown—was filled with the sweet aroma of spring. The sun poured down warmly, the skies were a clear blue, and the temperature hovered around a pleasant 72 degrees.

The melodious songs of American goldfinch birds filled the atmosphere. In the background, the soothing sounds of the nearby stream's flowing water mingled beautifully with the gentle flow of the waterfall, creating idyllic and romantic scenery for our special day.

As the clock struck 2:30 p.m., a sense of anticipation filled the air. It was time for a moment to unfold, a moment that would forever alter the course of our lives. Kindalle and her small team were in place, ensuring everything was nearly perfect. I lovingly observed our dear loved ones, just about fifteen of them, surrounding us. The building was heavenly, radiating a dreamlike quality. Looking up and around, I felt as though I was outdoors, immersed in a serene forest filled with lush green plants and the sound of birds chirping. Delicate strings of lights and pearls were entwined gracefully along the walls, surrounded by robust vines, enhancing the enchanting atmosphere.

One of our favorite worship songs filled the venue, creating an atmosphere we interpreted as a love song from God to us, just as I began my walk down the aisle. My father walked beside me but suddenly stopped, taking my hand in his while my bouquet rested in the other. With tears in his eyes, he kissed my hand warmly. He then glanced at my stepfather and whispered, "Thank you for taking care of my baby." As my stepfather took my hand, we locked our arms and continued down the aisle, moving toward my king, Demery. I looked up into his sweet, loving eyes, feeling the warmth of his affection. A giggle escaped my lips as I noticed the way he undressed me with his sweet brown eyes.

Demery stood there, swaying lightly, his hands casually resting in front of him. I took in his appearance, starting from the bottom: his deep, hidden forest-green shoes peeking out beneath his tailored ivory pants. He wore a perfectly tailored ivory double-breasted suit jacket adorned with gold paisley buttons. A crisp white shirt, unbuttoned at the neck and free of ties or bow ties, showcased how I loved to see him. Gold cufflinks mirrored the buttons of his jacket, glimmering with every movement. He didn't need a handkerchief; his elegance spoke for itself.

My eyes ventured up to meet his stunning, deep chestnut-brown eyes. A wave of emotion showered over me and tears formed in my eyes as a soft smile rested on his lips. "This man is ready, ready! God, thank you," I whispered. I paused to allow Rya to take my bouquet and she handed me a tissue. Another person came to pin a mic on me. My two bridesmaids, Sasha and my cousin Andie, with Rya as my maid of honor, all accompanied me in stunning ivory dresses, while the groomsmen looked dapper in their suits.

As I stood at the altar, my eyes tracing Narra's every delicate movement, the towering trees surrounding the glass house created a lush canopy, filtering the sunlight and giving us the feeling of being in a rainforest or jungle. Birds perched on the branches above and gentle lights twinkled among the leaves, while butterflies gracefully fluttered about, occasionally landing softly against the transparent walls of our gathering space. Next to me, my best man, Chris, along with my two closest friends, Benny and Aaron, shared in this intimate moment of pure anticipation. My groomsmen were sharply dressed in deep forest-green tuxedos, paired with crisp white shirts, their top buttons undone for a casual yet polished look, standing proudly by my side. In a tranquil hush, I paused to utter a sincere prayer for Narra. "Dearest Heavenly Father, I am profoundly grateful for the gift of this day. I ask that you shower Narra with the peace and comfort she seeks as she readies herself to unite with me at the altar. In Jesus' name, Amen."

As the soft melody of music filled the air, it sent my heart into a wild race. I gazed down the aisle, and our eyes met. Narra continued approaching me with captivating grace. As our gazes intertwined, bright smiles broke across our faces, pure joy illuminating our features and filling us with a glowing peace. I was mesmerized by her presence, savoring the sight of her taking in our treasured friends and family who had come to witness this special moment with us. Her eyes returned to mine and they remained anchored there until the officiant began the ceremony.

In that blink of an eye, I was overwhelmed with awe. There she was, wearing the hairstyle I had always told her I adored on her. Narra's hair was elegantly arranged in a loose curly bun. At the same time, a few long curls softly flowed beside her face, framing her features, which were beautifully accented by her mom's stunning pearl earrings that resembled delicate chandeliers. I was captivated by her enthralling, sweet, honey-brown eyes. "God, thank you!" I whispered silently, overwhelmed by her beauty. "She is the loveliest person I have ever seen. A Queen. My Queen. The one whom God has entrusted to me, the one my spirit recognized the moment I met her."

As she walked toward me, now within a short distance, I could smell the herby cinnamon homemade natural perfume she loved to wear.

I greeted her with my eyes, but my mouth could not utter a single word.

I felt a sense of spiritual and emotional rest whenever we were in God's presence together.

Her makeup was beautifully minimal, allowing her natural beauty to shine through. She carried a fresh bouquet of pure white flowers that perfectly complemented her elegant pure white satin gown. The gown flowed gracefully with a train that flowed perfectly about two feet behind her, harmonizing beautifully with her delicate veil. The thick, transparent straps wrapped gently around her neck, adding a delicate touch as they tied in a soft bow that rested on her bare back. "I can't wait to untie that bow," I playfully whispered.

She glided in translucent shoes that perfectly matched the glasshouse venue, creating an enchanting aura around her. She was absolutely stunning. Every time her wonderful eyes met mine, she gave a gentle smile.

Pastor Jack shared heartfelt insights about godly marriage that resonated deeply with everyone. It was a wonderful moment, but the one we had all been anticipating finally arrived. "It's now time for your personal vows, Narra and Dem." At that announcement, our eyes remained committed to each other's gaze, our spirits glowing with love and excitement for this special moment we would share together.

I took a deep breath and looked out at our wedding guests and asked, "Are y'all ready?" Laughter filled the space.

"My sweet Narra, the mystery of 'when' has been solved in my heart and in reality. While I was searching for the missing piece to my puzzle, I found something that was never missing— something that could never be apart from me. It was there all along, wrapped in God's loving timing.

"Narra, from the very first moment I began praying for you I cared about what your spirit and heart looked like the most. I cared that your soul was safe in Jesus. But also shoutout to God, for when I gaze upon you with my earthly eyes, I see a stunning angel before me, and deep down, I know that this beauty is a reflection of His grace.

"I've never encountered anyone like you; you are genuinely different. You own a divine nature that captivates me, drawing me closer with every spiritual movement you make. "Righteousness is found within your eyes, glowing from your beautiful spirit. It's like a warm hug from Jesus. I can't help but think about how your obedience to God makes your beauty shine even more. The softness of your spirit drew me even closer to you physically, enhancing the softness of your beautiful skin even more.

"Only God could have brought you into my life, Narra. Our life is a love poem, with God as the master poet. You're an 'Only God could have sent you' kind of wife. The moment I recognized your worth, it was as if God revealed His finest creation to me, made with various forms of love. Loving you has become one of the most effortless joys I have ever experienced.

"Here are the beautiful moments I look forward to sharing with you: sweet conversations, daily prayers and Bible studies, serving God together, growing alongside you, starting a family, kissing you, counseling, breaking generational curses, and creating generational love.

"Narra, your softness is beautiful and I'm attracted to you in so many ways. You are the favor that I know could only be possible through God. I crave to love you as Christ loves the Church. I promise to submit to God to demonstrate the beauty of mutual submission in our marriage. Though we have prayed for one another countless times, we will continue to grow and progress into the best versions of ourselves.

"Narr, I yearn to hear the sweet sound of your voice in our prayers and conversations. I will always pray for you and the woman you are becoming. You are my forever prayer partner.

I love experiencing God with you and want us to do so every day of our lives. No matter what trials we encounter, we shall face them together, with God guiding us through it all. I vow to protect your heart and provide a safe place for you.

"Narra," I said, my eyes sparkling with admiration, "you are truly a beautiful woman, one who resembles God's heart and His love. That's true beauty.

"Girl, you look like your Heavenly Father.

"When I look at you, I see my purpose reflected in your eyes, all I aspire to become.

"It is my purpose to love you properly, to protect you mightily," I said, my grip on her hand gentle yet firm, "and to offer you the love, tools, and resources that God has blessed us with."

I paused, captivated by the spirit that radiated through her. "Narra, you have been a wife long before we met. Meeting you taught me that being a wife isn't just a title but a true reflection of commitment to God. Though we may be imperfect, you possess the qualities of a Proverbs 31 wife, exemplifying grace and strength. God has been preparing us for this beautiful journey ahead."

With sincerity stamped on my face, I added, "I promise to hold you when you need comfort and to create a safe space in our marriage where you can truly express yourself and flourish— spiritually, emotionally, and mentally." I leaned closer, whispering, "You are covered and safe with me. Together, we are secure because God is our protector.

"The joy of serving God alongside you enlightens my spirit. Together, we will grow stronger through the challenges life presents." With contagious enthusiasm, I said, "I vow to pray with you and for you every day. We're going to pray Heaven on Earth, girl!"

My promise swelled with depth, a commitment that resonated from the very core of my being. "I promise to love you kindly, patiently, and boldly for the rest of my life, and I mean every word from the depths of my heart."

I looked up to the sky, a smile gracing my lips as I said, "This promise is to God first. This is His daughter." Returning to Narra's eyes, I continued with unwavering determination. "As long as I draw breath, I will lovingly lead you as I follow Christ." In that moment, I expressed a desire for our marriage—the sacred union—to be a constant reminder of God's grace, glory, and love for us every day. "You're the favor that I've been praying and waiting for—just what I needed."

A playful smile crossed her face as she added, "I told y'all, this man is so eloquent with his words! Lord! How?"

Our families erupted in gentle laughter. With a tender touch, I tucked a strand of hair behind her ear, my expression earnest. "Narra, you are worthy of this divine marriage."

"Okay, Dem!" Narra exclaimed with an impressed expression, her voice brimming with excitement at my vows. The room echoed with loud laughter.

I exhaled softly.

"Demery, my husband, your name means 'rare' and 'unique,' and that's you.

"Your discipline draws me closer to you, making you more attractive spiritually and physically.

"I didn't need to know your name to pray for you. I prayed for your spirit, character, and heart. I prayed for your mindset and mental well-being. I prayed for your strength in the Lord. I prayed for your soul and safety. I prayed for your health overall.

"I prayed for your peace.

"I prayed for your financial stability.

"I prayed for your spiritual awareness.

"I prayed that you would recognize me as your wife when we met.

"I also know that you aren't perfect.

"The person I prayed for is not perfect.

"The man I prayed for is not perfect. But he's prepared to pray and grow with me.

"The day I met you, I knew you were rare, my greatest gift from God thus far.

"Since day one, you have effortlessly been a tender, loyal, and loving man.

"It's as if God placed His love within you and stamped that love with my name.

"You have been kind, patient, and faithful to me.

"You are a man of your word, and, most importantly, a man of God's Word.

"I've seen your growth in the Lord; your efforts have not gone unnoticed.

"When I look at you, I see God as your strength, joy, and peace.

"I promise to pray with you, for you, and over our marriage every day, even in challenging times."

Tears began to crowd my eyes again.

"I promise to represent the definition of a Proverbs 31 wife through my character and deeds as best I can.

"Though we may occasionally get on each other's nerves, I vow to speak gently to your spirit; to uplift you using kindness as my first language.

"I promise to submit softly to you and support you as you submit to God and follow His ways.

"You are a natural leader and servant of God and I vow to follow you as you follow Jesus Christ humbly.

"I have dreamt of this moment with you—Hallelujah! My dreams have finally come true.

I love that we get to pursue our dreams together while remaining in God's will.

"Dreams do come true, and I know this to be true, for I am now becoming one with you.

"I love you with my entire spirit, Dem, and that will never change, no matter what.

"I often dream of praising God alongside you and I'm excited to love God with you.

"I know your heart was made to love me and be loved by me.

"I love you, Demery Foxer, my smooth, handsome dude. I want God to be the only one responsible for creating our love story, so I surrender my ways and my heart to Him.

"Soft dreams, soft love, soft songs, our sweet love.

"A safe home, a safe space, a safe union, a safe life.

"Life with you and getting to know you has been a safe journey. God has guided us through each step, from before we were born to where we stand now.

"My soul mate, the one who loves to worship God with me, my heart is full. Full of life, love, and so much more.

"The way you faithfully love God and follow Jesus, along with the gentle way you love me, makes it easy for me to submit to you. This is a once-in-a-lifetime love and marriage. Lord, thank you.

"May our beautiful marriage always remind us to be grateful for what we have.

"One of our gifts back to God is to mirror His love through our marriage—a thank you for blessing us with each other."

I handed Dem our last note of love before we said, "I do." It read, *Let's begin living in the marriage of our prayers without regrets.*

He realized it was a note of love, evident from its vibrant color, its noticeably small size, and the gentle stickiness. Looking at me, his eyes sparkled with a knowing expression that said, "Of course!" He chuckled, read the sweet note silently, folded it carefully, and tucked it away safely in his inside pocket.

Narra and I exchanged rings and said "I do's."Pastor Jack glanced at me and said, "Dem, you may kiss your bride."

In that precious moment, we both leaned in, our lips met softly, and it felt as if God and all of Heaven rejoiced with us and our loved ones, covering us in love and joy!

Narra raised her hand and I noticed she was wearing her double chain bracelet inscribed with the words, "And suddenly, it's your turn, and God makes it all happen for you." I pulled out my matching chain from under my shirt to reveal it. We laughed together and kissed passionately again, savoring the moment as I rubbed her rose-pink lipstick off my lips.

"I now pronounce you husband and wife." As Pastor Jack raised our joined hands into the air, he announced, "Ladies and gentlemen, Mr. and Mrs. Demery Robert Foxer!"

Chapter Twenty

❤

Secured Secrets

"I'd love to contribute to your honeymoon," Landen said, his eyes sparkling with joy at seeing his daughter happy. Narra and I exchanged a knowing glance; we had a different plan in mind. At 8:30 a.m., we gathered at the Loofy Peegan Hotel, a cozy spot where Narra's dad, her stepmother Marie, and her little brother—affectionately called "LL" for Little Landen— were staying. Marie was still asleep, recovering from the recent wedding celebrations that had taken place over several days.

"Thank you, Dad, but we're considering postponing our honeymoon for a little while. We want to save up for a trip to one of our dream destinations—the kind of journey that will create memories we can cherish forever," Narra said.

I nodded in agreement, squeezing Narra's hand affectionately. Our love story was still unfolding, and while the idea of a honeymoon was tempting, we knew that the adventure of saving together would only strengthen our bond. Landen understood; I could see his heart swelling with pride for the thoughtful couple we had become. He smiled back, fully supportive of our choice, knowing that our shared dreams would take us farther than any extravagant getaway ever could. For us, this was not a pressing concern. As a couple who valued simplicity, we preferred to focus on building our life together before taking an expensive journey. We kept in touch with Narra's father, stepmother, and brother, and we planned to visit them in the future.

For Narra, it was perfect; she got her dream intimate wedding almost exactly as she had envisioned it, with God's blessing ensuring everything was paid for. Narra was a simple girl and a small, intimate wedding was her dream—she didn't desire lavish accolades or attention. Unfazed by what others might think, she accepted that people would need to adjust to our wishes; after all, it was our wedding and should reflect what we desired. To keep our special day intimate, we decided to share pictures with the public a month later. Although some guests posted pictures on Facebook before we could, we made it clear that the fifteen guests and wedding party could share everything except for photos of the bride and groom until we were ready. And we indeed waited a little over a month.

With Narra recently graduating and me transitioning into full-time work, the realities of adult life had hit us at different times. We understood that these experiences are part of life and they ultimately strengthened our marriage and deepened our faith in Jesus. As a full-time employee, Narra had to adapt to her new routine; however, I appreciated the flexibility to work from home occasionally when needed.

Narra finally accepted an entry-level writing position at a small local company in my hometown. She began producing short stories for business owners aiming to advertise their services. And after weeks of endless scrolling online, she eventually found an apartment she loved and we decided to visit it together, inviting our parents for support. Throughout this experience, I was holding back an exciting secret.

As we toured the apartment, Narra asked questions and delighted in our parents' insights. After the tour, we all gathered in the parking lot near our cars, eager to share the news.

"Narra, there's something we need to tell you," my mom began.

Narra narrowed her eyes at me first, then at my parents.

"Don't worry, it's nothing bad," my dad reassured her with a laugh.

She took a deep breath. "Thank God."

With a warm smile, I faced her and took her hands in mine. "Narra, I love you. You've been an amazing wife and a wonderful person."

She furrowed a brow. "I've been holding on to some news," I confidently stated. "The Foxer residence is now ours."

"What? Wait—how? How does that work?" Her jaw dropped.

"I've been keeping a secret… My parents are moving into one of their smaller properties about thirty minutes away. The house is being handed over to us."

As I released her hands, my mom placed a brown folder full of paperwork into them, nodding with a smile.

During the stressful apartment search, my parents were busy with their own move, hiring a private moving company to assist them. It would take at least three months for them to entirely relocate as they were also handling the deed and paperwork to transfer everything over to Narra and me. My mom had informed the Potters about our situation when they came to meet us at the apartment. Just before Narra and I arrived, they met and discussed everything. Mr. John and Ms. Nikki were astonished and immensely grateful, especially since they had visited my parents' extravagant home during Narra's bridal shower, which featured an intimate dinner with a select few guests just weeks before our wedding. They recognized how remarkable our new home was, seeing it as a generational blessing to pass down to our children in the coming decades. This also meant one less primary concern for Narra regarding finding a new place to live. Additionally, the Foxer residence had enough space for both my parents and Narra's family to visit without infringing on our privacy. It was comforting to know that they could live with us later in life if needed.

"The big house we love so much is ours, babe."

Mouth agape, she gasped, "Seriously?"

"Yes, you haven't been there in a few weeks, but we hired movers months ago to start the process. Their job is almost done."

"You knew all along?" She beamed at me. "And I was stressed over apartment hunting?"

"Well, I wasn't sure if you'd agree."

"Seriously! Of course I agree!"

"Wait." She looked and smiled at me, reflecting on all the precious moments we'd spent together at my parents' house, especially those weekends when they were away on vacation. In that haven, we could truly be ourselves—just married, enjoying our time together, and experiencing all the joys of our new life while praying and worshipping God daily. We went from simply waving hi and bye to one another to raising our hands in worship together. The only time we felt completely free was at the Foxer residence, which now felt like a divine setup in retrospect.

I thought about all the love we'd shared in that house, amused as we exchanged knowing glances—an inside joke about the memories we'd already created in our new home. There was so much untouched space, from rooms to showers, waiting for more cherished experiences. We'd truly embraced life there and I suspected my parents had an inkling of what had been happening when they were there, and especially when they'd been gone.

"So, Narr, we're at a crossroads: should we move into our new apartment or our new home? There is a catch though. If we move into the house now, we would need to live with my parents for a while, all of us together, which won't be easy. It could take up to six months for them to be fully settled into their new place."

"Narra, consider that carefully," her mother urged, eyes widened.

"I still find it a bit strange being married and living in my parents' basement, which is why I've been actively searching for a new place."

"Honey, you can stay as long as you need; it doesn't bother us at all, but I know it must feel odd splitting your time between two homes," Ms. Nikki said reassuringly.

Mr. John chimed in, "And you're always welcome to visit. We can turn your old space into a guest suite for Levi and Micah and their wives, or for you and your husband."

I chimed in, "Like a couple's suite, huh?" We all chuckled, sharing a brief moment of lightness amid the conversation.

"On the bright side, this situation could save us the cost of a down payment, allowing me to focus on buying new furniture and other essentials for our future home."

"Oh, Narra, we'll be taking some items, such as dishes and cooking utensils, but not everything. You'll have a solid foundation, both spiritually and physically, to start with," my mom said.

"Oh! I am so in!"

I looked at her, smiled, and grabbed her hand, asking, "Are you sure, Narra?"

"Let's do it, my handsome husband!" she exclaimed, gazing into my eyes.

"Are you sure this is what you want?" Ms. Nikki asked again.

"I don't care! I'll chalk it up for four to six months." Narra said playfully, lifting her eyebrows as she looked at my parents. "And guess what. We don't need separate rooms this time."

We all laughed.

"Yeah, keep it down this time, Narra," my dad mumbled. "I'm kidding. The room you've already stayed in a few times is on a different level and side of the house, so we can't hear anything if we're on a different floor. However, you never know when we might be on the same floor, walking by your room. Haha."

Laughter from our group echoed outside the apartment complex, drawing the attention of onlookers. "If it were Dem's old childhood room, that would be different as it's close to our bedroom on the same floor."

I looked at Narra with a knowing smile, recalling moments when we'd blessed my room.

"Don't worry; the six or maybe four months will pass quickly, and then it will all be yours," my dad reminded us.

The experiences we'd shared in the theater lingered in my mind. I could hear Narra whispering to me, "All ten seats may have been used," and we giggled.

By then, during our brief meeting, we had all migrated to a long, bright orange bench outside the Crud and Beel apartment building, across from the parking lot, with Narra sitting on my lap, as there was only enough space for five people to sit. I felt a wave of gratitude flow over me as the Potters offered Narra and me their heartfelt advice. They reminded us that our union

John and Ronette Johnson   337 was still a vital part of God's plan, something that resonated deeply within me. I recalled the prayers I had for our marriage, understanding that the path ahead wouldn't always be easy. Even when we faced challenges, I believe that our marriage could still be profoundly beautiful. I even saw difficult moments as forms of beauty—a true testament to the strength of our love.

"If circumstances around school, work, or even the wedding had altered, I know life would still present its challenges. But hold on to the belief that God will guide and support you both through it all. His plan is for your success and His designs for you will never falter," Mr. John added.

I stole a glance at Narra, her eyes glistening with unshed tears. She spoke softly. "I'm overwhelmed by the profound love we share and the strong family bonds that support us. Being surrounded by all of you who love us and keep us in your prayers as we navigate this beautiful journey together is such a blessing. I appreciate every one of you. Y'all are wonderful parents and in-laws."

I expressed to our parents, "This is truly the marriage of my prayers."

We exchanged warm goodbyes, them lovingly urging us to take our time but to bless them with a grandchild eventually. Our focus shifted to adjusting to life together and building our careers. "Just go be married and we'll see you both at church Sunday," my mom said with a smile.

"And Narra, our church family misses you, y'all should come visit one Sunday!" Mr. John stated.

"We will!" she replied with a smile.

This moment was both overwhelming and exhilarating. I had already begun packing half of my room at the Potter residence, eagerly anticipating my upcoming move. All that remained was transferring my belongings.

As we settled into the car, I turned to Dem and said, "Let's celebrate before we dive into our new life together."

He beamed at me. "Exactly, you read my mind! First, let's enjoy some lunch and then we'll gather as much of your stuff as we can. We'll fill our cars and move in, taking our time unpacking in the days to come. Hopefully, our parents can lend a hand as we unload.

"Narra, you've done so much already. I know it's a lot. Let's relax together tonight and cherish this moment. It's going to be wonderful—a perfect evening to unwind with each other. Maybe we can watch a movie or do whatever we feel like!" We laughed together, excitement bubbling between us as we enjoyed the night.

Almost a year later, we were all moved in, but Dem's parents ended up staying a whole year due to renovations. They took their time, enjoying our presence more than we ever expected; they'd warned us it might be a more extended stay. Living with his parents felt strange, especially when all we craved was privacy. The house only felt like ours when they weren't home.

We savored home-cooked meals and both Dem and I took time to learn to cook our favorite dishes from Mr. and Mrs. Foxer, eventually preparing meals for the house instead of relying on his parents.

I discovered all the necessary details about the house—information that Dem had never come across. Meanwhile, he was once again enrolled in online school at Rovane, where he was expected to graduate that year. Although it may have taken him a little longer than anticipated, he was doing well, and we were all dedicated to supporting him in this decision.

"Narr! Did you know Sasha and Benny were dating?" Dem yelled from the living room while I was unpacking some bags from the store.

"Benny?"

"Yes, Benny!"

"Benny who?"

"Benny Reese!"

I dropped what I was doing.

"It's on Instagram!"

"What? Um, I just talked to Sasha a week ago and she didn't mention Benny at all."

Dem's phone rang. "Benny is video calling me now, Narr!"

I ran to the living room and there they were—Benny and Sasha on video!

We all laughed aloud.

"I was just about to call you, Sash!"

"Narra, I learned from the best," Sasha said, blushing and pointing at me.

"Keep it a secret until you know she's a keeper," Benny advised.

Laughter erupted once more.

Sasha cleared her throat. "So, when are we going to start double-dating?"

Benny chimed in, "Let's start with a date at church this Sunday."

"Sounds good!" Dem and I said in unison.

"I just can't believe you all hid this from us! Haha."

"We only hid it for three months," Sasha replied.

"But I'd been trying to talk to her for over a year before that," Benny stated with a grimace.

"It's a date—this Sunday. We can have dinner here at our house afterward."

"Cool, it's a date with the Foxers!" Benny said. "Talk to y'all later!"

Dem and I exchanged glances, hardly able to process the sweetness of that moment.

"I'm so happy and proud of them," I said.

"Me too, Narr."

The next day, Dem and I ventured into the House, Yard, and Thangs store, which was surprisingly empty for a Tuesday afternoon. We picked up a few essentials for our new project— light bulbs, tools for Dem's carpentry, a new hose, and a selection of paints and brushes.

As Dem focused on selecting wood, I wandered the aisle filled with vibrant paint colors. I felt an unexpected sense of maturity, as if I were in my 30s, even though I wasn't quite 25 yet. I was drawn to the array of colors, contemplating whether to choose fuchsia, lavender, or a deep plum. Dem came skipping down the aisle with a cart, playfully mimicking the sound of a racing car with his playful noises. We didn't need much more for this project, but paint, brushes, goggles, tape, and rollers were essential. Suddenly, Dem crept up behind me, his lips brushing softly against my neck. "That's the one, babe," he whispered, making my heart prance like a pony. I realized I had been taking too long in my color selection.

"Alright, let's go with the shade you suggested then," I replied, feeling a mix of affection and excitement as we continued our shopping together.

Back at home, Dem worked in the wood shop on the bottom floor every weekend and sometimes at night, making whatever small things we needed and some for customers.

As I slipped into my most unworn jeans, Dem and I embarked on a journey of transformation. I chose my faded black jean overalls, their comforting embrace reminding me of simpler times.

With crisp plastic sheets and painter's tape in hand, we sealed the windows with care, turning to YouTube for guidance to ensure we captured every detail of our preparation. Dem connected the Bluetooth, and soon, soft, enchanting worship music flowed through our home, filling every corner with a peaceful tone.

With brushes poised, we dove into painting, losing ourselves in a therapeutic flow. His childhood room began to morph into a sanctuary, bathed in a calming lavender hue. The deep purple doors, gateways to our tranquil retreat, promised peace for our souls. As I painted the baseboard with white paint, I felt Dem's warm presence behind me. He gently helped me off my knees, turning me into his embrace for a passionate kiss that sent butterflies flapping in my stomach. In this moment of holiness, we danced to the rhythm of our favorite worship songs, our laughter mingling with the melodies as the world outside drifted away.

Some more time passed and we finally replaced the furniture with stylish, deep-plum sofas, a cozy fuchsia recliner, and elegant gold drapes, complemented by deep purple curtains that framed the windows, enhancing the room's sophistication. The crowning jewel was a stunning deep purple hanging light fixture, radiating exquisite appeal throughout the newly transformed sanctuary. And then there were the sticky notes, a delightful surprise from Dem: he had saved every love note I had written him over the years before our wedding day. We planned to keep this tradition alive by framing new love notes on the wall each year, honoring our journey together.

In a carefully crafted heart-shaped oak wood frame from the Lovers collection, made by the Foxer Handcrafts shop, we displayed love notes and prayers on sticky notes from our closet. We planned to hang it on the wall once the paint dried. I looked over at Dem, who was holding a small plaque.

"Can't forget this one, babe," he said, waving it playfully in the air.

"The Sweet Narra Poem!" I said as we both giggled, the memory always bringing laughter to our conversations.

We then transformed the smaller prayer closet into a spacious walk-in closet, perfect for storing our bags, jackets, shoes, and even a mini-fridge, a little slice of heaven just for us. Besides our bedroom, the in-house temple—our new prayer room—stood as a calm haven for us.

As we paused the music, Dem remarked, "It's taking us forever to finish this room," a hint of tiredness barely masking his joy.

"Well, four hours isn't eternity," I replied, trying to uplift his spirit with a chuckle. "Good thing we're almost finished." He smiled, satisfaction evident in his gaze as he took in our nearly completed masterpiece.

As we admired our progress, love spread through me. "If you weren't so eager to get touchy-feely while painting…" I teased, producing laughter from both of us. We shared another adoring kiss, maintaining unbroken eye contact, paint brushes in our hands the entire time.

"Save some of that lavender paint for later," he murmured playfully as he pulled back, biting his lower lip, a gentle love glimmering in his eyes.

"I don't think we need any more; there's hardly any left," I said, glancing up at him once more. He winked at me, a playful spark kindling in his eyes. "That's all the paint I need to spread this divine love all over you, Mrs. Narra Foxer."

End

Secured Secrets

Acknowledgements

Our deepest gratitude goes to You, our faithful Heavenly Father, our loving Lord and Savior Jesus Christ, and the Holy Spirit, our eternal Comforter. Your guidance leads us daily, inspiring us to serve and honor You in every aspect of our lives—through our writing, our marriage, and all we do within Your beautiful kingdom. Thanks to Your perfect divine timing, our dreams are becoming a reality by Your grace, and we are filled with appreciation and love for You.

Thank you to everyone who has believed in us from the very beginning, supported us, and prayed for us: Dearist (Mom), Ronere, Des, Aunt G, Aunt Marla, Ykesha, Kierra Jacobs, De'Raye, Jackie, Aunt Neicy, Aunt Nay Nay, along with all our family and close friends who have shown their support and prayers. Apostle Owen, Lady Mimie, and TLC—you all are like family to us, and we sincerely value your prayers, love, and support. To our online community, Divine Heart Couples, your support means a great deal to us. We gratefully thank you from the bottom of our hearts.

About the Authors

———————— ♥ ————————

Ronette's journey began in Chester, Pennsylvania, and has unfolded into a vibrant life near Philadelphia, Pennsylvania, in the United States. Guided by her faith in Jesus Christ, she is an entrepreneur, business owner, writer, and author sharing a beautiful journey with her husband, John. With over 13 years woven into the fabric of the IT industry, her true passion blooms in the art of writing and the world of books. Possessing a creative mind, a spirited heart, and a profound love for godly storytelling, she has long cherished the dream of becoming a fiction romance author—a dream now unfolding into reality.

In 2016, Ronette wrote the heartfelt quote, "When the Person You Prayed for Becomes the Person You Pray With," which she initially jotted down in her notes about a year after their wedding. By 2017, she shared it on their Instagram and Facebook pages, @divineheartcouples. The message resonated widely, also becoming a touching sensation across TikTok, Pinterest, and YouTube. Now, after nine years, the romance novel is here.

Together, Ronette and John poured their love and faith into their debut book, *A Husband and Wife's Love Letter to God*, a beautiful testament to their journey and devotion to God. Their stories beautifully express divine love and deep romance, captivating readers with heartfelt quotes.

John, the co-author of Ronette's books and co-founder of Divine Heart Couples, pours his heart into inspiring both singles and married couples. With a deep love for God and the Bible, he passionately shares their heartfelt journey of love alongside his wife, Ronette, spreading hope and faith to others along the way. Join them and stay connected on IG, TikTok, YouTube, and Facebook at @divineheartcouples and learn more about them and their ministry on their website: www.divineheartcouples. com. **Get your book merch, featuring some of our favorite quotes from this book on T-shirts and more, available at** www.prayedforpraywithapparel.com.

The authors of **A Husband and Wife's Love Letter to God** *release their debut Christian romance novel.*

In a world where nurturing love meets the power of heartfelt prayer, a captivating love story unfolds, revealing God's divine plans. This dreamy romance novel weaves a beautiful narrative rich in sweetness, comfort, grace, and enchanting romance.

Dem Foxer and Narra Jones are both in their early twenties, currently navigating the final years of college—Dem as a junior and Narra as a senior. Dem has a wild group of friends, and with his charming personality, he often says all the right things. Narra is a hopeful romantic who dreams of a loving, safe, and godly relationship. However, her past experiences have made her cautious, and she finds it difficult to trust fully.

"This book is divine and passionate, filled with surprising banter, and just the right touch of swoon-worthy steam!"

Set against the backdrop of Rovane University, this romance novel by the husband-and-wife duo John and Ronette Johnson tells the captivating story of Narra Jones and Dem Foxer. Their chemistry is undeniable, and their instant attraction isn't merely physical; it's a profound, divine connection that shines from their first meeting. Narra, a gentle dreamer, and Dem, a charming romantic deeply devoted to Jesus, embark on a heartfelt journey as college sweethearts. Yet, their idyllic romance faces unforeseen challenges that test their bond and love.

Dem Foxer has a way with his words.

Dem is a remarkable young man—intelligent, kind, humorous, and handsome, embodying the qualities of a true charmer and prayer warrior. Initially, Narra finds it hard to believe the beautiful words Dem speaks. Yet, she remembers her prayers for a husband who loves God profoundly, prompting her to approach this budding romance with a cautious heart and discerning mind.

Narra Jones had heard it all before, until she met Dem.

Narra is strikingly attractive, which might create the impression that she is aloof. However, she is quite the opposite. She finds herself falling deeply in love with the beautiful uncertainty of God's plans for her, eagerly embracing the enchanting mystery surrounding her romantic life and all that it might entail.

As graduation approaches, their faith in love is challenged by concerns such as age, timing, friendships, external opinions, doubts, trust, and lingering past relationships.

As they navigate life's sudden shifts and challenges, one constant remains: God's will.

When you surrender your heart and ways to God, life unfolds in unexpected and favorable ways, even when circumstances appear daunting.